A step sounded in the corridor to Sten's left. He turned . . . And faced a figure that had likewise stopped still, one robed in black, the robes glittering with many small discs. Mri. Kel'en. The golden eyes above the veil were astonished. A slim bronze hand went to the knife at his belt and hesitated there.

The enemy. The destroyers of Kiluwa and Talos and Asgard. Sten had never seen one in the flesh at this range. Only the eyes, the hands were uncovered. The tall figure remained utterly still, wrapped in menace and in anger.

"I am Sten Duncan," he found courage to say. "I'm the assistant to the Federations envoy."

"We should not have met," said the other, and with that the mri turned on his heel and stalked off in the direction from which he had come, a black figure that vanished into shadows at the turning of the corridor. Duncan found himself trembling in every muscle. He had seen mri that close only in photographs, and all of those were dead.

We should not have met, the mri had said . . .

Someone was being deceived.

THE FADED SUN: KESRITH

C. J. Cherryh

DAW BOOKS, INC.
DONALD A. WOLLHEIM, PUBLISHER

1633 Broadway, New York, NY 10019

FIRST DAW PRINTING, AUGUST 1978

6 7 8 9

DAW TRADEMARK REGISTERED
U.S. PAT. OFF. MARCA
REGISTRADA, HECHO EN U.S.A.

PRINTED IN U.S.A.

Chapter One

Wind-child, sun-child, what is Kath?
Child-bearers, laugh-bringers, that is Kath.

IT WAS a game, *shon'ai*, the passing-game, Kel-style, in the dim round hall of the Kel, the middle tower of the House—black-robed men and a black-robed woman, a circle of ten. Warriors, they played the round not like children, with a pair of stones, but with the spinning blades of the *as'ei*, that could wound or kill. On the name-beat, the snap of fingers, the *as'ei* flew across the seated circle of players, and skilled hands seized the hilts in mid-turn, to beat the time and hurl the blades on in the next name-beat.

Fire-child, star-child, what is Kel?
Sword-bearers, song-weavers, that is Kel.

They played without words, with only the rhythm of their hands and the weapons, flesh and steel. The rhythm was as old as time and as familiar as childhood. The game had more meaning than the act, more than the simplicity of the words. The Game of the People, it was called.

Dawn-child, earth-child, what is Sen?
Rune-makers, home-leaders, that is Sen.

A kel'en who flinched, whose eye failed or whose wits wandered, had no value in the House. The boys and girls and women of the Kath played with stones to learn their skill. Those who became kel'ein played thereafter with edged steel. The Kel, like the mothers and children of the gentle Kath,

5

laughed as they played. They of Kel-caste were brief and bright as moths. They enjoyed life, because they knew this.

> *Then-child, now-child, what are we?*
> *Dream-seekers, life-bearers, we are—*

A door opened, echoing, the sound rolling through the hollows and depths of the tower. Sen Sathell broke in upon them, suddenly and without warning or courtesies.

The rhythm ceased. The blades rested in the hands of Niun, the youngest kel'en. The Kel as a whole inclined their heads in respect to Sathell s'Delas, chief of Sen-caste, the scholars. Gold-robed he was, like light breaking into the dark hall of the martial Kel, and he was very old—the oldest man of all in the House.

"Kel'anth," he said quietly, addressing Eddan, his counterpart in the Kel, "—kel'ein—news has come. The rumor is the war has ended. The regul have asked the humans for peace."

There was utter silence.

An abrupt move. The *as'ei* whirred and buried points in the painted plaster of the far wall.

The youngest kel'en rose and veiled himself, and stalked from the gathering, leaving shock in his wake.

The sen'anth and the kel'anth looked at each other, old men and kinsmen, helpless in their distress.

And from the deepest shadows one of the dusei, a brown, slope-shouldered mass larger than a man, stirred and rose, ambling forth into the light in that mournful, abstracted manner of dusei. It pushed its way irreverently between the two elders, thrusting its massive head at the kel'anth, who was its master, seeking comfort.

Kel'anth Eddan patted the beast with age-smooth fingers and looked up at the old scholar who, outside the divisions of caste and duty, was his half-brother. "Is the news beyond any doubt?" he asked, the least trace of hope yet remaining in his voice.

"Yes. The source is regul official communications, no city rumor. It seems completely reliable." Sathell gathered his robes about him and, tucking them between his knees, settled on the carpeted floor among the kel'ein, who eased aside to make room for him in their circle.

They were, these ten, the elders of the House, save one.
They were mri.

In their tongue, when they made this statment, they were merely saying that they were of the People. Their word for other species was tsi'mri, which meant not-people, and summed up mri philosophy, religion, and the personal attitudes of the elders at once.

They were, as a species, golden-toned. Mri legends said that the People were born of the sun: skin, eyes, coarse shoulder-length manes, all were bronze or gold. Their hands and feet were narrow and long, and they were a tall, slender race. Their senses, even in great age, were very keen, their hearing in particular most sensitive. Their golden eyes were lid-folded, double-lidded as well, for a nictitating membrane acted on reflex to protect their vision against blowing dust.

They were, as outsiders believed, a species of warriors, of mercenaries—for outsiders saw the Kel, and rarely the Sen, and never the Kath. Mri served outsiders for hire—served the regul, the massive tsi'mri merchants native to Nurag of the star Mab. For many centuries, mri kel'ein had hired out to protect regul commerce between-worlds, generally hired by one regul company as defense against the ambitions and ruthlessness of some business rival, and mri had therefore fought against mri. Those years and that service had been good for the People, this trying of one kel'en of a certain service against the kel'en of another, in proper and traditional combat, as it had always been. Such trials-at-arms refined the strength of the People, eliminating the weak and unfit and giving honor to the strong. In those days the tsi'mri regul had recognized themselves to be incapable of fighting and unskilled in planning strategies, and sensibly left all matters of conflict to the mri Kel to settle in the mri fashion.

But for the last forty years, mri had served all regul combined against all humans, a bitter and ugly conflict, lacking honor and lacking any satisfactions from the enemy. The mri elders were old enough to remember the life before, and knew therefore what changes had been wrought by the war; and they were not pleased with them. Humans were mass-fighters, animals of the herd, and simply understood no other way of war. Mri, who fought singly, had early suspected this, tested it with their lives, found it bitterly true. Humans rejected *a'ani*, honorable combat, would not respect challenge, un-

derstood nothing but their own way, which was widespread
destruction.

Mri had bent themselves to learn humanity, the way of the
enemy, and had begun to adjust their operations and their
manner of service to the regul accordingly. Mri were profes-
sionals when it came to combat. Innovation in the yin'ein, the
ancient weapons that were used in *a'ani*, was dishonorable
and unthinkable; but innovation in the zahen'ein, in modern
arms, was a simple matter of retooling and adjusting methods,
a matter of competency in the profession they followed for a
livelihood.

Regul, unfortunately, were not as capable of adapting to
new tactics. Regul had vast and accurate memories. They
could not forget what had always occurred, but conversely
they could hardly conceive at all of what had not yet happened, and did not make plans against it happening. Hitherto
the regul had depended on mri entirely in the matter of their
personal safety, and mri foresight—for mri could imagine—
had shielded them and compensated for that regul blindness
to the unexpected; but in latter days, when the war began to
take regul lives and threaten regul properties, regul took matters into their own unskilled hands. Regul issued orders,
prudent in their own estimation, for actions which were militarily impossible.

The mri had attempted to obey, for honor's sake.

Mri had died in their thousands, for honor's sake.

In the House, on this world, there lived only thirteen mri.
Two were young. The rest were the makers of policy, a
council of the old, the veteran. Long centuries ago the House
had numbered more than two thousand in the Kel alone. In
this present age all but these few had gone their way to the
war, to die.

And their war had been lost, by regul, who asked the humans for peace.

Sathell looked about him and considered these old ones,
kel'ein who had lived beyond their own years of service,
whose memories gave them in some matters the perspective
of sen'ein. They were Husbands to the she'pan, masters-of-
arms while there had been Kath children to teach; and there
was Pasev, the only surviving kel'e'en of the House, she most
skilled in the yin'ein next Eddan himself. There were Dahacha and Sirain of Nisren; Palazi and Quaras and Lieth of

Guragen, itself a dead House, taking refuge with the Mother of this one and adopted by her as Husbands. And from yet another dead House were Liran and Debas, truebrothers. These were part of an age that had already vanished, a time the People would not see again. Sathell felt their sadness, sensed it reflected in the beasts that huddled together in the shadows. Eddan's dus, whose species was reputedly never friendly with any caste but the warrior Kel, sniffed critically at the scholar's gold robes and suffered himself to be touched, then heaved his great bulk a little closer, wrinkled rolls of down-furred flesh, shamelessly accepting affection where it was offered.

"Eddan," said Sathell, stroking the beast's warm shoulder, "I must tell you also: it is very likely that the masters will cede this world if the humans should demand it as part of the peace."

"That would be," said Eddan, "a very large settlement."

"Not according to what we have just heard. It is rumored that the humans have secured the whole front, that the regul lords are in complete withdrawal, that the humans are in such a position now that they can touch all the contested areas. They have taken Elag."

There was silence. Elsewhere in the tower a door closed. At last Eddan shrugged, a move of his slender fingers. "Then the humans will surely demand this world. There is very little that they will miss in their desire for revenge. And the regul have left us open to it."

"It is incredible," said Pasev. "Gods! there was no need, no need at all for the regul to have abandoned Elag. The People could have held there—could have turned the humans, if they had been given the equipment."

Sathell made a helpless gesture. "Perhaps. But held for whom? The regul withdrew, took everything that was needed there for the defense, pulled ships from under their control. Now we—Kesrith—have become the border. You are right. It is very likely that the regul will not resist here either; in fact, it is not reasonable for them to do so. So we have done all that we could do. We have advised, we have warned—and if our employers refused to take that advice, then there is little we can do but cover their retreat, since we cannot restrain them from it. They took the war into their own management against our advice. Now they have lost their war; we have not. The war ceased to be ours some years ago. Now you are guiltless, kel'ein. You may justly reckon so. There is simply nothing further that can be done."

"There was something once that might have been done," Pasev insisted.

"The Sen attempted many times to reason with the masters. We offered our services and our advice according to the ancient treaty. We could not—" Sathell heard the footsteps of the youth downstairs as he spoke, and the disturbance disrupted his train of thought. He glanced hallward involuntarily as the door downstairs slammed with great violence. The sound echoed throughout all the House. He cast the Kel a look of distress. "Should not one of you at least go speak with him?"

Eddan shrugged, embarrassed in his authority. Sathell knew it. He presumed on kinship and friendship and stepped far out of bounds with Eddan when he made that protest. He loved Niun; they all did. But the autonomy of the Kel, even misguided, was sacred regarding the discipline of its members. Only the Mother could interfere within Eddan's province.

"Niun has some small cause, do you not think?" asked Eddan quietly. "He has trained all his life toward this war. He is not a child of the old way, as we are; and now he cannot enter into the new either. You have taken something from him. What do you expect him to do, sen Sathell?"

Sathell bowed his head, unable to dispute with Eddan in the matter, recognizing the truth in it, trying to see things as a young kel'en might see them. One could not explain to the Kel, could not refute them in debate nor expect foresight of them: children of a day, the kel'ein, brief and passionate, without yesterday and without tomorrow. Their ignorance was the price they paid for their freedom to leave the House and go among tsi'mri; and they knew their place. If a sen'en challenged them to reason, they must simply bow the head in their turn and retreat into silence: they had nothing with which to answer. And to destroy their peace of mind was unconscionable; knowledge without power was the most bitter condition of all.

"I think I have told you," said Sathell at last, "all that I know to tell you at the moment. I will advise you immediately if there is any further news." He arose in that silence and smoothed his robes into order, gingerly avoiding the reflexive grasp of the dus. The beast reached at his ankle, harmless in intent, but not in potential. The dusei were not to be treated with familiarity by any but a kel'en. He stopped and looked at Eddan, who with a touch rebuked the beast and freed him.

He edged round the massive paw, cast a final look at Eddan; but Eddan looked away, affecting not to be interested any further in his departure. Sathell was not willing to press the matter publicly. He knew his half-brother, and knew that the hurt was precisely because there was affection between them. There was a careful line drawn between them in public. When caste divided kinsmen, there had to be that, to save the pride of the lesser.

He gave a formal courtesy to the others and withdrew, and was glad to be out of that grim hall, heavy as the air was with the angers of frustrated men, and of the dusei, whose rage was slower but more violent. He was relieved, nonetheless, that they had listened to all that he had said. There would be no violence, no irrational action, which was the worst thing that needed be feared from the Kel. They were old. The old might reason together in groups, might consult together. The kel'en was, in youth, a solitary warrior and reckless, and without perspective.

He thought of going after Niun, and did not know what to say to him if he should find him. His duty was to report elsewhere.

And when the door closed, aged Pasev, kel'e'en, veteran of Nisren and Elag's first taking, pulled the *as'ei* from the shattered plaster and merely shrugged off the sen'anth. She had seen more years and more of war than any living warrior but Eddan himself. She played the Game all the same, as did they all, including Eddan. It was a death as honorable as one in war.

"Let us play it out," she said.

"No," said Eddan firmly. "No. Not yet."

He caught her eyes as he spoke. She looked at him plainly, aged lover, aged rival, aged friend. Her slim fingers brushed the fine edge of the steel, but she understood the order.

"Aye," she said, and the *as'ei* spun past Eddan's shoulder

to bury themselves in the painted map of Kesrith that decorated the east wall.

"The Kel bore the news," said sen Sathell, "with more restraint than I expected of them. But it was not welcome, all the same. They feel cheated. They conceive it as an affront against their honor. And Niun left. He would not even hear it out. I do not know where he went. I am concerned."

She'pan Intel, the Lady Mother of the House and of the People, leaned back on her many cushions, ignoring a twinge of pain. The pain was an old companion. She had had it forty-three years, since she lost her strength and her beauty at once in the fires of burning Nisren. Even then she had not been young. Even then she had been she'pan of homeworld, ruler over all three castes of the People. She was of the first rank of the Sen, passing Sathell himself; she was above other she'panei as well, the few that still lived. She knew the Mysteries that were closed to others; she knew the name and nature of the Holy, and of the Gods; and the Pana, the Revered Objects, were in her keeping. She knew her nation to its depth and its width, its birth and its destiny.

She was she'pan of a dying House, eldest Mother of a dying species. The Kath, the caste of child-bearers and children, was dead, its tower dark and closed twelve years ago: the last of the kath'ein was long buried in the cliffs of Sil'athen, and the last children, motherless save for herself, had gone to their distinies outside. Her Kel had declined to ten, and the Sen—

The Sen was before her: Sathell, the eldest, the sen'anth, whose weak heart poised him constantly a beat removed from the Dark; and the girl who sat presently at her feet. They were the gold-robes, the light-bearers, high-caste. Her own robes were white, untainted by the edgings of black and blue and gold worn by the she'panei of lesser degree. Their knowledge was almost complete, but her own was entire. If her own heart should stop beating this moment, so much, so incalculably much could be lost to the People. It was a fearful thing, to consider how much rested on her each pulse and breath amid such pain.

That the House and the People not die.

The girl Melein looked up at her—last of all the children, Melein s'Intel Zain-Abrin, who had once been kel'e'en. At times the kel-fierceness was still in Melein, although she had assumed outwardly the robes and the chaste serenity of the scholarly Sen—although the years had given her different skills, and her mind had advanced far beyond the simplicity of a kel'e'en. Intel brushed at Melein's shoulder, a caress. "Patience," she advised, seeing Melein's anxiety; and she knew that the advice would be discarded in all respects.

"Let me go find Niun and talk to him," she asked.

Brother and sister, Niun and Melein—and close, despite that they had been separated by law and she'pan's decree and caste and custom. Kel'en and sen'e'en, dark and bright, Hand and Mind; but the heart in them was the same and the blood was the same. She remembered the pair that had given them life, her youngest and most beloved Husband and a kel'e'en of Guragen, both lost now. *His* face, his eyes, that had made her regret a she'pan's chastity, gazed back at her through Melein's and Niun's; and she remembered that he also had been strong-willed and hot-tempered and clever. Perhaps Melein hated her; she had not willingly received the command to leave the Kel and enter the Sen. But there was no defiance there now, though the she'pan searched for it. There was only anxiety, only a natural grief for her brother's pain.

"No," said Intel sharply. "I tell you to let him alone."

"He may harm himself, she'pan."

"He will not. You underestimate him. He does not need you now. You are no longer of the Kel, and I doubt that he wants to be faced by one of the Sen at this moment. What could you tell him? What could you answer if he asked you questions? Could you be silent?"

This struck home. "He wanted to leave Kesrith six years ago," said Melein, her eyes bright with unshed tears; and possibly it was not only her brother's case she pleaded now, but her own. "You would not let him go. Now it is too late, she'pan. It is forever too late for him, and what can he imagine for himself? What is there for him?"

"Meditate upon these things," said Intel, "and tell me your conclusions, sen Melein s'Intel, after you have thought a day and a night on this matter. But do not intrude your advice into the private affairs of a kel'en. And do not regard him as your brother. A sen'e'en has no kin but the whole House, and the People."

Melein rose, and stared down at her, breast heaving with

her struggle for breath. Beautiful, this daughter of hers: Intel saw her in this instant and was amazed how much Melein, who was not of her blood, had become the things her own youth had once promised—saw mirrored her own self, before Nisren's fall, before the ruin of the House and of her own hopes. The sight wounded her. In this moment she saw clearly, and knew the sen'e'en as she was, and feared her and loved her at once.

Melein, who would hardly mourn her passing.

So she had created her, deliberately, event by event, choice by choice, her daughter-not-of-the-flesh, her child, her Chosen, formed in Kath and Kel and Sen, partaker of the Mysteries of all castes of the People.

Hating her.

"Learn restraint," she earnestly wished Melein, in a still, soft voice that thrust with difficulty into Melein's anger. "Learn to be sen'e'en, Melein, above all else that you desire to have."

The young sen'e'en let go a shuddering breath, and the tears in her eyes spilled over. Thwarted for now, the sen'e'en for a moment being child again: but this child was dangerous.

Intel shivered, foreknowing that Melein would outlive her and impose her own imprint on the world.

Chapter Two

————••———— ••• ————••————

THERE WAS a division in the world, marked by a causeway of white rock. On the one side, and at the lower end, lay the regul of Kesrith—city-folk, slow-moving, long-remembering. The lowland city was entirely theirs: flat, sprawling buildings, a port, commerce with the stars, mining that scarred the earth, a plant that extracted water from the Alkaline Sea. The land had been called the Dus plain before there were regul on Kesrith: the mri remembered. For this reason the mri had avoided the plain, in respect of the dusei; but the regul had insisted on setting their city there, and the dusei left it.

Uplands, in the rugged hills at the other end of the causeway, was the tower of the mri. It appeared as four truncated cones arising from the corners of a trapezoidal ground floor—slanted walls made of the pale earth of the lowlands, treated and hardened. This was the Edun Kesrithun, the House of Kesrith, the home of the mri of Kesrith, and, because of Intel, the home of all mri in the wide universe.

One could see most of Kesrithi civilization from the vantage point Niun occupied in his solitary anger. He came here often, to this highest part of the causeway, to this stubborn outcrop of rock that had defeated the regul road and made the regul think otherwise about their plans to extend it into the high hills, invading the sanctity of Sil'athen. He liked it for what it was as well as for the view. Below him lay the regul city and the mri edun, two very small scars on the body of the white earth. Above him, in the hills, and beyond and beyond, there were only regul automatons, that drew minerals from the earth and provided regul Kesrith its reason for existence; and wild things that had owned the world before the

15

coming of regul or of mri; and the slow-moving dusei that
had once been Kesrith's highest form of life.

Niun sat, brooding, on the rock that overlooked the world,
hating tsi'mri with more than the ordinary hatred of mri for
aliens, which was considerable. He was twenty-six years old
as the People reckoned years, which was not by Kesrith's or-
bit around Arain, nor by the standard of Nisren, nor by that
of either of the two other worlds the People had designated
homeworld in the span of time remembered by Kel songs.

He was tall, even of his kind. His high cheekbones bore the
seta'al, the triple scars of his caste, blue-stained and indelible;
this meant that he was a full-fledged member of the Kel, the
hand of the People. Being of the Kel, he went robed from
collar to boot-tops in unrelieved black; and black veil and
tasseled headcloth, *mez* and *zaidhe*, concealed all but his
brow and his eyes from the gaze of outsiders when he chose
to meet them; and the *zaidhe* further had a dark transparent
visor that could meet the veil when dust blew or red Arain
reached its unpleasant zenith. He was a man: his face, like
his thoughts, was considered a private identity, one indecent
to reveal to strangers. The veils enveloped him as did the
robes, a distinguishing mark of the only caste of the People
that might deal with outsiders. The black robes, the *siga,* were
held about the waist and chest with belts that bore his
weapons, which were several; and also they should have held
j'tai, medallions, honors won for his services to the People:
they held none, and this lack of status would have been obvious to any mri that beheld him.

Being of the Kel, he could neither read nor write, save that
he could use a numbered keyboard and knew mathematics,
both regul and mri. He knew by heart the complicated gene-
alogies of his House, which had been that of Nisren. The
name-chants filled him with melancholy when he sang them:
it was difficult to do so and then to look about the cracking
walls of Edun Kesrithun and behold only so few people as
now lived, and not realize that decline was taking place, that
it was real and threatening. He knew all the songs. He could
foresee begetting no child of his own who would sing them,
not on Kesrith. He learned the songs; he learned languages,
which were part of the Kel-lore. He spoke four languages flu-
ently, two of which were his own, one of which was the
regul's, and the fourth of which was the enemy's. He was ex-

pert in weapons, both the yin'ein and the zahen'ein; he was taught of nine masters-of-arms; he knew that his skill was great in all these things.

And wasted, all wasted.

Regul.

Tsi'mri.

Niun flung a rock downslope, which splashed into a hot pool and disturbed the vapors.

Peace.

Peace on human terms, it would be. Regul had disregarded mri strategists at every crucial moment of the war. Regul would spend mri lives without stinting and they would pay the bloodprice to edunei that lost sons and daughters of the Kel, all because some regul colonial official panicked and ordered suicidal attack by the handful of mri serving him personally to cover his retreat and that of his younglings; but far less willingly would that same regul risk regul lives or properties. To lose regul lives would mean loss of status; it would have brought that regul instant censure by regul authorities, recall to homeworld, sifting of his knowledge, death of himself and his young in all probability.

It was inevitable that humans should have realized this essential weakness of the regul-mri partnership, that humans should have learned that inflicting casualties on regul would have far more effect than inflicting those same casualties on mri.

It was predictable then that the regul should have panicked under that pressure, that they would have reacted by retreat, precipitous, against all mri counsel to the contrary, exposing world after world to attack in their haste to withdraw to absolute security. Consequently that absolute security could not exist.

And that regul would afterwards compound their stupidity by dealing directly with the humans—this too was credible, in the regul, to buy and sell war, and to sell out quickly when threatened rather than to risk losing overmuch of their necessary possessions.

The regul language contained no word for courage.

Neither had it one for imagination.

The war was ending and Niun remained worldbound, never having put to use the things that he had learned. The gods knew what manner of trading the merchants were doing, what disposition was being made of his life. He foresaw that things might revert to what they had been before the war, that mri might again serve individual regul—that mri would fight mri again, in combat where experience mattered.

And gods knew how long it would be possible to find a regul to serve, when the war was ending and things were entering a period of flux. Gods knew how likely a regul was to take on an inexperienced kel'en to guard his ship, when others, war-wise, were available.

He had trained all his life to fight humans, and the policies of three species conspired to keep him from it.

He rose up of a sudden, mind set on an idea that had been seething there for more than this day alone, and he leaped to the ground and started walking down the road. He did not look back when he had passed the edun, unchallenged, unnoticed. He owned nothing. He needed nothing. What he wore and what he carried as his weapons were his to take; he had this by law and custom, and he could ask nothing more of his edun even were he leaving with their blessing and help, which he was not.

In the edun, Melein would surely grieve at such a silent desertion, but she had been kel'e'en herself long enough to be glad for his sake too, that he went to a service. A kel'en in an edun was as impermanent as the wind itself, and ought to own no close ties past childhood, save to the she'pan and to the People and to him or her that hired him.

He did feel a certain guilt toward the she'pan too, to her who had mothered him with a closeness much beyond what a she'pan owed a son of her Husbands. He knew that she had particularly favored Zain his father, and still mourned his death; and she would neither approve nor allow the journey he made now.

It was, in fact, Intel's stubborn, possessive will that had held him this long on Kesrith, kept him at her side long past the years that he decently should have left her authority and that of his teachers. He had once loved Intel, deeply, reverently. Even that love, in the slow years since he should have followed the other kel'ein of the edun and left her, had begun to turn to bitterness.

Thanks to her, his skills were untried, his life unused and now perhaps altogether useless. Nine years had passed since the *seta'al* of the Kel had been cut and stained into his face, nine years that he had sat in heart-pounding longing whenever a regul master would come up the road to the edun and seek a kel'en to guard a ship, be it for the war or even for commerce. Fewer and fewer of these requests came in the passing years, and now there came no more requests to the edun at all. He was the last of all his brothers and sisters of the Kel, last of all the children of the edun save Melein. The others had all found their service, and most were dead; but Niun s'Intel, nine years a kel'en, had yet to leave the she'pan's protective embrace.

Mother, let me go! he had begged of her six years ago, when his cousin Medai's ship had left—the ultimate, the crushing shame, that Medai, swaggering, boastful Medai, should be chosen for the greatest honor of all, and he be left behind in disgrace.

No, the she'pan had said in the absolute, invoking her authority, and to his repeated pleading for her understanding, for his freedom: *No. You are the last of all my sons, the last, the last I shall ever have. Zain's child. And if I will you to stay with me, that is my right, and that is my final decision. No. No.*

He had fled to the high hills that day, watching and not wishing to watch, as the ship of the regul high command, *Hazan,* that ruled the zone in which Kesrith lay, bore Medai s'Intel Sov-Nelan into manhood, into service, into the highest honor that had yet befallen a kel'en of Edun Kesrithun.

That day Niun had wept, though kel'ein could not weep. And then in shame at this weakness, he had scoured his face with the harsh powdery sand and stayed fasting in the hills another day and two nights, until he had to come down and face the other kel'ein and the Mother's anxious and possessive love.

Old, all of them. There was not a kel'en left now save himself that could even take a service if it were offered. They were all greatly skilled. He suspected that they were the greatest masters of the yin'ein in all the People, although they did not boast anything but considerable competency; but the years had done their subtle robbery and left them no strength to use their arts in war. It was a Kel of eight men and one woman past their reason for living, without strength to fight or—after him—children to teach: old ones whose dreams must now be all backward.

Nine years they had stolen from him, entombing him with them, living their vicarious lives through his youth.

He walked the road down to the lowlands, letting the causeway take him to regul, since regul would not come to the edun in these days. It was not the most direct route, but it was the easiest, and he walked it insolently secure, since the old ones of the Kel could not possibly overtake him on so long a walk. He did not mean to go to the port, which was directly crosslands, but to what lay at the causeway's end, the very center of regul authority, the Nom, that two-storied building that was the highest structure in Kesrith's only city.

He felt uneasy when his boots trod concrete and he found all about him the ugly flat buildings of regul. Here was a different world from the cleanliness of the high hills, even a different smell in the air, a blunting of the acrid flavor of Kesrith's chill winds, a subtle effluvium of oil and machinery and musky regul bodies.

Regul younglings watched him—the mobile ones, the young of regul. Their squat bodies would thicken further in adulthood, greyish-brown skin darken, loosen—fat accumulate until they found themselves enveloped in weight almost too great for their atrophying muscles to lift. Mri seldom saw elder regul; Niun himself had never seen an elder in the flesh, only heard them described by his teachers of the Kel. Adult regul kept to their city, surrounded by machines that carried them, that purified their air; they were attended by younglings that must wait on them constantly, who themselves lived precarious lives until they chanced to reach maturity. The only violence regul perpetrated was against their own young.

The younglings on the square looked at him now in sidelong glances and talked in secretive tones that carried to his sensitive hearing, more clearly surely than they realized it could. Ordinarily this spitefulness would not have troubled him in the least: he had been taught less liking for them, and despised them and all their breed. But here he was the petitioner, desperately anxious, and they held what he wanted and had the power to deny it to him. Their hate breathed about him like the tainted city atmosphere. He had veiled himself long before he entered the town; but with a little more encouragement he would have dropped the visor of the *zaidhe* also. He had done so on his last visit to this city, being a very young kel'en and uncertain of the proprieties of conduct between regul and mri. But now, older, a man in his own right, he had the face to leave the visor up and glare back at the younglings who stared too boldly; and most could not bear the direct contact of his eyes and flinched from meeting them. A few, older and braver than the others, hissed soft displeasure, warning. He ignored them. He was not a regul youngling, to fear their violence.

He knew his way. He knew the Nom's proper entrance, fronting the great square around which the city was built in concentric squares. It faced the rising sun, as main entrances of central regul buildings must. He remembered this. He had been here as escort to his father, who was about to take his last service; but he had not been inside. Now he came to the door before which he had waited on that day, and at his presence the regul youngling on duty in the vestibule arose in alarm.

"Go away," said the youngling flatly; but he paid no attention to it, and walked into the main foyer of the echoing place, at once stifled by the heat and the musky flavor of the air. He found himself in a great place surrounded by doors and windowed offices, all with titles written on them; he was quickly sick and dizzy from the air and he stood confused and ashamed in the middle of the hall, for here it was a matter of reading to know where he must go next, and he could not read.

It was the regul youngling from the vestibule desk that came to him in his distress, stumping across the floor in short, scuffing steps. The youngling was flushed dark with anger or with the heat, and breathing heavily from the exertion of overtaking him. "Go away," the youngling repeated. "By treaty and by law you have no business coming here."

"I will speak to your elders," he told the youngling, which he had been taught was the ultimate and unanswerable appeal among regul: no youngling could make an ultimate decision. "Tell them that a kel'en is here to speak with them."

The youngling blew air, fluttering, through its nostrils. "Come with me, then," it said, and cast him a disapproving glance, a flash of white, red-veined, from the corner of a rolling eye. It was—it, for regul could not determine their own gender until maturity—like all regul, a squat figure, body almost touching the floor even while it was standing. It was also a very young regul to have been given the (among regul) considerable honor of tending the Nom door. It still bore itself erect, bones showing through the skin, the brown, pebbly hide fine-grained yet and delicate with beige tones and a casting of metallic highlights. It walked beside him, a rolling gait that needed considerable leeway. "I am Hada Suraggi," it said, "secretary, guardian to the door. You are doubtless one of Intel's lot."

Niun simply did not answer this rudeness on the part of the tsi'mri guard, naming the she'pan by her name with such insolent familiarity. Among regul, elders would be *the reverence,* or *the honorable,* or *the lord* . . . , and he reckoned the familiarity for calculated insult, marking it down for a later date, if so happened he found himself holding what Hada Surag-gi desired. The youngling at present was doing what he wanted it to do, and this, between mri and tsi'mri, was sufficient.

Steel tracks ran the bowed edges of the walls, and a vehicle whispered past them at a speed so great the presence was only an instant. The tracks went everywhere, on the wall opposite the doors, and another and another vehicle passed, missing one another by a hand's breadth. He did not let himself appear amazed at such things.

And neither did he thank the youngling when it had shown him through a door and into a waiting room where another, seeming adult, kept a metal desk; he simply turned his back on the youngling when it had ceased to be of use, and heard it leave.

The official leaned back from its desk, cradling its body in the mobile chair that—amazingly—moved under power: another such vehicle, a gleaming steel device such as he had heard the adult regul used to move about without rising.

"We know you," the regul said. "You are Niun, from the Hill. Your elders have contacted us. You are ordered to return to your people immediately."

Heat rushed to his face. Of course they would have done this, forestalling him. He had not even thought of it.

"That does not matter," he said, carefully formal. "I am asking service with your ships. I renounce my edun."

The regul, a brown mass, folded and over-folded, its face a surprising bony smoothness within this weight, sighed and regarded him with small, wrinkle-edged eyes. "We hear what you say," it said. "But our treaty with your folk does not permit us to accept you with your elders protesting. Please return to them at once. We do not want to quarrel with your elders."

"Do you have a superior?" Niun asked harshly, out of patience and fast losing hope as well. "Let me speak to someone of higher authority."

"You ask to see the Director?"

"Yes."

The regul sighed again and made the request of an intercom: a grating voice refused, flatly. The regul looked up, rolling its eyes in an expression that was more satisfied and smug than apologetic. "You see," it said.

Niun turned on his heel and strode out of the office and out of the foyer, ignoring the amused eyes of the youngling Hada Surag-gi. He felt his face burning, his breath short as he exited the warm interior of the Nom and walked onto the public square, where the cold wind swept through the city.

He walked swiftly, as if he had a place to go and went there of his own will. He imagined that every regul on the street knew his shame and was laughing secretly. This was not beyond all possibility, for regul tended to know everyone's business.

He did not slow his pace until he was walking the long causeway back from the city's edge to the edun, and then indeed he walked slowly, and cared little for what passed his eyes or his hearing on the road. The open land, even on the causeway, was not a place where it was safe to go inattentive to surroundings, but he did so, tempting the Gods and the she'pan's anger. He was sorry that nothing did befall him and that, after all, he found himself walking the familiar earthen track to the entrance of the edun and entering its shadows and its echoes. He was sullen still as he walked to the stairs of the Kel tower and ascended, pushing open the door of the hall, reporting to kel'anth Eddan, dutiful prisoner.

"I am back," he said, and did not unveil.

Eddan had the rank and the self-righteousness to turn a naked face to his anger, and the self-possession to remain unstirred. *Old man, old man*, Niun could not help thinking, *the seta'al are one with the wrinkles on your face and your eyes are dimmed so that they already look into the Dark. You will keep me here until I am like you. Nine years, nine years, Eddan, and you have made me lose my dignity. What can you take from me in nine more?*

"You are back," echoed Eddan, who had been his principal teacher-in-arms, and who adopted that master/student manner with him. "What of it?"

Niun carefully unveiled, settled crosslegged to the floor near the warmth of the dus that slept in the corner. It eased aside, murmured a rumbling complaint at the disturbance of its sleep. "I would have gone," he said.

"You distressed the she'pan," Eddan said. "You will not go down to the city again. She forbids it."

He looked up, outraged.

"You embarrassed the House," Eddan said. "Consider that."

"Consider *me*," Niun exclaimed, exhausted. He saw the shock his outburst created in Eddan and cast the words out in reckless satisfaction. "It is unnatural, what you have done, keeping me here, I am due something in my life—something of my own, at least."

"Are you?" Eddan's soft voice was edged. "Who taught you that? Some regul in the city?"

Eddan stood still, hands within his belt, old master of the yin'ein, in that posture that chilled a man who knew its meaning: *here is challenge, if you want it.* He loved Eddan. That Eddan looked at him this way frightened him, made him reckon his skill against Eddan's; made him remember that Eddan could still humble him. There was a difference between him and the old master, that if Eddan's bluff were called, blood would flow for it.

And Eddan knew that difference in them. Heat rose to his face.

"I never asked to be treated differently from all the others," Niun declared, averting his face from Eddan's challenge.

"What do you think you are due?" Eddan asked him.

He could not answer.

"You have a soft spot in your defense," said Eddan. "A gaping hole. Go and consider that, Niun s'Intel, and when you have made up your mind what it is the People owe you, come and tell me and we will go to the Mother and present your case to her."

Eddan mocked him. The bitter thing was that he deserved it. He saw that this over-anxiousness was what had shamed him before the regul. He resumed the veil and gathered himself to his feet, to go outside.

"You have duties that are waiting," Eddan said sharply. "Dinner was held without you. Go and assist Liran at cleaning up. Tend to your own obligations before you consider what is owed to you."

"Sir," he said quietly, averted his face again and went his way below.

Chapter Three

————•◦•━━━◆━━━•◦•————

THE SHIP, a long voyage out from Elag/Haven, had shifted to the tedium that had possessed it before transition. Sten Duncan took a second look at the mainroom display and was disappointed to discover it had not yet noted the change. They had spent the longest normal-space passage he had ever endured getting out of Haven's militarily sensitive vicinity, blind and under tedious escort. That was suddenly gone. It was replaced likely by another passage as tedious. He shrugged and kept walking. The place smelled of regul. He held his breath as he passed the galley-automat, the door of which was open. He kept to the center of the corridor, scarcely noticing as a sled whisked past him; the corridors were built wide, high in the center and low on the sides, with gleaming rails recessed into the flooring to guide the conveyance sleds that the regul used to get about the long corridors of their ship.

It was not possible to forget for an instant that this ship was regul. The corridors did not angle or bow as they would in a human-made vessel; they wound, spiraled, amenable to the gliding course of the sleds that hugged the walls, and only a few of them could be walked. In those designed for walking, there was headroom in their center for humans—or for mri, who were the ordinary tenants of regul ships, but tracks ran the sides, for regul.

And about the whole ship there were strange scents, strange aromas of unpalatable food and spices, strange sounds, the rumbling tones of regul language that neither humans nor probably even mri had ever pronounced as regul might.

He loathed it. He loathed the regul utterly, and knowing

that that reaction was neither wise nor helpful in his position, he constantly fought against his instincts. It was clear enough that the reaction was mutual with the regul; they restricted their human guests to six hours in which they were supposedly free to roam the personnel areas to their hearts' content; and after that came a twenty-two-hour period of confinement.

Sten Duncan, aide to the honorable George Stavros, governor-to-be in the new territories and presently liaison between regul and humanity, regularly availed himself of that six-hour liberty; the Hon. Mr. Stavros did not—did not, in fact, venture from his own room. Duncan walked the corridors and gathered the appropriate materials and releases from the library for the honorable gentleman to read, and carried to the pneumatic dispatch whatever communications flowed from Stavros to Stavros' regul counterpart bai Hulagh Alagn-ni.

Regul protocol. No regul elder of dignity performed his own errands. Only a condemned incompetent lacked youngling servitors. Therefore no human of Stavros' rank would do so; and therefore Stavros had chosen an aide of apparent youth and fairly advanced rank, criteria that regul would use in selecting their own personal attendants.

He was, in effect, a servant. He provided Stavros a certain prestige. He ran errands. Back in the action that had taken Haven, he had held military rank. The regul knew this, which further enhanced Stavros' prestige.

Duncan gathered up the day's communications, laid others from Stavros down on the appropriate table, and delivered the food order to the slot that ultimately would find its way to the correct department, and bring an automated carrier to their door with the requested meal, at least as regul construed it, out of human-supplied foodstuffs that had come with them.

Like exotic pets, Duncan reflected with annoyance, with the regul trying, as far as convenient, to maintain an authentic environment. As in most wild-animal displays, the staging was transparently artificial.

He retraced his way down the hall, through the mainroom recreation area and library. He had never set eyes on any of the regul save the younglings that frequented this central personnel relaxation area. Curiously enough, neither had Stavros encountered Hulagh. Protocol again. It was likely that, in all the time they had yet to spend among regul, they would never meet the honorable, the reverence bai Hulagh Alagn-ni, only the younglings that served him as crew and aides and messengers.

Regul elders were virtually immobile; this was certain; and Hulagh was said to be of very extreme age. Duncan privately surmised that this helplessness was a source of embarrassment to the elderly regul in dealing face-to-face with non-regul, and that therefore they arranged to keep themselves in such total seclusion from outsiders.

Or perhaps they judged humans and mri unbearably ugly. It was certain that there was little that humans could find beautiful in the regul.

He opened the unlocked door that let him into the double suite he shared with Stavros. The anteroom was his, serving as sleeping quarters and all else he was supposed to desire during the long passage: regul revenge, he thought sourly, for human insistence on the long, slow escort. The reception salon and proper bedroom both belonged to Stavros. So did the sanitary facilities, which were in the adjoining bedroom and likewise not designed for human comfort: he wondered how Stavros, elderly as he was, coped with that. But it had not been deemed wise to make an issue of regul-human differences even in that detail. The theory was that the regul were *honoring* their guests by treating them precisely as if they were regul, down to the tradition of dealing only through youngling intermediaries, and the tradition that placed Duncan's own quarters uncomfortably in the tiny anteroom, between Stavros and the outer corridor.

Precious encouragement for confidence in regul civilization, Duncan thought sourly, when he thought about it: he was to defend the honorable human gentleman from harm, from contact with rude outsiders, from all unpleasantness. It seemed no insult to regul hospitality to assume that such rudenesses might be anticipated.

And Stavros remained a virtual prisoner of his exalted rank, pent within one room, without any contact with the outside save himself.

Duncan sealed the outer door and knocked on the inner, a formality preserved necessarily—first because listening regul (assuming regul listened, which they firmly believed) would not understand any informality between elder and youngling;

and second, because they had been at close quarters too long, and both of them cherished what privacy they could obtain from each other.

The door opened, controlled by Stavros' remote devices—incongruous to see a human, especially a frail and slight one, sitting in the massive chair-sled designed for regul elders. Desk, control center, mode of transportation: Stavros disdained to propel it across the room. Duncan went to him, presented the tapes and papers, and Stavros took them from him and began to deal with them at once, all without a smile or word of greeting or even a dismissal. Stavros had smiled a few times at the beginning of their association; he did not now. They lived under the continual witness of the regul. He was treated, he suspected, as if he were in truth a regul youngling, without courtesy and without consideration of himself as an individual: he hoped, at least, that this was the source of Stavros' coldness to him.

He knew that he was far from understanding such a man. He saw some qualities in Stavros that he respected: courage, for one. He thought that it must have taken a great deal of that to enter on such a mission at Stavros' age. An elderly human had been wanted, a diplomat who, aside from his duties as administrator of the new territories, could obtain greater respect from the regul that would be neighbors to humanity. Stavros had come out of retirement to take the assignment, not a strong man, or an imposing one physically. He was, Duncan had learned in their only intimate conversation, and that before boarding, a native of Kiluwa, one of the several casualties of the war in its earliest years; and that might explain something. Kiluwans were legendarily eccentric, of a fringe-area colony left too long on its own, peculiar in religion, in philosophy, in manners: like the regul, they had not believed in writing. For the years after Kiluwa's fall, Stavros had been in the XenBureau—retired to university life of late. He had children, had lost a grandson to the war at Elag/Haven. If Stavros hated regul either for Kiluwa or for the grandson's sake, he had never betrayed it. He seldom betrayed any emotion beyond a certain obsessive interest in the regul. Everything in Stavros was quiet; and there were depths and depths beneath that placidity.

The old man's pale eyes flashed up. "Good morning, Dun-

can," he said, and instantly returned to his studies. "Sit,"
he added. "Wait."

Duncan sat down, disappointed, and waited. He had nothing else to do. He would have gone mad already if he had
not had the ability to bear long silence and inactivity. He
watched Stavros work, wondering over again why the old
man had so determined to learn the regul tongue, which occupied his many hours. There were regul who spoke perfectly
idiomatic Basic. There always would be. But Stavros had
succeeded well enough on their voyage that now he could listen to the tape from the regul master of the ship, outlining
the day's schedules and information, and needed to glance
only occasionally at the supplied written translation—regul
propaganda, praising the elders of homeworld, Nurag, praising the correct management of the director of the ship—
Duncan found it all very dry, save for the small hints of the
progress the ship was making.

But from such things Stavros learned, and became fluent at
least in trivial courtesies—learned at a rate that began to
amaze Duncan. He could actually understand that confusion
of sound, that remained only confusion to Duncan.

Such a man, a scholar, an intelligent man, with grandchildren and great-grandchildren, had left everything human and
familiar, everything his long life had produced, and now took
a voyage with the enemy, into unknown space. Although a
governorship was a considerable inducement, the hazards for
Stavros were more than considerable. Duncan did not know
how old the man was: there had been rumors at Haven verg-
ing on the incredible. He did know that one of the great-
grandchildren was entering the military.

If Duncan had enjoyed any intimacy with Stavros he
would have been moved to ask him why he had come; he
dared not. But every time he was tempted to give way to the
pressures of their confinement, his own fear of the strangeness about them, he thought of the old man patiently
at his lessons and resigned himself to last it out.

He did not think that he contributed anything to Stavros,
be it companionship or service, only the necessary appearance of propriety in the regul's eyes. Stavros could have done
without him, for all the notice he paid him. Personnel had
chosen half a dozen men for interview, and he, one of the
Surface Tactical officers at Haven, had been the choice. He

still did not know why. He had admitted to his lack of qualifications for such a post: *Then he'll know that he has to take
orders,* Stavros had concluded in his presence. *Volunteer?*
Stavros had asked him then, as if this were a point of suspected insanity. *No, sir,* he had answered, the truth: *they
called in every SurTac in the Haven reach.* —*Pilot's rating?*
Stavros had asked. —*Yes,* he had said. —*Hold any grudge
against the regul?* Stavros asked. *No,* he had answered simply,
which was again the truth: he did not like them, but it was
not a grudge, it was war; it was all he knew. And Stavros had
read his record a second time in his presence and accepted
him.

It had sounded good at the time, fantastically desirable:
from a war where life expectancy was rated in missions
flown, and where he was reaching his statistical limit, to an
easy berth on a diplomatic flight under escort, with guaranteed retirement home and discharge in five years; discharge at
less than thirty on a pension larger than any SurTac could
reasonably dream of, or—and this was the thing that Duncan
pondered with most interest—permanent attachment to a new
colonial directorate, permanent assignment to Stavros' territories, wealth and prominence on a developing world. It was a
prize for which men would kill or die. He had only to endure
regul company for a while in either case, and to win Stavros'
approval by his service. He had five years to accomplish the
latter. He meant to do it.

He had not been much frightened when he stepped aboard
the regul ship: he had read the data known on the regul,
knew them for noncombative, nonviolent by preference, a
basically timid species. The warrior mri had done their fighting for them, and provoked further conflicts, and finally the
regul had called the mri into retreat, gotten them under firm
control. New regul were in power on their homeworld now, a
pacifist party, which also controlled the ship on which they
were travelling and the world to which they were bound.

But he had learned a different kind of fear over the long
slow voyage, a sullen, biding sort of fear; and he began to
suspect why they had wanted a SurTac as Stavros' companion: he was trained for alien environment, inured to solitude
and uncertainties, and above all he was ignorant of higher
policies. If something went wrong, and he began to appreciate ways in which it could, then Stavros was the only con-

siderable expenditure; but Sten Duncan was nothing, military personnel, without kin to notify, a loss that could be written off without worry. His low classification number signified that he could spill everything he knew to an enemy without damage to any essential installations; and Stavros himself had been long secluded in the university community of New Kiluwa.

Perhaps—the thought occurred to him—Stavros himself was capable of expending him promptly if he proved inconvenient. Stavros was a diplomat, of that breed that Duncan instinctively mistrusted, that disposed of the likes of Sten Duncan by their hundreds and thousands in war. Perhaps it was that which had stolen away Stavros' inclination to talk to him as if he were anything more than the furnishings. Regul dealt with rebellious younglings, even with inconvenient younglings, instantly and without mercy, as if they were an easily replaceable commodity.

It was a nightborn fear, the kind that grew in the dark, in those too-long hours when he lay on his bed and considered that beyond the one door was an alien guard whose very life processes he did not understand; and beyond the other was a human whose mind he did not understand, an old man who was learning to think like the regul, whose elders were a terror to the young.

But when they were in day-cycle, together, when he considered Stavros face to face, he could not believe seriously such things as he thought and imagined at night. So long pent up, so long under such stress, it was no strange thing that his mind should turn to nameless and irrational apprehensions.

He only wished that he knew what Stavros hoped he was doing, or what Stavros expected him to do.

The tape loop cycled its third time through. Duncan knew its salutation, at least, the few words in the regul language he knew. Stavros was listening and memorizing. Shortly he would be able to recite the whole thing from memory.

"Sir," he interrupted Stavros' thoughts cautiously, "sir, our—" the tape went off, "our allotted liberty is just about up if you want anything else from the library or the dispensary."

He wished Stavros would think of something he needed. He longed to enjoy that precious time outside their quarters, to walk, to move; but Stavros had forbidden him to loiter anywhere in regul view, or to attempt any exchange with any

of the crew. Duncan understood the reasoning behind that
prohibition, a sensible precaution, a preservation of human
mystique as far as regul were concerned: *Let them wonder
what we think,* Stavros would say to many a situation. But it
was unbearable to sit here while the liberty ran out, with the
ship newly arrived in regul space.

"No," said Stavros, dashing his hopes. Then, perhaps an af-
terthought, he handed him one of the tapes. "Here. An excuse. Look like you have important business and stay to it.
Find me the next in sequence and bring both back. Enjoy
your walk."

"Yes, sir." He rose, moved to thank the old man, to appreciate his understanding of his misery; but Stavros started the
tape again, looked elsewhere, making it awkward. He hesitated, then left, through his own room, to the outside.

He drew a few deep breaths to accustom himself to the
taint of the air, felt less confined at once, even faced with the
narrow halls. Regul living spaces were small, barren places,
accommodating only space for a sled's operation; most things
were grouped within reach of someone sitting. He suppressed
the desire to stretch, settled himself into a sedate walk, and
headed for mainroom through a corridor that was utterly
empty of regul.

Mainroom served all personnel for recreation and study; it
was the library terminal also. Simpler, Duncan thought, to
have included a library linkup to the console already in their
quarters and obviate the need for them coming out at all, but
he was desperately glad that they had not. It provided an excuse, as Stavros had said. And perhaps there were restrictions
on some passengers who could read and understand more
than they. He did not know. He studied the twisting regul
numbers on the cartridge he carried and carefully punched
the keys next in sequence.

Machinery clicked, the least delay, and the desired cartridge shot into position. He provided the library with their
special code, which changed the alphabet module, and, noti-
fied that humans desired the cartridge in question, the library
flurried through authorizations, probably went through another process to decide that printout was supposed to accompany the cartridge—actually three forms of printout, literal,
transliterated and translated came with each—and finally
from its microstorage it began to produce the printouts.

Duncan paced the room while the machine processed the print sheet by sheet and checked the time: close. He walked back to the machine and it was still working, slower than any human-made processing system he had used. It had reactions like those of the regul themselves, sluggish. To fill the seconds he counted the changes in the viewscreen mockup that was the center of the library wall. It showed their course through human space, curiously never once acknowledging the presence of the armed escort vessels that had been the source of so much controversy. It was out of date as of this morning. At every pulse it cycled through to other views, to landscapes fascinating in their alien character (carefully censored, he was sure, lest they learn too much of regul; there were no living things and no cities and structures in the views) to starfields, back to the progress mockup. It dominated the room. He had watched it change day by slow day during their approach to jump. He had ceased to think of the voyage as one with a particular destination. Their peculiar isolation had become an environment in itself that could not be mentally connected to the life he had lived before and from which it was impossible to imagine the life he would live after. They had only the regul's word for where they were going.

He watched through three such cyclings and turned back to the machine, which had stopped in the middle of its printing, flashing the Priority signal. Someone of authority had interrupted it to obtain something more important. His materials were frozen in the machine's grip. He pushed the cancel button to retrieve the cartridge, and nothing happened. The Priority was still flashing, while the library did what it was commanded to do from some other source.

He swore and looked again at the time. The printout was half in the tray, the tail of it still in the machine. He could go and keep scrupulously to the schedule or he could wait the little time it would take for the machine to clear. He decided to wait. Probably the stall was because of the printout, an unwieldy and awkward operation, printout surely a rare function of their library apparatus, inefficiently done. The rumor used to be that regul themselves did not write at all, which was not, as they had discovered, true. They had an elaborate and intricate written language. But the library was designed for audio replication. The majority of regul materials were oral-aural. It was said, and this seemed true according to their own observations, that the regul did not need to hear any tape more than once.

Instant and total recall. Eidetic memory. The word *lie* was, he remembered Stavros telling him, fraught with associate concepts of perversion and murder.

A species that could neither forget nor unlearn.

If this were so, it was possible that they could depend on the exact truth from the regul at all times.

It was also possible that a species that could not lie might have learned ways of deception without it.

He did not need to wonder how regul regarded humans, who placed great emphasis on the written word, who had to be provided special and separate materials to comprehend slowly what regul absorbed at a single hearing; who could not learn the regul language, while regul learned human speech as rapidly as they could be provided words, and never needed to be told twice.

When he thought of this, and of the regul younglings, so helplessly slow, so ponderous in their movements, and yet the piggish little eyes glittering with some emotion that wrinkled the corners when they beheld a human, he grew uneasy, remembering that these same younglings, unless murdered by their own parent, would live through several human lifetimes and remember every instant of it; and that bai Hulagh, who commanded them and the ship and the zone where they were bound, had done so.

He resented both their long lives and their exact memories. He resented the obstinacy of their ubiquitous machines, the bigotry and insolence that kept them confined and tightly scheduled as they were, surrounded by automation that made their regul hosts more than the physical equals of humans; and with all the accumulating frustration of long imprisonment, he resented most of all the petty irritations that were constantly placed in their way by their regul hosts, who clearly despised humans for their mental shortcomings.

Stavros was headed for failure if he sought accommodation with such neighbors. It was a mortal mistake to think that a human could become regul, that he won anything at all by slavishly imitating the manners of beings that despised them.

That was the worm that had eaten at his gut ever since the first days of this chromium-plated, silken-soft imprisonment.

All about them were regul and regul machines, hulking beasts
helpless but for that automation, like great shapeless parasites
living attached to appliances of steel and chromium; and
Stavros was utterly, dangerously wrong if he thought he became esteemed of regul by giving up the few advantages that
humans had. The regul looked with contempt on the species
whose minds forgot, whose knowledge was on film and paper.

He sought to say this to Stavros, but he could not come
close enough to the man to advise him. Stavros was an edu-
cated man; he was not: he was only an experienced one, and
experience cried out that they were in a dangerous situation.

He struck the library panel a blow with his hand, for the
time was out and he was defeated by the monstrosity—incredible that the thing could be so slow. It was as futile and
thoughtless as jostling any human-made machine; but he
knew in the second after that he should not have done it, and
when the Priority signal at once went off, he was for an instant terrified, believing that he had caused it somehow, an-
tagonizing some high-ranking regul.

But the machine started to feed out the rest of the paper
and shot the cartridge out in good order after, and he paused
to gather them up. And when, in turning to leave, he looked
up at the panel, he saw that the whole display had changed,
and that they had before them the visual of a star system
with seven planets, with their ship plotted in toward the second.

Their final destination.

As he watched, he saw another ship indicated on the simu-
lation, moving outward on a nonintersecting course. They
were in-system, in inhabited, trafficked regions, nearing Kesrith. Time began to move again. His heart quickened with
the elating surety that they had indeed arrived where they
were supposed to, that they were near their new world. Coming in to dock at Kesrith's station would be a process of more
than a week, by that diagram, but they were coming in.

The imprisonment was almost over.

A step sounded in the corridor to his left. For an instant
he ignored it, knowing that he was overtime and expecting a
surly rebuke from a youngling; and the ominous character of
it had not registered. Then it struck him that it did not belong here, the measured tread of boots on the flooring, not
the slow scuffing of the regul nor even Stavros' fragile tread.

He turned, frightened even before he looked, by a presence that was not of them nor of the regul.

And he faced a figure that had likewise stopped still, one robed in black, the robes glittering with many small discs. Mri. Kel'en. The golden eyes above the veil were astonished. A slim bronze hand went to the knife at his belt and hesitated there.

For a moment yet neither moved, and it was possible to hear only the slow changes of the projector.

The enemy. The destroyers of Kiluwa and Talos and Asgard. He had never seen one in the flesh at this range. Only the eyes, the hands were uncovered. The tall figure remained utterly still, wrapped in menace and in anger.

"I am Sten Duncan," he found courage to say, doubting that the mri could understand a word, but reckoning it time words intervened before weapons did. "I'm the assistant to the Federations envoy."

"I am kel Medai," said the other in excellent Basic, "and we should not have met."

And with that the mri turned on his heel and stalked off in the direction from which he had come, a black figure that vanished into shadows at the turning of the corridor. Duncan found himself trembling in every muscle. He had seen mri that close only in photographs, and all of those were dead.

Beautiful, was the strange descriptive that came to his mind, seeing the mri warrior: he would have thought it of an animal, splendid of its kind, and deadly.

He turned, and the blood that had resumed somewhat its normal circulation drained a second time, for a regul youngling stood in the mainroom, its nostrils flaring and shutting in rapid agitation.

It shrilled a warning at him, anger, terror: he could not tell which. Its color went to livid pallor. "Go to quarters," it insisted. "Past time. Go to quarters. Now!"

He moved, edged past the regul and hurried, not looking back. When he reached the sanctuary of his own doorway his hands were shaking, and he thrust himself through even while it was opening, then shut it at once, anxious until the seal had hissed into function. Then he sank down on his cot, knowing that, all too quickly, he must face Stavros and give an account of what he had done. The library materials tumbled from his cold hands and some of the papers fell on the floor. He bent and gathered them up, feeling nothing with his fingers.

He had committed a great mistake, and knew that it was not to be the end of it.

They were going to the world that was said to be the mri homeworld, to Kesrith of the star Arain.

Regul claimed title to it, all the same, and the right to cede it to humans. They claimed the authority to command the mri and to sign for them.

They betrayed the mri, and yet carried a kel'en on the ship that brought the orders that turned Kesrith over to humans.

We should not have met, the mri had said.

It was obvious that the regul at least, and possibly the mri, had not intended the meeting. Someone was being deceived.

He gathered himself up and expelled a long breath, rapped on Stavros' door and entered this time without permission.

Chapter Four

ANOTHER of the ships was leaving this evening, one of the several shuttles that ferried passengers and goods from the surface of Kesrith up to the station—and thence to starships: to freighters, liners, warships—anything that would remove panicked regul from the path of humans.

Niun watched, as he was accustomed to watch each evening, from that high rock that overlooked the sea and the flats and the city. It was true. He had accepted the fact of the war's end at last, although a sense of unreality still possessed him as he watched the ships go—never so frequent, not in his lifetime, nor, he thought, in that of his elders. The fact was that the regul city was dying, its life ebbing with every outbound ship. He obeyed the she'pan's order and did not go near the city or the port, but he thought if he were to go down now into the square, he would find many of the buildings empty and stripped of things of value; and day after day, by the road that wound along the seashore, the merest line visible from his vantage point, he could see traffic coming into the city, bringing regul from the outlying towns and stations; aircraft came to the city, and fewer and fewer left it again. He had a mental image of a vast heap of abandoned regul vehicles at the edge of town, of ships at the port. They would have to drag them into heaps and let them rust.

It was rumored—so Sathell had gleaned from regul communications—that the chief price of the peace the regul had bought had been the cession of every colony in the Kesrith reach.

Tsi'mri economics had finally proven more powerful than the weapons of the Kel, more important, surely, than the honor of the mri in the regul's estimation. Kesrith was a loss to the regul, to be sure, a mining and transport site, expensively automated; doubtless to lose such a colony was embarrassing to the regul elders; doubtless it was inconvenient for their business and commerce; doubtless for the regul in those fleeing ships the inconvenience ascended to tragedy. Regul valued many peculiar objects; variance in the quality and amount of these and their clothing and their comforts betokened personal worth in their eyes; and the loss of their homes and valued objects that could not be taken onto the ships would be grievous for them; but they had no Revered Objects, nothing that could afflict them to the degree that the loss of homeworld could affect the People; and the honors they coveted could be purchased anew if they were fortunate—unlike mri honors, that had to be won.

And therein Niun did not muster any great sympathy for any of them. His personal loss was great enough: all the life he had planned and desired for himself was departing from possibility with the violence and speed of those outbound ships. The migration had become a rout, night and day; and events gave clear proof that the personal plans of Niun s'Intel Zain-Abrin were nothing to the powers that moved the worlds. But the threat to the House: that was beyond his power to imagine; and that the powers that moved the worlds had no concern for the fate of the People—that was beyond all understanding.

He had tried to adjust his mind to this change in fortunes.

Where shall we make our defense? he had asked of Eddan and the kel'ein, assuming, as he assumed that sanity rested with his people, that there was to be a defense of homeworld, of the Edun of the People.

But Eddan had turned his face from his question, gesturing his refusal to answer it; and in the failure of the Kel, he had dared ask the she'pan herself. And Intel had looked at him with a strange sorrow, as if her last son were somehow lacking in essential understanding; but gently she had spoken to him in generalities of patience and courage, and carefully she had declined to give any direct answer to his question.

And day by day the regul ships departed, without mri kel'ein aboard. The she'pan forbade.

He was watching the end. He understood that now, at least

that. Of what it was an end he was not yet sure; but he knew the taste of finality, and that of the things he had desired all his life there was left him nothing. The regul departed, and hereafter came humans.

He wished now desperately that he had applied himself with even more zeal to his study of human ways, so that he could understand what the humans were likely to do. Perhaps the elder kel'ein, who had such experience with them, knew; and perhaps therefore they thought that he should know, and would not reward ignorance with explanation. Or perhaps they were as helpless as he and refused to admit the obvious to him; he could not blame them for that. It was that he simply could not admit that there was nothing to be done, that there were no preparations to be made, while the regul so desperately, so anxiously sought safety. He knew, with what faith remained to him in his diminishing store of things trustworthy, that the Kel would resist in the end; but they were to die, if that were the case. Their skill was great, greater than that of any kel'ein living, he believed; but the nine were also very old and very few to stand for long against the mass attacks of humans.

The imagination came to him over and over again, as horrid and unreal as the departure of regul from his life—of humans arriving, of human language and human tread echoing in the sanctity of the edun shrine, of fire and blood and ten desperate kel'ein trying to defend the she'pan from a horde of defiling humans.

Brothers, sister, he longed to ask the kel'ein, *is it possible that there is some hope that I cannot see?* And then again he thought: *Or, o gods, is it possible that we have a she'pan who has gone mad? Brothers, sister, look, look, the ships!—our way off Kesrith. Make our she'pan see reason. She has forgotten that there are some here who want to live.* But he could not say such things to his elders, to Eddan; and he would ultimately have to account for those words to Intel's face, and he could not bear that. He could not reason with them, could not discuss anything as they did among themselves, in secret: they, she—all save Melein and himself—remembered Nisren's days, the life before the war. They had taken regul help once, escaping the ruin of Nisren, and refused it now, resolved together in councils from which he, not of the Husbands, was excluded. He insisted on believing that his elders were rational. They were too calm, too sure, to be mad.

Forty-three years ago, the like had come to Nisren. A regul ship, rescuing she'pan Intel, had carried the holy Pana and the survivors of the edun to Kesrith. The elders did not speak of that day, scarcely even in songs: it was a pain written in their visible scars and in the secrecies of their silence.

Shame? he wondered, heart-torn at thinking ill of them. *Shame at something they did or did not do on Nisren? Shame at living, and unwillingness to survive another fall of Home-world?* Sometimes he suspected, with dread growing and gnawing in him like some alien parasite, that such was the case, that he belonged to a she'pan that had wearied of running, to an edun that had consciously made up its mind to die.

An edun which held the Pana, the Revered, the Objects of mri honor and mri history, to behold which was for the Sen alone, to touch which unbidden was to die; to lose which—

To lose the relics of the People—

It betokened the death, not alone of the edun, but of the People as a race. He held the thought a moment, turned it within his mind, then cast it aside in haste, and fearfully picked it up again.

O gods, he thought, mind numbed by the very concept, Another shuttle lifted. He saw it rise, up, up, a star that moved.

O gods, o gods.

It was *shon'ai,* the Passing-game. It was the flash of blades in the dark, the deadly game of rhythm and bluff and threat and reckless risk.

The Game of the People.

The blades were thrown. Existence was gambled on one's quickness and wit and nerve, for no other reason than to deserve survival.

He felt the blood drain from his face to his belly, understanding why they had looked through him when he asked his vain questions.

Join the rhythm, child of the People: be one with it; accept, accept, accept.

Shon'ai!

He cried aloud, and understood all at once. All over known space mri would react to the throw the she'pan of Kesrith had made. They would come, they would come, from all quarters of space, to fight, to resist.

The Pana was set in the keeping of Edun Kesrithun.

The circle was wide and the blades flew at seeming random, but each game tended to develop its unique pattern, and wisest the player who did not become hypnotized by it.

Intel had cast. It was for others to return the throw.

The first of Kesrith's twin moons had brightened to the point of visibility. The stars became a dusty belt across the sky. The air grew chill, but he felt no impulse to return to the edun, to resume the mundane routine of their existence. Not this evening. Not upon such thoughts as he carried. Eventually the kel'ein would miss him, and look out and see him in his favorite place, and let him be. He spent many evenings here. There was nothing to do in the edun of evenings, save to sleep, to eat, to study things no longer true. None of them had sung the songs since the day the news of the war's end came. They frequently sat and talked together, excluding him. Probably, he thought, it was a relief to them to have him gone.

The geyser named Sochau belched steam far across the flats, a tall plume, predictable as the hours of any regul clock. By such rhythms the world lived, and by such rhythms it measured the days until the humans should come.

But for the first time in all the days since he had heard of the war's ending, he felt a suspicion of gladness, a fierce sense that the People might have something yet to do, and that humans might find their victory not an accomplished fact.

A star grew in the sky as the other had departed, rapid and omen-filled. He looked up at it with quickening interest, enlivened by something, even a triviality, that was not part of the ordinary. The shuttles did not usually descend until morning.

He watched it grow, cherishing imaginings both dread and hopeful, a mere child's game, for he did not really believe that it would be anything but a variance in regul schedules for regul reasons, as ordinary as anything could be in the organized routine of Kesrith's dying.

He watched it descend and saw suddenly lights flare on at the port in the farthest area, realized suddenly that it was not coming down at the freighter or shuttle berths, but to the area given over to military landings, and it was no shuttle. It was a ship of size, such as the onworld port had not held in many years.

The ship was nothing in the dark and the distance but a shape of light, featureless, nameless. There was nothing to indicate what it was. Of a sudden he knew his people must have word of this—that doubtless they had already been alert to it and only he had not been.

He sprang down from his rock and began to run, swift feet changing course here and there at the outset where the fragile earth masked dangers of its own. He did not use the road, but ran crosslands, by an old mri trail, and came breathless to the door of the edun, chest aching.

There was silence in the halls. He paused only a moment, then took the stairs toward the she'pan's tower, almost running up the first turn.

And there a shadow met him—old Dahacha coming down, Dahacha with his great, surly dus lumbering downsteps after him. Everyone brought up short, and the dus edged down a step to rumble a warning.

"Niun," the old man said. "I was coming to look for you."

"There is a ship," Niun began.

"No news here," said Dahacha. *"Hazan* is back. Yai! Come on up, young one. You are missed."

Niun followed, a great joy in him: *Hazan*—command ship for the zone; and high time it came, among regul panicked and retreating in disorder. There was resolution in the regul after all, some authority to hold the disintegrating situation under control.

And *Hazan!* If *Hazan* came, then came Medai—cousin, fellow kel'en, home from human wars and bringing with him experience and all the common sense that belonged to the fighting Kel of the front.

He remembered other things of Medai too, things less beloved; but it made no difference after six years, with the world falling into chaos. He followed Dahacha up the winding stairs with an absolute elation flooding through him.

Another kel'en.

A man the others would listen to as they would never listen to him, who had never left the world.

Medai, who had served with the leaders of regul and knew their minds as few kel'ein had the opportunity to know them—kel'en to the ship of the bai of Kesrith zones.

Chapter Five

———•◦•◆•◦•———

THE DOOR was locked, as it was at every unpermitted period. Sten Duncan tried it yet another time, knowing it was useless, pounded his fist against it and went back to the old man.

"They refused to answer," said Stavros. He sat in the desk-chair, with the console screen at his left elbow a mono-tone grey. He looked uneasy, unusual for Stavros, even at the worst of times.

They were down, onworld. That was unmistakable.

"We were to dock," said Duncan finally, voicing the merest part of the concern boiling in his mind.

Stavros did not react to that piece of observation, only stared at him dispassionately. Duncan read blame into it.

"If there's been a change in plans, something could be wrong either on the station or onworld," Duncan said, trying to draw the smallest reassurance from the old man, a denial of his apprehensions—even outright anger. He could deal with that.

And when Stavros gave him nothing at all in reply he sank down at the table, head bowed against his hands, exhausted with the strain of waiting. It was their night. It was halfway through that night.

"Perhaps they're sleeping," Stavros said unexpectedly, star-tling him with a tone that held nothing of rancor. "If they chose to keep ship-cycle after landing, or if we're in local night, bai Hulagh could be asleep and his orderlies unwilling to respond to us without his authority. The regul do not in-convenience an elder of his rank."

Duncan looked back at him, not believing the explanation, but glad that Stavros had made the gesture, whether or not he had another in the back of his mind that he was not saying. It did not ease his feelings in the least that Stavros had never said anything to him in the matter of the encounter with the mri, had only asked quiet questions of what had happened there in the mainroom: no blame, no hint of what had passed in Stavros' mind. Nor had Stavros said anything when they were shortly afterward presented with another schedule, their hours of liberty cut in half, a regul youngling constantly watching their door and following at a distance when he left the room.

The retaliation fell most heavily on himself, of course, confining him more closely, while that did not much concern Stavros; but for their safety and for the future of regul/human cooperation it augured ill enough. The regul's official manner did not change toward them. There was still the formal manner, still the salutations in the day's messages. Characteristic of the regul, there had been no direct mention of the incident in the hall, only the notification, without explanation, that their hours had been changed.

"I'm sorry, sir," Duncan volunteered at last, out of his own frustration.

Stavros looked for once surprised, then frowned and shrugged. "Probably just regul procedure and some minor change in plans. Don't worry about it." And then with a second shrug, "Get some sleep, Duncan. There's little else to do at the moment."

"Yes, sir," he said, rose and went out to the anteroom, sat down on his own bunk and tucked his legs up. He set his elbows on his knees and head on his hands and massaged his aching temples.

Prisoners, thanks to him.

Stavros was worried. Stavros doubtless knew what there was to concern them and he was worried. Perhaps if the regul had accepted the offering, Stavros could have demonstrated the punishment of the human youngling who had created the difficulty. Perhaps he had not done so because, in the main, they were both human and Stavros felt an unvoiced attachment to him; or perhaps he had declined to do so because a regul elder would not have done so under the same circumstances.

But it was clear enough that they were under the heavy shadow of regul displeasure, and had been for many, many

days; and that they were not now where they had been told
at the outset they would land.

A sound reached him, a sound of someone passing in the
corridor, one of the sleds whisking along the tracks outside.
He looked up as it seemed to stop, hoping against hope that
the thing had stopped to bring them news.

The door opened. He sprang up, instantly correct. The sled
indeed had stopped before the doorway, and within it sat the
oldest, most massive regul that he had ever seen. Roll upon
roll of wrinkled flesh and crusting skin hid any hint of structure that lay within that grey-brown body, save the bony plat-
ing of the face, where eyes were sunk in circular wrinkles,
black and glittering eyes; and flat nose and slit mouth gave a
deceptive illusion of humanity.

It was the face of a man within the body of a beast, and
that body was lapped in brown robes, silver-edged and shim-
mering, gossamer enfolding a gross and wrinkle-crossed skin.
The nostrils were slanted, slits that could flare and close. He
knew this movement for an indication of emotion in the
younglings, one of the few expressions of which their bone-
shielded faces were capable—a roll of the eyes, an opening or
closing of the lips, a flutter of the nostrils. But had he not
known that this being was of precisely the same species as the
younglings, he would have doubted it.

Incredibly the elder arose, heaving his body upright, then
standing, on bowed and almost invisible legs, within the sled.

"Stavros," it—he—said, a basso rumble.

Humans could not imitate regul expression: the regul perhaps could not read courtesy or lack of it among humans, but
Duncan knew that courtesy was called for now. He made a
bow. "Favor," he said in the regul tongue, "I am the youngling Sten Duncan."

"Call Stavros."

But the door was open. Duncan turned, about to comply
with the order, and saw of a sudden Stavros in the doorway,
standing, coming no farther.

There was a rumbling exchange of regul politenesses, and
Duncan took himself to the side of the room against the wall,
bewildered in the flow of language. He realized what he had
suspected already, that this was the bai himself who had
come to call on them, bai Hulagh Alagn-ni, high commander
of the ship *Hazan*, successor to the Holn, and provisional

governor of Kesrith's zones during the transfer of powers from regul to human.

He made himself unnoticed; he would not offend a second time against regul manners, complicating things which he could not understand.

The exchange was brief. It was concluded with a series of courtesies and gestures, and the bai subsided into his sled and vanished, and Stavros closed the door for himself, before Duncan could free himself of his confusion and do so.

"Sir?" Duncan ventured then.

Stavros took his time answering. He looked around finally, with a sober and uneasy espression. "We are grounded on Kesrith," he said. "The bai assures us this is quite a natural choice for a ship of this sort, landing directly at the port—that it was a last-moment decision and without reason for concern to us. But I also gather that there is some instability here, which I do not understand. The bai wants us to remain on the ship. Temporary, he says."

"Is it," Duncan asked, "trouble over that business with the mri?"

Stavros shook his head. "I don't know. I don't know. I think that the whole crew is expected to remain aboard until things sort themselves out. This, at least—" Stavros' eyes went to the ceiling, toward venting, toward lighting, toward installations they did not understand and did not trust. The glance warned, said nothing, carried some misgiving that perhaps he would have voiced if he were safe to do so. "The bai assures us that we will be taken to the central headquarters in the morning. It is planetary night at the moment; we are already on Kesrith main time, and he advises us that the weather is fair and the inconvenience minor and we are expected to enjoy our night's rest and rise late, with the anticipation of a pleasant advent to Kesrith."

The bai is being courteous and formal, Stavros' expression thrust through the words themselves. There was no credibility there. Duncan nodded understanding.

"Good night, then," said Stavros, as if the exchange had been aloud. "I think we may trust that we are delayed aboard for some considerable number of hours, and there is probably time to get a night's sleep."

"Good night, sir," said Duncan, and watched as the old man went back to his quarters and the door closed.

He wished, not for the first time, that he could ask the old man plainly what he thought of matters, and that he could reckon how much the honorable Stavros believed of what he had been told.

In the time that they had been on scant favor among regul, Duncan had begun to apply himself to learning the regul tongue with the same fervent, desperate application he had once applied to SurTac arms and survival skills. He had begun with rote phrases and proceeded to structure with a facility far above what he had ever imagined he could achieve. He was not a scholar; he was a frightened man. He began to think, with the nightmare concentration that fears acquired in their solitude, that Stavros was indeed very old, and the time before humans would arrive was considerable, and that regul, who disposed of their own younglings so readily, would think nothing of killing a human youngling that had survived his elder, if that human youngling seemed useless to them.

Stavros' age, that had been the reason for his being assigned this mission, was also against its success. If something should befall the Hon. Mr. Stavros, it would leave Duncan himself helpless, unable to communicate with the general run of younglings, and, as Stavros had once pointed out, regul younglings would not admit him to contact with the likes of bai Hulagh, who were the only regul capable of fluent human speech.

It was not a possibility he cared to contemplate, the day that he should be left alone to deal with regul.

With hours left before debarkation on Kesrith, and with his nerves too taut to allow sleep, he gathered up his notes and started to study with an application that had his gut in knots.

Dag—Favor, please, attention. The same syllable, pronounced instead with the timbre of a steam whistle, meant: honorable; and in shrill tone: blood. *Dag su-gl'inh-an-ant pru nnugk*—May I have indirect contact with the reverence. . . . *Dag nuc-ci:* Favor, sir.

He studied until he found the notes falling from his nerveless hands, and collapsed to sleep for a precious time, before regul orderlies opened the door without warning and began shrilling orders at him, rudely snatching up their baggage without a prior courtesy.

None of the courtesies did these youngling regul use with

him, even when he protested their rough handling of their belongings; they maintained a surly silence toward him, a fe-
vered haste, interspersed with a chittering among themselves,
as they loaded baggage on the transport sled that was to
carry it away; another vehicle waited, a passenger sled.

"Now, now," one said, probably the extent of the human
vocabulary he had troubled to hear, urging their haste; and
only when Stavros himself appeared did the younglings assume decorum.

Even an elder human had his honor from the regul: they
seemed to regard Stavros with a healthy fear.

But Duncan, when he looked back as they were boarding,
chanced to look directly into the face of one of the younglings that bent, assisting them into the sled, and nostrils
snapped shut and lips clamped, a look of hate that transcend-
ed species.

They were on Kesrith, among regul, who would be their
companions and counselors in dealing with the evacuation of
other regul who had made their homes here for centuries.
They had come to take this world as conquerors, conquerors
who, at least for thirty days, were only two, and vulnerable.
The world had belonged to regul and to mri; and it was likely
that certain of the crew of *Hazan* had called Kesrith their
home.

It dawned upon him with immediacy that there could be
more than simple racial or political hatred among regul
toward their presence on Kesrith.

And perhaps there were many residents on Kesrith who
had never consented to the treaty that disposed of their world
and brought humans to it.

The inconvenience is minor, Stavros had translated the
bai's assurance. Perhaps in the bai's eyes it was minor: the
regul were not supposed to be able to lie; but in the eyes of
the regul younglings that attended them there was no lie either, and it told a different story.

While they were on Kesrith, they would be housed in a
building called the Nom, in the center of the chief city of
Kesrith, and they would be thus protected for the first and
most critical days against the irritations of Kesrith's natural
atmosphere and the other minor inconveniences of the local
climate: they would be expected to adapt.

And he saw Stavros' face when they first broke out of the ship's warmth into the wide world, and had their first sight of the place: hills, mountains, white plains, strangely lit by a ruddy pink sun.

For Stavros this was home, forever. His assignment was to prepare for other humans, to direct them after they had come, to build civilization again; and already Duncan was considering that five years here might be a very long time.

Regul, and alkali flats, and geysers, dust and mines and a sun that looked sickly and too large in the sky. He had been on half a score of worlds in his travels in the service, from bare balls of rock to flowering wildernesses, but he had never been on one so immediately alien as Kesrith.

Forbidding, unfriendly to humans. The very air smelled poisonous, laden with irritants.

If Stavros felt regret, he did not show it. He let himself be handled like a regul elder, already playing the part, and the younglings handed him down to the land sled that waited below. It was well after dawn, the sun a quarter of the way up the sky. There was, instead of the welcome they had expected—like most regul courtesies, carefully controlled and managed—a still and ghostly quiet about the port, as if they and the younglings were the only living things about the premises.

And far away, on the heights, was visible something that set Duncan's heart to beating more rapidly, a clutch of fear at the stomach that had nothing to do with reason, for there was the peculiar silhouette of four slanted towers that formed a flat-topped, irregular pyramid.

A mri edun. He had known there was one onworld. He had seen pictures of the ruins of Nisren. He was unprepared for it to be here, so close. It overlooked the city in such a way that nothing that was done on the plains could be hidden from it.

It brooded, an ominous and alien presence, reminding them all that there was a third party to the transaction that promised peace.

"Now. Now!" the regul repeated, impatient of the delay or at the object of his attention, it was unsure; but Duncan did not want to contest the matter, and he lowered his head and entered the sled, where the air was filtered and cleaned of the acrid biting taste that contaminated the air of Kesrith.

The sled lumbered off toward the city on pavement made rough by inroads of sand from the flats, taking them to what he thought with increasing conviction was a confinement only wider in space than their last.

Chapter Six

———••———••———

THE SUN was climbing the east, and on another day Niun would have been out about the hills, walking, hunting, practicing at arms, all other such things as he used to fill the solitary hours and relieve the sameness of his days.

But on this day nothing could have persuaded him from the vicinity of the edun. He haunted the communications station in the top of the Sen tower, where, in an edun grown informal by reason of its small size, he was permitted to be on occasion; he hovered about the main entrance; and finally, consumed by his impatience, he went to the rock at the top of the causeway, to stare into the growing glare off the white flats and strain his eyes for any movement from the direction of the port.

He had for so very, very long had nothing good to anticipate. Now he savored the feeling, hating the waiting, and yet relishing the feeling of waiting: with mixed feelings about the meeting, and yet longing desperately for the comradeship it promised. He had not loved Medai. He remembered the rivalry with his cousin, his—he could be honest with himself after so many years—jealousy of his cousin; and he strove to forget any such feelings he had ever cherished: he wanted Medai's presence, wanted it desperately, fervently. Anything was better than this long loneliness, this knowledge that the edun was slowly, irrevocably perishing.

And there was, at the foundation of all the thoughts, the least stirring of hope, the suspicion that Medai had been summoned, that he was the first of many to come—that the she'pan had stirred to action, and that something was moving in the future of the People.

On a thousand previous days, he had sat as he sat now,

54

seeking any tiny deviation in events to occupy him, the struggles of an insect, the slow, perilous blooming of a windflower, the rise or descent of ships at the port—ill-wishing such ships, imagining disasters, imagining important arrivals that would somehow change the pattern of his existence. He had done this so often that it was hard to realize that this time it was real, that the game was substance on this morning so like a thousand other mornings. The very air seemed alive. His heart beat so strongly, his muscles were so taut that his chest and stomach hurt, and he almost forgot to breathe whenever his eyes would deceive him into believing that he had seen movement below.

But in the full light of noon, there was a plume of dust on the flats, at the beginning of the causeway, a line of dark figures moving slowly upward. He sat upon his rock at the top of the causeway and lowered his visor to remove the haze of daylight, trying to discern the figures individually.

He had seen vehicles come up the road years before. Judging the distance and the size of the objects and the amount of dust, that was what it looked to be. A sense of wrongness grew in him, a weight in his stomach counterpoised against the beating of his heart. He clenched his limbs together, long arms wrapped about his knees, and watched, unwilling to run and tell the others. Regul. Regul were coming up.

Once he would have been delighted at such an unaccustomed visitation; but he was not so on this morning of all mornings. Not now. Not with mri business afoot that was more important than regul.

Not with mri business in the working, in which regul might seek to interfere.

Of a sudden he realized that the she'pan desperately needed to know what was coming up the hill: he made them out—six vehicles and a moving dot further back that his eyes could not resolve; but it looked to be a seventh.

No such number of regul had ever called on the edun in his memory.

He slid down from his rock and started downhill, his long strides carrying him at what swiftly became an uncontrollable run, undignified, but he was too alarmed to care for appearances. He raced toward the edun, breathless.

Others were coming out the doorway even before he arrived with his warning—black-robes of the Kel, and none of gold: he slowed his pace and came to them, out of breath and trying to conceal his pain. Sweat filmed his skin, quickly dried as the moisture-hungry air stole it. One did not run on Kesrith: a hundred times he had been taught so, the sober necessities of the world imposed over the nature of youth. His lungs burned; there was the sharp edge of blood in the air he breathed. None of the Kel rebuked him for his rashness; and he felt the mood of them, saw it in the attitude of the attendant dusei that had come out of the edun with them. One of the dusei reared up, towering, snuffing the wind. It came down heavily on all fours again, an action that stirred the white dust, and blew a snort of distress.

"Yai, yai!" kel Dahacha rebuked the lot of the dusei, that meaningless word that had a thousand meanings between dus and kel'en. They shied away, the nine of them, dismissed, hovering in a knot near the edun, ears pricked. Some sat. Now and then one would rise and walk the circuit of the group of dusei, a different one each time, and constantly that one would eye the advancing caravan of regul vehicles and utter small whuffs of warning.

The Kel was veiled, for meeting outsiders. Niun secured the *mez* a proper degree higher, and took his place in their black rank, one among others; but kel'anth Eddan took him by the elbow and drew him to the front of the group.

"Here," said Eddan, and no more. A man would not jabber questions with the Kel in such a mood. Niun held himself silent, his heart constricted with panic at Eddan's gesture. He was a novice, even at his age; he did not belong in the fore of question-and-answer with regul, here between Eddan and kel Pasev, oldest masters of the Kel.

Unless it involved him personally.

Or a kinsman.

Of a sudden he knew a message must have been passed to the edun through the Sen-tower, some intelligence of events that the edun possessed and that he had missed, sitting alone, vainly anticipating pleasure in this day.

Something was fearfully amiss, that regul had intervened between mri kinsmen.

The regul caravan ground its slow way upward, the sound of its motors audible now. The sun beat down, wanly red. Out on the flats a geyser spouted: Elu, one of the dangerous random ones, that kept no schedule. The plume continued a time, ten times the height of a man, and with its characteristic slant. Then it quickly dissipated. It was possible to recognize each of the geysers of the flats by its characteristic pattern and location. Niun reckoned that if Elu had erupted, Uchan would not be long after. It was a precious moment of distraction, in which it was not necessary to consider the sinister line of dark vehicles laboring their way upslope.

One—two—three—four—five—six.

Six landsleds. No more than two had ever come to the edun at once. He did not make this observation aloud. The Kel about him stood utterly rigid, like images against which black robes fluttered in the strong wind. Each kel'en's right hand was at the belt where the *as'ei* were sheathed, fingers slipped within the belt. This was a warning, to another kel'en. The regul, being mere tsi'mri, had likely not the sense to recognize it; but it was courtesy all the same, to advise intruders that they were not wanted, whether or not the intruder had the wit to recognize a warning.

The sleds bounced over the final ruts in the ascending road, came at last to a dusty halt even with the front entry to the edun, fronting the Kel. Motors were cut off, leaving sudden silence. Regul opened doors and began laboriously to disembark: a full ten of regul younglings, sober and joyless, without even visible arrogance. One of them was the Nomguard, Hada Surag-gi: Niun recognized that one by the badges and the robes, which was the best way to recognize any individual regul. It was also likely, he reflected bitterly, that the regul Hada Surag-gi recognized him by his distinctive lack of badges; but the youngling came forward to face Eddan, and consequently himself, and gave no sign of recognizing him. Hada's eyes did not even linger. There was no hint of insolence. Hada Surag-gi sucked air and rocked forward, a regul courtesy.

There was a proper mri response to this, a gesture of reciprocal goodwill. Eddan did not make it, and therefore no mri moved. Hands stayed by the *as'ei*.

"Favor," said Hada Surag-gi. "We bring most tragic news."

"We are prepared to hear what you say," said Eddan.

"We trust that our elder informed you—"

"Do you bring us Medai?" asked Eddan harshly.

Hada turned, an awkward motion for a regul, a shifting of feet. It closed its hands and made the gesture that wished its assistants to perform their duties. They shuffled about the second sled and opened its storage, lifted out a white, plastic-encased form on a litter. They bore it forward and carefully set it down at the feet of Hada Surag-gi, before the Kel.

"We have brought the remains of Medai," said Hada.

Niun knew, already, had known from Hada's first words; he did not move, nor even lower his visor. This steadiness might be mistaken by some of his brothers for self-control. It was numbness. He heard their movings, their stirrings about the scene as if they and he were in different places, as if, divorced from the scene, he watched from elsewhere, leaving the flesh of Niun s'Intel, like that of Medai s'Intel, senseless and unparticipant.

"Are the humans then that close?" asked Eddan, for it was the custom to give the dead of the People who had died in the war, to cold space where they had died, or, better still, to the fires of suns, recalling the birth of the People, rather than to make a long and inconvenient journey from the fighting front to inter them in earth. All the People would choose, if they had the choice, to avoid earth-burial. It was strange that regul, knowing mri even slightly as they did, could have misunderstood this and made the mistake of returning a dead mri to his edun.

The regul younglings—no arrogance at all in their manner now—let air flutter their nostrils and by other signs looked uncomfortable in their mission.

Guilty, was the bitter thought that came to Niun, watching them. He came back to his own body and fixed his eyes on the eyes of Hada Surag-gi, willing that youngling to meet his gaze directly. For an instant Hada did so, and flinched.

Guilty and uncomfortable in this whole meeting, and trying not to say the half of what they knew. Niun trembled with anger. He found his breath short. There was no move from the Kel. They stood absolutely still, one with the mind of Eddan, who led them, who with a word could lead them to a thing no mri had ever done.

Hada Surag-gi shifted weight on bowed legs and backed a little from the shrouded corpse between them. "Kel'anth Eddan," Hada said, "be gracious. This kel'en wounded himself and would not have the help of our medical facilities, although we might perhaps have saved him. We regret this, but we have never attempted to violate your beliefs. We bring you the regrets also of bai Hulagh, in whose service this kel'en gained great distinction. It is bai Hulagh's profound regret—his most profound regret, that this meeting is an inauspicious one, and that he makes the acquaintance of the People in such a sad moment. He sends his condolences and offers his extreme personal distress at this most unhappy event—"

"Bai Hulagh is then the new commander of this zone. What of bai Solgah? What of the Holn?"

"Gone." The word was almost swallowed, momentum quickly resumed. "And the bai wishes, kel'anth, to assure you—"

"I surmise," said Eddan, "that the death of kel Medai is very recent."

"Yes," said Hada, deterred from the prepared speech: Hada's mouth worked, seeming to search for words.

"Suicide." Eddan used the vulgar regul word, although regul knew the meaning of the mri word *ika'al*, where it regarded the ritual death of a kel'en.

"We protest—" In gazing directly at the kel'anth, the youngling seemed to lose its thread of thought, which was an impossibility with the eidetic regul. "We protest vehemently, kel-anth, that this kel'en was in deep melancholy that had nothing to do with the accession of bai Hulagh to command or the fall from power of the Holn. We fear that you are drawing the wrong inference. If you suppose that—"

"I did not advance any statement of inference," said Eddan. "Do you suggest that one might be made?"

The regul, interrupted more than once, confounded by argument that was no argument, confused as regul easily were when dealing with mri, blinked rapidly and tried to regroup. "Kel'anth, I protest, be gracious, we only stated that this kel'en was in deep melancholy prior to his act, that he had been confined in his quarters by his own choice, refusing all attempts to inquire into his needs, and this had nothing to do with the accession of bai Hulagh, in no wise, sir, in no wise. Bai Hulagh became employer to this kel'en and this kel'en served him with great distinction in several actions. There was nothing amiss. But after the peace was announced, kel Medai evinced an increasing melancholy."

"You are of the Nom," Niun interrupted, unable to bear it longer, and Hada Surag-gi looked in his direction, black eyes wide, showing whites in amazement. "How is it that you report accurately on the state of mind of a kel'en who was on a ship far removed from you?"

It was not his place to have spoken. From a kel'en youth before strangers, it was an outburst, not an acceptable behavior; but the Kel stood firm, and as for Hada Surag-gi, its mouth flew open and shut again in a taut line.

"Elder," it protested to Eddan.

"Can the bai's spokesman answer the question?" asked Eddan, a vindication that sent a flood of fierce gratitude through Niun.

"Most gladly," said Hada. "I know these things to be fact because they are exactly as given to me by the bai himself, face to face, by his word. We had no idea that the kel'en contemplated such an action. It was not due to any animosity toward his service."

"Yet it is abundantly evident," said Eddan, "that kel Medai considered that he had sufficient reason to quit your service, such strong reason that he chose *ika'al* to be free of you."

"This was doubtless because of the end of the war, which this kel'en did not desire."

"It is," said Eddan, "curious that he would have elected *ika'al* when he knew that he was returning to homeworld."

"He was despondent," said Hada Surag-gi, illogicality that the regul did not seem to comprehend as illogical. "He was not responsible for his actions."

"You are speaking before his kinsman," said Eddan sharply. "This was a kel'en, not a dus, to go mad. He was bound for homeworld. What you say he did is not reasonable unless the bai offended against his honor. Is it possible that this was what happened?"

The regul, under the sting of Eddan's harsh voice, began to retreat slightly, a sidling backward by the hindmost.

"We are not done with questions," Eddan said, fixing Hada Surag-gi with his stare. "Tell us where and when kel Medai died."

The regul did not want to answer at all. It sucked air and visibly changed color. "Favor, kel'anth. He died during the previous evening on the ship of the bai."

"On the ship of bai Hulagh."

"Kel'anth, the bai protests—"

"Was there any manner of discussion passed between the bai and the kel'en?"

"Be gracious. The kel'en was despondent. The end of the war—"

"The bai made this mri despondent," Eddan said, discomfiting the youngling utterly.

"The bai," said Hada, nostrils dilating and contracting in rapid breaths, "requested of this mri that he remain in the ship and remain in service; the kel'en refused, wishing to leave at once, a privilege the bai had denied to everyone, even himself. There were matters of business to attend. It is possible—" the skin of the youngling went paler and paler as it spoke: its lips faltered upon the words. "Kel'anth, I realize that there is possible blame in your eyes; yet we do not understand the actions of this kel'en. The bai commanded him to wait. Yet the kel'en found fault with the order sufficient that he committed this act. We do not know why. We assure you we are greatly distressed by this sad event. It is an hour of crisis for Kesrith, in which this kel'en would have been of great service to the bai and to yourselves, surely. The bai valued the service of kel Medai. We protest again that we do not understand the source of his bitterness with us."

"Perhaps you did not inquire or listen," said kel'anth Eddan.

"Be gracious. Kesrith has been ceded to humans. We are in the process of the evacuation of all residents of Kesrith. Arrangements are being made also for the mri of Kesrith. The bai wishes his ship manned at all hours, and he wishes the crew, naturally—" The youngling moved uneasily, looking at Eddan, who did not move. "These are affairs over which we have no control. If the kel'en had only informed the bai of his extreme desire to have an exception granted in his case—"

"Kel Medai chose to leave his service," said Eddan. "It was well done. We do not want to talk to youngling regul on this subject any longer. Go away now."

And this was plainly put, and the regul, degree by degree, retreated, more rapidly as they neared their sleds. Hada was neither the first nor the last seated. Hatches were closed, engines started; the landsleds lumbered clumsily into a turn on the narrow and rutted roadway and retreated down the long slope as slowly as they had come.

No one moved. There was a numbness in the air now that the regul had gone, leaving them alone with their dead.

And suddenly in the doorway, gold-robes and white, the sen'anth and Melein, and the she'pan herself, on their arms.

"Medai is dead," said Eddan, "and the world is going to humans soon, as we suspected." He lifted his robed arms to shield the she'pan from the sight; and Melein started forward a step, only a step: it was forbidden her. She veiled herself and turned her face away, bowing her head; and likewise the she'pan and the sen'anth veiled, which they did not do save in the presence of the unacceptable.

They went away into the edun. Death was the peculiar domain of the Kel, either in inflicting it or mourning it; and it was for them to attend to the proprieties.

For a kinsman within the Kel it was a personal obligation.

Niun knew that he was expected in this to take charge; and he saw that the others longed to help, to do something, and he opened his hands, gave them leave. He had only heard the rites, had never done them, and he did not wish to shame himself or Medai by his ignorance. They gathered up the litter, he and all who could find space to help, and passed within the doors of the edun, toward the Pana'drin, the Shrine, to present Medai at his homecoming, where he would have presented himself first if he had lived.

Niun's hands felt the warm metal of the litter frame; he looked down on the object in white that had been his cousin, and the shock that had held him numb until now began to meld into other feelings, into a deep and helpless rage.

It was not right that this had happened. There was no justice in things if this could happen. He found himself almost trembling with anger, a violence in which he could kill, if there were anyone or anything against which to direct that rage.

There was no one. He tried to feel nothing; that was easier, than to try to find a direction for the resentment that boiled in him. He had hoped: he schooled himself not to hope, henceforth. The world was mad, and Medai had added himself to the madness.

My last son, the she'pan had called him. Now it was true.

Chapter Seven

THERE WAS a screen in the Shrine of the Edun of the People, worked in metals and precious stones and over-written with ancient things. It was old beyond reckoning, and in every Shrine that had ever existed, this very screen had stood, between the lamps of bronze that were of equal age with it. In life it marked the division between the Kel and the Sen, the point past which the Kel might not tread: in death it was no more crossable.

Before the screen, at its very base, they laid the white-shrouded body of Medai s'Intel Sov-Nelan, as close to the dividing line as a kel'en could ever come. Incense curled up from burners on either side of the screen, heavy and cloying, overhanging the room and obscuring the ceiling like an immaterial canopy.

For Niun, attendant to his cousin, that scent of incense held its own memories, of being in the Kath and of watching holy rites from that least, outermost room, when he had been a child with Melein and Medai beside him, and others now gone, whose deaths he knew: from that outer room the small shrine of the Kel had seemed mysterious and glorious, a territory where they might not yet venture, where warriors in their *sigai* might move, disdaining the Kath.

His mind ran to a later day, when they three had been taken among the black-robes, one with the Kel, and had been allowed for the first time to enter the middle shrine, and to realize that yet another barrier lay between them and the Pana, the Mysteries; and a day later yet, that they had prayed the welfare of Medai, who was leaving the edun for service, greatly honored—and Niun had died inwardly that night with jealousy and bitterness, his prayers insincere and

63

hating and mingled with thoughts that came back now like
guilty ghosts.

He felt no differently now than then. Medai had taken another departure, leaving him the ugliness, the loneliness of
Kesrith.

Medai had never endured the things he had endured, left
here, last guard to the House, servant to the others.

Medai was counted a great kel'en for what he had done.

There was a whisper of robes in the holiness dimly visible
beyond the screen, where the Sen met and tended the Holy
Objects. Melein would be there, with Sathell.

Three children an age ago had stood within the outer
Kath-hall, and longed for honor; and they had gotten their
prayers in strange and twisted ways: Niun within Kel-shrine,
where they had all longed to go; Medai possessing the honors
of a warrior, newly wandering the Dark; and Melein, Melein
the light-hearted, had passed through Kel-shrine to the place
beyond, to the Mysteries that were never for a kel'en to see.

He bowed down, shaking with rage and frustration, and remained so for a time, trying to take his breath back again
and compose himself.

A hand touched his shoulder. A dark robe brushed him
with shadow as Eddan sank down beside him. "Niun," the
kel'anth said in a soft voice. "The she'pan calls you. She does
not want you to have to sit this watch. She says that she
wants you to come and sit with her this night, and not to go
to the burial."

It took him a moment to be sure of his voice. "I do not believe it," he said after a moment, "that she will not loose me
even for this. What did she say? Did she give no reason?"

"She wishes you to come, now."

He was stunned by such an attitude. There had been no
love between himself and Medai: the she'pan knew that well
enough; but there was no decency in what she asked him to
do, publicly. "No," he said. "No, I will not go to her."

The fingers dug into his shoulder. He expected rebuke
when he looked up. But the old man unveiled to him,
showing his naked face, and there was no anger there. "I
thought you would say so," Eddan said, which was incredible,
for he had not known himself: it was impulse. But the old
man knew him that well. "Do as you think right," Eddan said
further. "Stay. I will not forbid you."

And the old man rose and ordered the others, who moved about their separate tasks. One brought the vessels of ritual, given by the Sen, that were for burying, and set them at Medai's feet; Pasev brought water; and Dahacha, cloths for washing; and Palazi filled the lamps for the long vigil; and Debas whistled softly to the dusei and took them from the outer hall, herding them away into the tower of the Kel so that they should not disturb the solemnities. In the midst of the activity Niun sat, conscious finally that he had torn his robe in his haste for descending from the hills, and that he was dusty and his hands were foul with dirt. Feet pattered about him. Sirain came, half-blind Sirain, and gave him a damp cloth, and Niun unveiled and washed his face and veiled again, grateful for his thoughtfulness. Liran brought a robe for him, and he changed his *siga* in the very Shrine, for it was not respect to sit the watch in disorder. He sat down again, and began to be calmer at their quiet, efficient ministering.

Then at Eddan's whispered word, they began to take the ugly white shroud from Medai, and patiently, patiently the fingers of one and the other of them tore the webbing that was as close-spun as a cocoon and well-nigh impenetrable— like *cho*-silk it was, having to be unravelled with the fingers. But Pasev knew to touch the regul fiber with a burning wick, and so to part the strange web. The material burned sullenly, but it gave way, shedding its chemical smell into sickening union with the incense that lowered overhead.

It was something on which they all silently agreed, that they would not give to burial a kel'en in a regul shroud, whatever the inconvenience; and gradually they recovered Medai from the web, a face that they remembered, a countenance still and pale. The body was small and thin in death, pitifully so; it weighed very little, and Medai had been a strong man. The honors that they found laced to his belts were many, and the *seta'al* were weathered to pale blue on his face. He had been a handsome youth, had Medai s'Intel, full of the life and the hope of the edun in brighter days. Even now he was very fine to see. The only marring of him was the blood that stained the fiber under his central ribs, where he had dealt himself his death wound.

Suicide.

Niun worked, not looking at Medai's face, trying not to

think what his hands did, lest they tremble and betray him. He was trying to remember better days, could not. He knew Medai too well. His cousin was in his dying as he had been in life: selfish, arrogant to match regul arrogance, and stubborn with it all. It was wrong to hold anger with the dead, impious. But in the end Medai had been as useless to his kinfolk as he had always been. Medai had lived for himself and died for his own reasons, nothing regarding what others might need of him; and there was precious little honor for a cold corpse, whatever the high traditions of the Kel.

They had parted in anger. He remembered, each day of his life for six years he had remembered, and he knew why the she'pan had wanted him upstairs, and what was surely in the minds of his brother kel'ein who sat with him. There had been a quarrel, the *av'ein-kel*, the long blades drawn; it had been his own fault, drawing first, in the Shrine hall, outside. It was the day that Medai had laid hand on Melein.

And Melein had not objected.

The she'pan herself had put an end to that quarrel—abler in those days six years gone—had descended the tower stairs and intervened. Had called him *eshai'i*, lack-honor, and *tsi'daith'*, un-son, and because then he had loved her, it had crushed him.

But not a word, never a word of rebuke to Medai.

And for Medai within a hand of days came the honor of service to the bai of the regul, an honor that might have gone to one of the Husbands; and for Melein came the chastity of the Sen.

And for Niun s'Intel came nothing, only a return to study, a long, long waiting, crushed to the Mother's side and held from any hope of leaving Kesrith.

There had never been a way to undo that one evil day. Intel would not let him go. He had hoped for peace with Medai, for a change in the affairs of the People.

But Medai had robbed him of that too. It was on him alone, the service of homeworld, and there had never been any justice in it.

When you have made up your mind what it is the People owe you, Eddan had said, *come and tell me*. He would have settled for half of what Medai had had.

But then, beginning with Eddan, the Kel spoke of Medai, each praising him: ritual, the *lij'aiia*, beginning the Watch of the Dead; and the voices of the old kel'ein shook in the telling of it.

"It is hardest," said Liran, "that the old bury the young."

And last of all but himself, Pasev: "It is certain," she said, touching the medallions, the *j'tai* that glittered in the lamps' golden light, the honors that Medai had won in his services, "that though he was young, he has travelled very far and seen a great deal of war. I see here the service of Shoa, of Elag, of Soghrune, of Gezen and Segur and Hadriu; and it is certain that he has served the People. Surely, surely he has done enough, this brother of ours, this child of our house; I think that surely he was very tired. I think he must have been very weary of service to the regul, and he would have come home as best he could, with what of his strength he had left. I understand this. I am also very tired of the service of regul; and if I knew my service was at an end, I would go the road he took."

And then it should have been Niun's time to speak, praising Medai, his cousin. He had gathered angry words, but he could not, after that, speak them or contradict the feelings of Pasev, whom he loved with a deep love. He sank down and lowered his head into his crossed arms, shaking with reaction.

And the Kel allowed him this, which they seemed to take for a kinsman's grief. But theirs was a true, unselfish sorrow for a child they had loved. His was for himself.

In this he found the measure of himself, that he was capable of meanness and great selfishness, and that he was not, even now, the equal of Medai.

The others talked around him, whispering, after such a time as it became clear that he would not choose to speak in the ritual. They began finally to speak of the high hills, the burial that they must accomplish, and woven into their speech and their plans was a quiet desperation, a shame, for they were old and the hills were very far and the trail very steep. They wondered unhappily among themselves whether the regul might not, at their request, give them motorized transport; but they felt at heart that they dishonored Medai by asking such help of the regul. They would not, therefore, ask. They began to consider how they might contrive to carry him.

"Do not worry," said Niun, breaking his long silence. "I can manage it myself."

And he saw in their faces doubt, and when he thought of the steep trails and the high desert he himself doubted it.

"The she'pan will not allow it," said Eddan. "Niun, we might bury him close at hand."

"No," said Niun, and again, thinking of the she'pan, "no." And after that there were no more suggestions to him. Eddan quietly signed at the others to let be.

And they left him, when he asked of them quietly and with propriety to be left alone. They filed out with robes rustling and the measured ring of honors on their garments. The tiny high sound of it drew at Niun's heart. He considered his own selfishness, lately measured, and the courage of his elders, who had done so much in their lives, and was mortally ashamed.

But he began to think, in the long beginning of his night-long watch, in the silences of the edun, where elsewhere others were in private mourning—and knew that he was not willing to die, whatever the traditions of his caste, that he did not want to die as Medai had died, above all else; and this ate at him, for it was contrary to all that he was supposed to be.

Medai had been able to accept such things, and the she'pan had accepted Medai. And this was what it had won him.

It was blasphemy to entertain such thoughts before the Shrine, in the presence of the gods and of the dead. For himself he was ashamed, and he longed to run away, as he had done when he was a child, going into the hills to think alone, to try himself against the elements until he could forget again the pettinesses of men, and of himself.

But he was reckoned a man now, and it had been long since he had had that freedom. Dangerous times were on the edun, hard times, and it was not an hour that Niun s'Intel could afford to play the child.

There was a matter of duty, of decencies. Medai had lived and died by that law. He could not manage the inner part of him, but he could at the least see to it that the outer man did what was dutiful to those who had to depend on him.

Even if it were totally a lie.

"Niun."

The stir, the whisper from beyond the screen he had taken for the wind that blew constantly through the shrine. He looked up now and saw a hazed golden figure through the intricate design, and knew his sister's voice. She crossed the floor as far as the screen that divided them, religiously, though they could meet face-to-face elsewhere in the edun and outside its limits.

"Go back," he wished Melein, for she violated the law of her caste by being in the presence of the dead, even a dead kinsman. Her caste had no debts of kinship; they renounced them, and all such obligations. But she did not leave. He rose up, stiff from kneeling on the cold floor, and came to the grillwork. He could not see her distinctly. He saw only the shadow of her hand on the lacery of the screen and matched it with his own larger one in sympathy, unable to touch her. He was unclean and in the presence of the dead, and would remain unapproachable until he had buried his kinsman.

"I am permitted to come," she said. "The she'pan gave me leave."

"We have done everything," he assured her, struck to the heart remembering that there had been affection between Melein and Medai, cousinwise, and at the last, perhaps more than cousinly. "We are going to take him to Sil'athen— everything that we can do we will do."

"I had not thought you would watch here," she said. And then, with an edge of utter bitterness. "Or is it only because you were directly ordered not to?"

Her attack confused him. He took a moment to answer, not knowing clearly against what manner of assumption he was answering. "He is kin to me," he said. "Whatever else— is no matter now."

"You would have killed him yourself once."

It was the truth. He tried to see Melein's face through the screen; he could only see the outline, golden shadow behind gold metal. He did not know how to answer her. "That was long ago," he said. "And I would have made my peace with him if he were alive. I had wanted that. I had wanted that very much."

"I believe you," she said finally.

She left silence then. He felt it on him, an awkward weight. "It was jealousy," he admitted to her. The thing that he had pondered took shape and had birth, painfully, but it was not as painful as he had thought it would be, brought to light. Melein was his other self. He had been as close as thought to her once, could still imagine that closeness be-

tween them. "Melein, when there are only two young men
within a Kel, it is impossible that they not compare themselves and be compared by others. He had first all the things
I wanted to excel in. And I was jealous and resentful. I inter-
fered between you. It was the most petty thing I have ever
done. I have paid for it, for six years.

She did not speak for a moment. He became sure that she
had loved Medai, only daughter of an edun otherwise fading
into old age, it was inevitable that she and Medai should once
have seemed a natural pairing, kel'en and kel'e'en, in those
days when she had also been of the Kel.

Perhaps—it was a thought that had long tormented him—
she would have been happier had she remained in the Kel.

"The she'pan sent me," she said finally, without answering
his offering to her. "She has heard of the intention of the Kel.
She does not want you to go. There is disturbance in the city.
There is uncertainty. This is her firmest wish, Niun: stay.
Others will see to Medai."

"No."

"I cannot give her that answer."

"Tell her that I did not listen. Tell her that she owes Medai
better than a hole in the sand and that these old men cannot
get him to Sil'athen without killing themselves in the effort."

"I cannot say that to her!" Melein hissed back, fear in her
voice, and that fear made him certain in his intentions.

It made no more rational sense than the other desires of
Intel, this she'pan that could gamble with the lives of the
People, that could bend and break the lives of her children in
such utter disregard of their desires and hopes. *She has given
me her virtues,* he thought, with a sudden and bitter insight:
*jealousy, selfishness, possessiveness, . . . ah, possessive, of
myself, of Melein, the children of Zain. She sent Melein to
the Sen and Medai to the regul when she saw how things
were drifting with them. She has ruined us. A great she'pan,
a great one, but flawed, and she is strangling us, clenching us
against her until she breaks our bones and melts our flesh and
breathes her breath into us.*

Until there is nothing left of us.

"Do as you have to do," he said. "As for me, I will do him
a kinsman's duty, truesister. But then you are sen'e'en and
you do not have kinsmen anymore. Go back and say what
you like to the she'pan."

He had hoped, desperately, to anger her, to pierce through her dread of Intel. He had meant it to sting, just enough. But her hand withdrew from the screen and her shadow moved away from him, becoming one with the light on the other side.

"Melein," he whispered. And aloud: "Melein!"

"Do not reproach *me* with lack of duty," her voice came back to him, distant, disembodied. "While he lived, I was a kinswoman to him and you were grudging of everything he had. Now I have other obligations. Say over him that the she'pan is well pleased with his death. That is her word on the matter. As for me, I have no control over what you do. Bury him. Do as you choose."

"Melein," he said. "Melein, come back."

But he heard her footsteps retreat up hidden stairs, heard doors close one after another. He stayed as he was, one hand against the screen, thinking until the last that she would change her mind and come back, denying that answer she had made him; but she left. He could not even be angry, for it was what he had challenged her to do.

Intel's creation. His too.

He hoped that somewhere in Sen-tower Melein would lay down her pride and weep over Medai; but he doubted it. The coldness, the careful coldness that had been in her voice was beyond all repentance, the schooled detachment of the Sen.

He left the screen finally, and sat down by the corpse of Medai. He locked his hands behind his neck, head bowed on his knees, twice desolate.

The lamps snapped and the fires leaped, the door of the edun having been left open this night, an ancient tradition, a respect to the dead. Shadows leaped and made the writings on the walls seem to writhe with independent life, writings that the she'pan said contained the history and wisdom of the People. All his life he had been surrounded by such things: writings covered every wall of the main hall and the Shrine and the she'pan's tower, and the accesses of Kath and Kel— writings that the she'pan said were duplicated in every edun of the People that had ever existed, exact and unvaried. Through such writings the sen'ein learned. The kel'ein could not. He knew only what had happened within his own life and within his sight, or those things he heard his elders recall.

But Melein could read the writings, and knew what truth

was, as did the she'pan, and grew cold and strange in that knowledge. He had asked once, when Melein was taken into the Sen, if he could not be taken too: they had never in their lives been separated. But the she'pan had only taken his hands into hers, and turned the calloused palms upward. Not the hands of a scholar, she had said, and dismissed his appeal.

Something stirred out in the hall, a slow shuffling, a click of claws on stone—one of the dusei that had strayed from the Kel-tower. They generally went where they chose, none forbidding them, even when they were inconvenient or destructive. It was not even certain that one could forbid them, for they were so strong that there could be no coercion. They sensed, in the peculiar way of dusei, when they were wanted and when not, and rarely would they stay where they were not desired.

They understood the kel'ein, the belief was, whose thoughts were unfearing and uncomplex, and for this reason each dus chose a kel'en or kel'e'en and stayed lifelong. One had never set affection on Niun s'Intel, though once he had tried—shamefully desperate—to trap a young one and to coerce it. It had fled his childish scheme, smashing the trap, knocking him unconscious.

And never after that had he found any skill to draw one after him, as if that one, betrayed, had warned all its kind of the nature of Niun s'Intel.

The elder kel'ein said that it was because he had never truly opened his heart to one, that he was too sealed up in himself.

He thought this false, for he had tried; but he also thought that the sensitive dusei had found him bitter and discontent and could not bear it.

He believed so, hoping that this would change; but in the depth of his heart he wondered if it were possibly because he was not a natural kel'en. For a woman of the People all castes were open; for a man, there were only Kel-caste and Sen; and he had been both deprived in one sense and overindulged in others, simply because he was the last son of the House. It had meant that he received the concentrated efforts of all his teachers, that they had worked with him until he had understood, until his skill was acceptable. But in an edun full of sons and daughters, he thought that he might have failed to survive; his stubbornness would have brought him early challenge, and the People might then have been rid of his irritance in the House. He thought that he might have been a better kel'en if not for the Mother's interference; but then many things might have been different if he were not the last; and so might she.

Medai had pleased the Mother; and Medai was dead; but he sat here living, a rebel son to the Mother. She would have somewhat to say to him after Medai's burying in the hills, when he must come back and face her. Thereafter would be bitter, bitter words, and himself without argument, and Melein on the she'pan's side in it. He shrank from what the she'pan might say to him.

But she would have to say it. He would not unsay what he had said.

Again the scrape of claws. It was a dus. The explosive sough of breath and the heavy tread made it clear that the intruder was coming closer, and Niun willed it away from the Shrine, for dusei were not welcome here. Yet it came. He heard it enter the outer room, and turned and saw it in the dark, a great slope-shouldered shadow. It made that peculiar lost sound again, and slowly edged closer.

"Yai!" he said, turning on one knee, furiously willing it out.

And then he saw that the dus was dusty and that its coat was patched with crusted sores, and his heart froze in his chest and his breath caught, for he realized then that it was not one of their own tame beasts, but a stranger.

Sometimes wild dusei would come down off the high plains to hover round the lands of the edun and create havoc among the tame ones; in his own memory kel'ein had died, trying to approach such an animal, even armed. Dusei sensed intentions, uncannily prescient: there were few animals more dangerous to stalk.

This one stood, head lowered, massive shoulders filling the doorway, and rocking back and forth, uttering that plaintive sound. It forced its way in, making the plaster crumble here and there, though the door was purposely made small and inconvenient for them, to protect the Mysteries from their mindless irreverence.

It came, irresistible, thinner than the well-fed dusei of the edun. Niun edged aside, one of the lamps crashing down as

the dus shouldered it. It whined and whuffed and fortunately
the spilled fire went out, though the hot oil stung its foot and
made it shy aside. Then it approached the body of Medai and
pawed at it with claws as long as a man's hand—poisonous,
the dewclaw possessing venom ducts, the casual swipe of
them capable of disemboweling mri or regul. Niun crouched
in the shadow by the overturned lamp, as immobile as the
furniture. The beast's body filled much of the room and
blocked the doorway. It had a fearsome, sickly stench that
overrode even the incense; and when it turned its massive
head to stare at the frail mri huddled in the corner, its eyes
showed, running, dripping rheum onto the hallowed floor.

Miuk! The Madness was on him. The secretions of his
body were out of balance and the *miuk,* the Madness of his
kind, was to blame for his behavior, sending him into a mri
dwelling. There was nothing Niun knew, neither beast nor
man, more to be feared than this: if the dusei of the edun
had not been locked upstairs this night, they would never
have let a *miuk'ko* dus come near the edun; they would have
died in defense of that outer doorway, rather than let that
beast in.

And Niun s'Intel prepared himself to die, most horribly, in
a space so small that the dus could not even cast his body
from underfoot; his brothers would find him in shreds. It
prodded at the body of Medai, as if in prelude to this, but it
hesitated. Grotesque, horrid, the beast rocked to and fro,
straddling the corpse, its eyes streaming fluid that blinded it.
From some far place in the Kel-tower there was a deep
moan, a dus fretting at its unaccustomed confinement, at the
mood of the mourning Kel—or sensing invasion downstairs,
trying desperately to get out. Others joined in, then fell
abruptly silent, hushed perhaps by the order of the kel'ein.

Niun held his breath while the rogue lifted his rheum-
blinded eyes toward that sound, mobile lips working nervously. It rocked. It gave another explosive snort and shifted
its weight, easing aside. The shoulder hit the screen. It
toppled with a brazen crash, and the beast whirled, bathed in
the glow from the inner shrine. Niun flung his arm over his
eyes in horror lest he see the Forbidden, and then, surety in
his heart, he reached for his gun, futile against a dus.

He must attack whatever threatened the Forbidden, to prevent, if he could, the invasion of the Sen-shrine. He sighted

for the brain, the first of the two brains, knowing full well the following convulsions would destroy him with the dus.

But the dus did not take that step beyond. It lowered its weeping head and nosed at the corpse, disarranging the veil; and when it had done so, it moaned and slowly, almost distractedly, swung its head about, putting its shoulder between its head and the gun, and began to withdraw from the Shrine.

And when it had done so, when it walked the hall outside, still giving that lost-infant sound, for the first time Niun clearly knew it.

Medai's dus.

There was no mri who could claim, other clues removed, to know any dus but his own, and not even that one, given much passage of time. Dusei were too similar and too mutable, and one could only say that this one was *like* the dus he knew.

But that this particular one had not killed him, that it had been primarily interested in the body, and departed unsatisfied—that action he understood. Dusei were troubled at death. Other animals ignored the dead, but dusei did not understand, did not accept it. They grieved and searched and fretted, and eventually died themselves, more often than not. They rarely outlived their masters, pining away in their search.

And this one was hunting something it had not found.

Medai's dus, come looking for him.

A dus that was sickly and covered with sores and deep in the throes of a madness that did not come on swiftly, although regul said that Medai had died but a night ago.

A dus that was thin and starved as its dead master.

A chill feeling grew in Niun, until he was physically shivering, not alone from dread of the dus. He holstered his gun and glanced fearfully at the nakedness of the inner shrine, on which he ought never to have looked.

It should not have happened. He washed his hands with the water of the offerings, and without setting foot across the forbidden line, he set the screen in place again, his fingers reverent on the inanimate metal. He had lived. The gods, like men, could forgive the irreverence of dusei; and he had looked within the Sen shrine, and felt shaken, but not to the death. He had seen brightness, but nothing of the Objects, or nothing that he could identify as the Holy. He tried to put

this from his mind. It was not for a kel'en to have seen. He
did not want to remember it.

And Medai—

He set up the lamp again, and refilled it, and lighted it, restoring its comforting glow. Then on his knees he mopped up
the spilled oil that by the mercy of the gods had not kept
burning; and all the while he worked, exhausted and trembling from his vigil, he thought, and nursed that cold feeling
that lodged under his heart.

At last he washed his hands for respect and laid hands on
Medai for the irreverence he had to commit: the thought
borning in his mind gave him no peace otherwise. He did it
quickly, once he had gathered his courage, carefully unfastened the clothing and examined the wound, and found it—
shaming his suspicion and his act—as the regul had said.

Ika'al.

"Forgive me," he said to the spirit of Medai; and reverently reclosed the robes and washed the face and replaced the
veils. Then he cast himself on his face before the shrine and
made the proper prayers to the several ancestor-gods of his
caste for rest for the soul of Medai, with more sincerity than
he had ever used on his cousin when he was living.

This should have absolved him and given him peace, having surrendered to that which was proper and honest, but it
did not.

He had in him a gathering certainty that, whatever the evidence of his eyes and the testimony of the regul, Medai had
not laid down his life willingly.

The dus, so close to a kel'en's mind, was *miuk'ko* and
grown so thin that it could pass shrine doors; and the body of
Medai, once solid with muscle, was thin as the mummified
dead.

Kel-quarters were independent units within the regul ship
plan, because of the dusei, which the regul feared beyond all
logic; and because of the stringent caste laws that a kel'en
must observe with respect to contact with outsiders.

But essentially that kel'en was always at the mercy of the
regul, who supplied that unit with food, water, even the air
he breathed. All that a kel'en could do to assert his independence was lock the door.

Had they wanted him dead, they could have stopped the
air and cast him into cold space afterward. But these were

tsi'mri, and more than that, they were strangers to the People, a strange new branch of regul; and they might not have known enough to deal with a kel'en. Regul were not fighters.

Not directly.

Consumed by the thought that took shape in him, he rose up and left the Shrine, took an offering vessel of water and a pannikin, and went out to the outer hall, to the door, where the mad dus still crouched before the edun.

He had known it must be there, waiting. It was near what it desired, but could not find it. He had been as sure of its lingering there as he was sure how it had been driven mad. It was no less dangerous for its once having been tame; it could still rise up and kill on impulse. But when he set the water before it, it sniffed at the offering curiously and at last bestirred itself, nosing down into the water. The contents of the pannikin disappeared. Niun filled it a second and a third and a fourth time, and only at the fourth did the beast suddenly avert its head in refusal.

He sank down on his heels and studied the creature, thin as it was and its fur gone in patches. A great open wound was fresh on its side.

Medai's dus, come from regul care, from violence, from starvation. It would not have left Medai of choice even after he was dead.

Regul would not act as mri would act. They were capable of collusion, of bribery, of deceit, of slaughter of their own young, but never of murder of an adult, never of that. They could neither kill nor lie in cold blood; they hired mri to attend to their enemies.

So he had always been taught, by those who knew the regul better than he, by those who had dealt with regul lifelong.

So he had implicitly believed.

As had Medai.

He rose and walked inside, back to the Shrine, and sat down beside the body of his cousin, arms locked about him, staring without comprehension at the serpentine writings that recorded and concealed the history of the People.

Murder had been done, in one manner or another, whatever name the regul gave it. A kel'en had been killed by his own employers, and his dus weakened to the point that they could drive it out to die naturally—one body to return to the

Kel, the act of ignorant regul; another disposed of by predators and scavengers, or at best those incapable of betraying
what had happened. Regul hands and regul conscience were
doubtless clean. Medai had finally done as they had wished.

He wished desperately to go upstairs and tell someone. He
wished to run to Eddan for counsel, to alert the she'pan. But
he had nothing for proof but a beast that lay outside the
door. He had nothing on which to hang such an accusation,
no shape to his suspicion, no motive he could reckon which
would have driven the regul to compel a kel'en to such an action.

It was irony of a kind, he thought, that of all whom Medai
might have trusted to see to his avenging, he had come to the
hands of his oldest rival; and the only likely witness of the
truth was a *miuk'ko*.

Dusei, it was said, lived in the present; they had no
memories for what had happened, only for persons and
places. It had sought home, the House where it had first
lived; it had sought Medai; it had found the one, and not the
other.

Chapter Eight

NIUN HAD BEGUN, before the others had even stirred, to prepare for the journey to Sil'athen. There was the water drawn, and the ritual store of food, a token only, and the real provisions that were for the living.

With much effort he took the body of Medai from the small Shrine and bound it with cords to the regul litter on which it had come. The dus that waited by the doorway saw, but paid no heed to what he did.

Then the others began to come: Eddan and Pasev and Dahacha and the rest of the Kel. The dusei came down too, and the *miuk'ko* by the door withdrew a space. There in the sunlight it subsided, massive head between its paws, sides heaving. It was deep in shock.

"*Miuk*," murmured Debas, horrified to see what sat at their gates.

But Pasev, who was, despite having killed many humans, a gentle soul, went and tried to call to it, staying out of its reach. It reared aside with a plaint of rage and sank down again a little distance away, exhausted by its effort. The dusei of the edun drew aside from it, agitated, sensing the distress of their fellow and the danger he posed. They formed a tight knot about the Kel and commenced that circling action by the guard dus, protecting the Kel from the threat of the rogue.

And eyes were on Niun, questioning. He shrugged and picked up the ropes of Medai's improvised sled. "It came," he said, "into the shrine last night." He looked at Eddan. "It was hunting someone."

And he saw the ugly surmise leap into the kel'anth's eyes: a wise man, Eddan, if he were not kel'en. And quietly Eddan

79

turned and gestured to Pasev, to Liran and Debas and Lieth. "Stay here," he said. "Guard the she'pan."

"Eddan," said Pasev, "the she'pan forbade——"

"Any who wish to stay besides these may stay. Guard the she'pan, Pasev."

And Niun, not waiting for them, started out, knowing already by the resistance of the sled that he was going to pay dearly for his obstinacy, when the she'pan and all the rest had given him a way to escape this kinsman's duty.

Slowly, painfully, the *miuk'ko* heaved itself up and tried to follow the sled. It went only as far as the roadway, and there sank down, exhausted, at the end of its strength.

The other dusei flanked it, one still pacing between the dus and the remaining Kel, watching the rogue. They did not follow the burial party. They were not wanted. They guarded the edun.

And Eddan and the other kel'ein overtook Niun on the slope that led to the hills, and offered their hands to the rope. He did not object to this. He felt pained that they must make this gesture, showing him their fellowship, as if that needed to be shown.

He veiled himself, one-handed, lowered the visor, already conserving the moisture his panting breaths tended to waste. He had taken along more than the usual quota of water, knowing the toll it would exact of them. One did not work on Kesrith: this was for youngling regul and for regul machines. Exertion would wring the moisture from the body and bring hemorrhage without proper caution.

But none of them said the obvious, that the journey was ill-advised.

Never had the Kel defied the Mother, not directly.

And it came to Niun then that the Mother had recourse available: she might have directly ordered Eddan. She had not done this.

Uncharitably, he attributed it not to love, but that she drank again of *komal*, and therefore could not be awakened when Melein brought his refusal back to her: such was Intel, she'pan of Kesrith. It had happened before.

He held to this irreverent anger, refusing to believe that she had relented, for this, at least, had never happened before, not in all the years that he had made requests of her.

He did not think that she would begin now, that he defied her.

He refused to repent his stubbornness even when the trail grew steeper, and the rocks tormented his feet and the air came like cold fire into his lungs.

In the sky, the regul ships continued to come and go, their speed making mock of the agony of the small figures of mri—ships carrying more and more of their kind into refuge before humans should come and claim the world.

The trail to Sil'athen was no trail, but a way remembered by all mri that had ever walked it. There was no real trace of it among the rocks, save that it was devoid of the largest obstacles and tended from landmark to landmark. Niun knew it, for burials had been common enough in his life, though he had never seen the ceremonies surrounding a birth; he had been too young for Melein's. He drew on the sled's ropes alone now, following after Eddan's tall slim figure, wrestling the sled along among the small rocks until he had to wrap a fold of his robes about his torn hands to save them. His breath came hard and his lungs ached; he was accustomed to weapons-work, not to labor like tsi'mri; and every few paces of altitude gained made breathing that much more difficult.

"Niun," one and another of the brothers would say, "let me take it a time." But he shook off their offering hands here. Only the oldest, save Pasev, whom Eddan had placed in command back at the edun, had come on this trek. His conscience tormented him now, that his stubbornness might prove the death of one of these brave old men; and surely, he thought, the she'pan had foreseen this, and he had been too blind with his own self-importance to consider that her reasons might not have involved him. He had thought the worst of Medai, and repented it now; and it began to dawn on him that he might have been mistaken in other things.

But it would shame these men now, having begun, to turn back. He had brought them out here, he with his stubborn pride; he welcomed the pain, that drove clear thought from his mind, atonement for his pettiness, against them, against the dead. Medai had been no coward, no man light-of-thought; he was certain of that now, that his cousin had held a long time, against perfidy of his masters, against the gods knew what else.

And why these things had been: this was still beyond him.

"Eddan," he said quietly, when they rested in the shadow of a high crag, and the sand beyond them rippled in the ruddy light of Arain's zenith. A burrower had his lair out on the flat beyond. He had seen it pock the surface, sand funnelling down as it reacted to the breeze, thinking it had prey.

"Ai?"

"I think you believe Medai's death was not what the regul said."

Eddan, veiled, moved his hand, a gesture that agreed.

"I think," Niun continued, "that the Kel has already discussed this, and that I was probably the only one in the Kel who was surprised to find that so."

Eddan looked at him long. The membrane nictitated across his eyes, flashed clear again. "Niun," he said, "that is an uncharitable thing, to assume that we would willfully keep you from our thoughts in such a matter."

"But perhaps it is still so, sir, that you had reasons."

Eddan's hand closed on Niun's wrist, a hard grip. Eddan had taught him the yin'ein; there was none more skillful than Eddan and Pasev, to divide a man body from soul with delicacy; one could not see the blade move. And the strength was still in his hand. "Do not look to serve regul, Niun s'Intel Zain-Abrin. You serve the she'pan; and one day you will be in my place. I think that day is coming soon."

"If I should be kel'anth," said Niun, cold at the words of omen, and unsure what he meant by that, "then it will be a very small Kel. Everyone else is senior to me."

"You will have your honor, Niun. There was never doubt of this in our minds, only in yours. It will come."

He was disturbed to the heart by the deadly urgency of this, at Eddan's pressing this upon him. "I have never fought," he objected. "How am I fit for anything?"

Eddan shrugged again. "We are the Hand; others do the planning. But be sure that you have a use and that the she'pan has planned for it. Remember it. Medai was considered and rejected. Remember that too."

He sat stunned, all his surmises torn down and laid waste at once. "Sir," he said, but Eddan thrust away from him and rose, turning his face from him, making it plain that he wanted no further question on the matter. Niun rose to his feet, seeking some way to ask, let his hand fall helplessly:

when Eddan would not answer, he would not answer, and quite probably it was all Eddan could say, all that he knew how to say.

The she'pan is well-pleased with his death, Melein had said; the coldness of that still chilled him. And: *Medai was considered and rejected,* Eddan had told him.

For the first time he pitied his cousin, saw everything turned inside out.

Himself, in his youthful jealousy—Medai, whose crime had been only that he had looked on Melein, and that the she'pan had planned otherwise. Kesrith was a hard and unforgiving world. The Mother of Kesrith was like her world, without mercies.

His own stubbornness had run counter to her will. He had defied her, knowing nothing of her reasons. He had done a thing which kel'ein did not do and tested her resolve to stop him, at a time when the People could least afford division.

It was possible, he thought, that not alone the regul had killed Medai—that the she'pan and even Melein had had their part in it.

He pitied Medai, fearing for himself. He would have wished to have spoken with his cousin, both of them men now, and not one only—to have learned of Medai the things Eddan could not tell him. He looked at the black-shrouded form on the litter as he took up the ropes again, and found that all his confidence had left him.

He need not have been alone these years, he thought suddenly, and Medai need not have died, and so many things need not have happened, if he had not made the she'pan choose between them.

It was not alone the regul that had killed Medai.

It was evening when they reached the holy place, the cliffs, the windy recesses where the caves of Sil'athen hid the dead of the People that had died away from sun-burial. There were many, many graves, the oldest dating from before Kesrith had known regul, the last those that had been born on Nisren, and had fled here for refuge.

The valley was a long retreat where the cliffs marked a new level of the uplands. Here the sands were red, beginning with the cliffs, in contrast to the pale lowlands, and the red rock was banded at times with white. Where rock formed a hard cap, erosion by wind and the burning rains had made strange pillars and hulking shapes that guarded the way through Sil'athen, and cast strange shadows in the setting light of ruddy Arain. A windflower had occupied one of the crags; its tendrils glistened like threads of glass, red-stained, in the sunset. On the left of the entry a burrower had laired for many years: they swung wide, avoiding this guardian.

It was shaming to stumble here, at the end: Niun felt the sand shift underfoot and caught himself, fearing at first a smaller burrower, undetected; but it was an old hole, only soft sand. He gathered himself up, dusting the knee on which he had fallen, and leaned against the ropes, shaking off the several offered hands. There was a black shadow over his vision, tinged with red; the membrane half closed, no longer responsive to conscious will. The air he breathed was salt with his own evaporating moisture.

They passed the old graves, the thousands of the old Kath, from days before the regul. Then there were the lonely twelve of their own Kath, buried westward according to tradition, facing the rising sun, dawning hope: they were the child-bearers, and with them were buried the few sad children, those too gentle for Kesrith's harsh winds, lives that should have preserved the People, had Intel not chosen Kesrith for homeworld. Many worlds the regul had offered, fair, green worlds; but Intel had desired Kesrith. She had told them this. *The forge of a new people,* she had said of Kesrith. But the gentle Kath had died in that forging, leaving them desolate.

Facing the sun's setting were the Sen in their thousands, and the nineteen recent graves of their own Sen. These also, in their way, gentle and vulnerable, had failed in Intel's refining, leaving Melein and Sathell alone to serve.

In the highest cliffs were the graves of she'panei and the kel'ein who guarded them in death. It was not certain how many she'panei had been on Kesrith. Niun knew of fifty-nine. He also knew that no kel'en knew a whole truth. He thought on this through the red and black haze of other thoughts, as they turned toward the graves of the Kel.

There were only a few hundred, to the others' thousands, almost as few as the graves of the she'panei—on Kesrith. Their dead would many times outnumber the Sen; but very, very few found their graves in earth.

They stopped at the newest cave, where the veterans of

Nisren were entombed; and Niun forced himself to stay on his feet, to help them in unsealing it, moving rock until his hands were numb, for these stubborn old men would do everything if he did not forestall them. He ached and his own blood was on the rocks with which he made place for Medai.

Kel'ein were not buried like others: other castes faced into the valley of Sil'athen; but the Kel faced outward, toward the north, the traditional direction of evil. Row on row the other dead lay in the dark. When they lit their single lamp they could see them, musty black shadows in veils and robes moldering into ruin, veiled faces turned toward the north wall of the cave.

The air inside was cold and strange with decay. The dark oppressed. Niun stood, content for a moment only to stand, and let the old men set Medai in place among the others. They stopped then and faced north, and spoke over him the *Shon'jir,* the Passing ritual. Niun repeated the words—spoken at birthings and burials, heralding a life of the People into the world and out of it.

> *From Dark beginning*
> *To Dark at ending,*
> *Between them a Sun,*
> *But after comes Dark,*
> *And in that Dark,*
> *One ending.*

The words echoed in the cavern, in darkness wrapped about them; and Niun looked at the dead, and at his companions, and considered the frailty of them that chanted of the Dark; and the fragile breath's difference between lips that moved and those that could not. Terror possessed him, rebellion, to rush out into the open; but he did not give way. His lips continued to form the words.

> *From Dark to Dark*
> *Is one voyage.*
> *From Dark to Dark*
> *Is our voyage.*
> *And after the Dark,*
> *O brothers, o sisters,*
> *Come we home.*

He had never thought the words. He had mouthed them;
he had never felt them. He felt them now, looking about him.
Home.
This.
He held himself still while the others filed out, forced himself to be the last, mastering his fear; but even when he had
the light of stars and Kesrith's first moon overhead, he felt
that cold inside him, that many suns would never warm
away.
"Seal it," said Eddan.
He gathered up the rocks one by one, and fitted them into
place, making tight their joinings, sealing them between himself and Medai. His breath came hard. He found himself with
tears flooding his cheeks, for his shame before Medai.
Not like you, cousin, not like you, he kept thinking, as he
set each stone in place, a determination, a wall that he built,
a protection for the hallowed dead against the winds and the
sands and the prying fingers of the suruin that ranged the
high hills: a protection for himself, against the truth inside.
And they were done, all debts paid. The brothers blew dust
upon the wind; he gathered up his handful and did likewise,
bidding farewell. Then they rested a time, before beginning
the long, hard trek back to the edun.
Soah joined the first moon overhead, making their passage
safer, and they set forth. Eddan went first, using his staff to
probe for windflowers in the dark air, wary as those who
walked the wilds of Kesrith dus-less had to be; but Niun lent
his company to Sirain, who was half blind and very frail, and
too proud to accept help. Often he gave way to exhaustion
himself to slow their progress, as if the sores on his hands
and the long walk and the sleeplessness had utterly undone
him; but of a sudden pride was not important to him: it was
only important that Sirain's pride be saved, that he not die.
He did not flaunt his youth at them any longer. He found
comradeship with them, as if they and he had finally understood a thing that he should have understood long ago.
They shared water and food together—sat, the six of them,
in the dark after the moons had set, and broke fast; and the
brothers were sorry for his hands, and offered of their own
experience various advice to heal them. But Eddan cut the
stalk of a young luin and rubbed the juice of it on the sores,

which was a remedy counted sovereign for every wound: it eased the pain.

In the journey after that the pace was slower still, and perhaps Sirain had seen through his careful pretense from the beginning, for at last he clasped Niun's arm in a feeble grip and admitted that this time it was himself who must rest a time.

By such degrees they came homeward.

And it was evening again when they returned, and the edun's entry was lit for them, and the great bulk of the ailing dus still was to be seen at the door.

In the end there was no hurrying. Niun had been anxious lest he have to take up Sirain and carry him, which would have been a crushing shame to the old warrior. And for Sirain's sake, and for Eddan's, who labored now, they walked slowly despite their anxiety to reach the edun, their dread of things that might have gone amiss in their absence.

But there in the doorway Melein waited, and gave them gentle welcome, unveiled, as they unveiled themselves, coming home.

"Is all well?" Eddan asked of her.

"All is well," she said. "Come in. Be at ease."

They entered, footsore and cold, and passed the long hall to the Shrine, that first of all, making their individual prayers and washing of the hands and face. And when they were done they turned toward the steps of the Kel-tower, for they were exhausted.

But Melein waited, outside the Shrine.

"Niun," she said. "The Mother still sends for you."

He was tired. He dreaded the meeting. He turned his shoulder to her rudely and walked out of the hall, to the step, to see how the dus fared. He gave it a scrap of meat that he had saved from his own rations on the journey; but someone else had filled the pannikin with water.

It turned from his gift, and would have none of him. He had thought that this would be the case, but he had tried. He sank down in exhaustion on the step and stared at the dus helplessly.

Never would the beasts tolerate him, and this one, bereaved and suffering, he could not help.

He gave a great sigh that was almost a sob, and stared at his bloody hands in the light, so sensitive, so delicate to wield the yin'ein, and reduced to this. There was no warrior here, none that the dus could detect. It chose to die, like Medai. It found nothing in him to interest it in living.

He had the *seta'al* and the weapons and the black robes; he had the skill, but the heart in him was terrified, and angry, and the dus, being sensitive to such things, would not have him.

He swept off *mez* and *zaidhe*, bundled them into the crook of his arm, and with his right hand he gathered a handful of dust from the side of the step and smeared his brow with it, a penance for his jealousy.

Then he went inside, ascended the stairs of the inmost tower, that of the she'pan. He opened the door to the she'pan's hall cautiously, and saw that Melein knelt at the she'pan's left hand, arranging the cushions.

"Hush," said Melein, accusing him with her eyes. "She has just now fallen asleep. You are too late tonight. Be still."

But the she'pan stirred as he came near her, and her golden eyes opened and the membrane receded, leaving them clear.

"Niun," she said very softly.

"Little Mother." He sank down on her right, and offered his bowed head to her gentle touch, an intimacy the Kel offered no others but the she'pan or a mate. Her hands were warm against the chill of his skin.

"You are safe," she said. "You are back safely." And as if that were all the burden of what she desired, like a child sleeping with a favorite toy at hand, she settled back into her dreams.

Niun stayed still, leaned his head against the arm of her chair, and gradually gave himself to sleep, her hand still resting on his shoulder. His dreams were troubled. At times he woke, seeing the cave and the dark; and then he saw the golden light that surrounded them, and felt the weight of the she'pan's hand, and knew where he was.

She dreamed, did the Mother, and reclaimed him; possibly she confused him with another. He did not know. He was kel'en, like the other. He sat at her side and slept at times, and knew that the sum of his duty to her was to live, to stay by her. She had rejected Medai, and never from her had come a word of regret, of sorrow for him.

You are safe, she had said.

The bonds, so lately slipped, ensnared him again; and at last he gave up his struggle and knew that he must serve to the service that had claimed him.

The *su-she'pani kel'en a'anu*.

The she'pan's kel'en, like those in the cliffs.

In the whispered long-ago days, when there was no war, there had been such, when mri fought against mri and house against house, when she'pan contended against she'pan.

Her last kel'en, the one—he foresaw with what he thought was a true vision—would never indeed know the Dark of the caves of Sil'athen: the one to seal the barrier for the others, and to remain outside, a guardian.

He slid a glance toward Melein, saw her awake also, her eyes staring into the shadows; he realized what it had surely been for her, alone here, with Intel.

For her also, he was afraid.

Chapter Nine

———◆◆◆———

It was, in the Nom, the twentieth day.

It was possible finally for human nerves to adjust to Kesrith's longer day. Duncan rose and wandered to the private bath—that luxury at least their onworld accommodations had afforded him, though he must content himself with the recycled ration of water available within the Nom's apparatus.

The Nom depended entirely on life-support systems like those of a ship: regul did not find surface existence comfortable, although it was tolerable.

Neither was it, he suspected, comfortable for humans.

Filtered air, recycled water, and that originally reclaimed from a sea so laden with alkali that nothing would live in it. The world's little animal life was confined to the uplands, and from what information he had obtained from the translated regul advisories on that score, there was little born of Kesrith that was harmless.

The interior of the Nom held gardens that somewhat humidified their air and provided pleasantness, but the alien harshness of the foliage and the accompanying scent of regul made the gardens less pleasant than they might have been.

He was, he reckoned, growing used to regul. He was learning to tolerate a number of things he had once thought impossible to accept, and that in twenty days of close contact.

It was close contact. There were no restricted hours, no confinement to quarters, but the regulations forbade them to leave the Nom at any time. Stavros, of course, would not do so as long as regul remained on Kesrith—a reasonably brief time to wait: ten days until the first human ships should come in and replace the regul.

Duncan reckoned, at least, that their sanity might hold that long. He had a mental image of their first encounter with those humans incoming: that the landing party would find them both changed, bizarre and altered by their stay on Kesrith. He was not the man that had begun the voyage; SurTac Sten Duncan on Haven had been capable of far more impulsive behavior than Sten Duncan, aide to the new governor of Kesrith. He had acquired patience, the ability to reckon slowly; and he had acquired something of regul manners, ponderous and unwieldy as their conventions were. They began to come as naturally as yes, sir and no, sir: Favor, my lord; and, Be gracious, elder.

They had promised him retirement after five years; but five years in this sullen environment would make him unfit for human company: five years from now he might find clean air a novelty and Haven daylight strange to the eyes—might find human manners banal and odd after the stark, survival-oriented settlement that men would have to make of Kesrith. He was in the process of adapting: any world, any climate, any operation in hostile terrain that wanted human hands directly at work onworld was a SurTac's natural job, and he was learning the feel of Kesrith.

Stavros was doing the same thing in his intellectual way, absorbing every oddity within his reach—like the regul, never seeming to need notes, simply looking and listening, on his rare excursions from his room to the gardens.

This morning he had an appointment in Hulagh's offices. It was an important occasion.

Something rumbled outside, different from the accustomed thunder of departing ships. Duncan switched the view to let light through the Nom's black windows. They had a view of the whole horizon from the sea at the right to the hills at the left, save that they could not see the mri edun and could not see the port, the two things in which they had the greatest interest: it was of course no accident that they were arranged as they were. Nothing in that desolation had changed in twenty days; but now above the hills there was a change. A storm was moving in, the clouds grey, red-tinged, shadowing the sea in one quarter. Lightning flashed with impossible rapidity.

The weather, said the prepared statements of the bai's staff, *is unpredictable by season, and occasionally violent. The rain is mildly caustic, especially in showers following duststorms. It will be desirable to bathe if one is caught in the rain. Above all it is necessary to seek suitable cover at the earliest indication of a storm. The winds can achieve considerable violence. If fronts converge on the seaward and hillward sides, cyclonic action is frequent.*

The red light in the ceiling mount flared, summoning him. Stavros was awake. Duncan quickly obtained a cup of soi from the wall dispenser—soi being the regul liquid stimulant, and only mildly flavored, unlike most regul foods. It was one of the few regul graces they had come to enjoy. A touch of sweetener made it completely palatable. He added the two drops, set the cup on a small tray, gathered up the morning dispatches from the slot, and carried the offering in to Stavros' quarters—again accessible only from his own apartment.

"Good morning, sir," he murmured, courtesy which was regularly answered with only a civil nod, and that sometimes belated. Stavros was in exceptional spirits this morning. He actually smiled, a gesture which made his thin mouth the tighter.

"Do the windows," Stavros said. It was thundering again.

Duncan switched them over and let in the day's sullen light.

The first drops began to spatter the dust on the panes. A crack of thunder made the glass bow and rattle, and Stavros walked over to enjoy the view. Duncan himself felt a heightening of senses, a stimulation unaccustomed in their carefully controlled environment. This was something the regul could not schedule or censor, the violence of nature. He could see it sweep down on the sea, where the waves whitecapped, dyed pink. The whole day was enveloped in reddish murk, and fitful with lightning.

"This," said Stavros, "is going to be one of the major obstacles to settlement here."

Duncan felt he was called on to discuss the matter. He did not know precisely how; his training was not in civilizing worlds, but in taking them. "The regul gave us an edge there," he said, "with this city for a base."

"There's considerable attrition in machinery on Kesrith, so I'm told; and for some idiotic reason they've followed the mri example and built a number of outposts out of rammed earth and binder, cheap but remarkably unsuited for the climate."

"If you have a lot of labor you can keep rebuilding, I suppose."

"Humans can't run a colony that way." Stavros went off on another tangent of thought, sipping at the warm drink. Thunder rattled at the glass again. Wind hit with a force that sent a sheet of water between them and the world, obscuring everything. Duncan swore in surprise and awe.

"The storm shields," Stavros advised him. It was hailing now, a rapid patter that threatened the windows. It was coming from their direction.

Duncan quickly activated the shutters. They whisked across and cut off the daylight; the room lights compensated. Then he went back at once to see to the windows in his own quarters, appalled, even afraid to approach the glass under the violence that battered against it.

The thunder broke overhead as he reached for the switch. His heart was pounding as the storm shield slid over the window. Distantly he could hear an alarm in the building, and for a moment the hiss of air in the ducts ceased and he could feel a pressure in his ears like ascent in an aircraft.

He went to the door, opened it. Regul were whisking about in sleds along the corridors in mad confusion. The pressure eased then. He heard a sound that was too deep for sound, shuddering through the building.

"*Nai chiug-ar?*" —What is it?—he asked the first regul he saw afoot. "*Nai chiug-ar?*"

"*Sak noi kanuchdi hoc-nar,*" the youngling spat back, which had something to do with the port, but nothing else he could understand. "*Sa-ak toc dac,*" it hissed at him then. Keep to quarters, favor.

He retreated, closed the door and called the main desk for information. No one would respond to his calls. Eventually everything seemed to grow calm outside, only a rush of rain against the storm shields. He ventured finally to open the shields and saw nothing but a wash of water, distorting everything outside. He closed them again.

And from Stavros' room, long silence.

He gathered together his shaken faculties, berating himself for his panic, and went in to see about the old man, expecting cynical amusement at a SurTac who feared storms.

The cup was on the floor, a brown stain on the carpet. He saw the old man half across the bed, still in his nightclothes.

"Sir?" he exclaimed. He went and touched his shoulder fearfully, then turned him over and obtained faint movement, a gasp for breath, a flutter of the right eye. The left remained drawn, that side of the mouth peculiarly distorted. Stavros tried to talk to him, unintelligible.

In the next instant Duncan ran from the room, from his quarters to the hall and the duty desk, trying every word that would come to mind to express his need.

"Stavros," he said at last, "Stavros!" and this finally seemed to impress itself on the youngling. It rose, lumbering in its gait, and came with him.

It stood, for a considerable time, at the foot of the bed. "Elder," it said finally, with the regul equivalent of a shrug. Here was an elder. It did not seem capable of rising; this was natural for an elder. Duncan seized its massive arm and raised his voice.

"Sick," he insisted.

Slowly, with ostentatious slowness, the youngling turned and went to the console, coded in a call and spoke to higher authority.

Authority responded, in a bewildering patter of words. Duncan sank down and bowed his head into his hands, despair knotted in his stomach.

And when an array of important regul arrived, and began with dispatch to load Stavros into one of the sled transports, Duncan stayed nearby constantly, and insisted with forceful gestures that he intended to come with Stavros.

A regul seized him, firmly but without violence, and held him, while the sled moved and departed. Then the regul let him go. It was all the restraint that need have been applied; there was no way for him to follow down that web of tracks.

He sank into a chair in his quarters, shivering with anger and terror, and utterly, utterly helpless to do anything for Stavros.

Outside the storm pattered against the shields. It continued for an hour or more. He left the room four times during that period to go down to the duty desk and demand information on Stavros' condition, each time arming himself with applicable phrases from his dictionary and lesson sheets.

The regul on duty had learned quickly enough that it need not be silent to express disdain; it needed only to shower words at him as rapidly as it could speak, impressing on him his incapacity to understand.

"*Dal*," it said finally, "*seo-gin*."

Go away. It repeated it several times more.

He turned away, not for the apartment, but for the forbidden first-level ramp, down which bai Hulagh had his offices. Words shrilled after him. A trio of regul closed in on him and marched him firmly enough to his door, pushing at him to make him enter.

"Stavros sick," one said finally.

It was the sum of information available until the morning, an entire night in sleepless anxiety.

But with dawn they came in numbers, and transferred a brown wrapped bundle from a sled to the bed; and Duncan, roughly thrusting himself into their midst, saw Stavros conscious, but still with that deadness about his left side.

And then there was deference in plenty among the younglings, for a hum sounded at the door and a sled console eased through the ample doorways to rest in their midst.

Bai Hulagh.

Words came from Stavros, distorted, unrecognizable in either language.

"Honorable Stavros. Rest now." The bai rose within his sled with great effort and looked directly upon Duncan. "Youngling, the affliction is to the nervous system."

"Bai," Duncan said, "help him."

The regul shrugged. "Human structure is strange to us. We regret. We are in the midst of considerable disaster. The storm toppled a tower at the port. There was great loss of life. Our facilities are strained by this emergency. Our information on the human system is very scant."

"I can provide you—I can provide you myself, bai, if your medics would—"

"Youngling," said the regul, a basso profundo that vibrated with disdain, "we do not have information. We do not experiment on living beings. This moderate restoration of function we could accomplish, no more. This is an elder of your people. He will be made comfortable to the utmost of our abilities. Do you, youngling, question this statement?"

"Be gracious," he murmured, reserving decisions to others;

he moved to Stavros' side, took the good hand in his. A mild pressure answered. Stavros' pale eyes glittered wetly, alive, fully cognizant and trying to command him something, a stern and reprimanding look. He tightened his hand in reassurance and looked up at the bai.

"Favor, reverence," he said. "I am distressed for him."

The bai gestured him to come. He let slip Stavros' fingers and did so, submitted to the touch of the regul bai, whose rough fingers rested on his shoulder, a considerable weight.

The bai spoke curtly to his servitors, who hastened about their business. Then the wrinkle-enfolded eyes looked into Duncan's, and the bai's fingers tightened until it was hard not to wince.

"Youngling, I am informed you have neglected food and drink. This is an expression of grief? This is religion?"

"No, reverence, I will eat."

"Good." The word rumbled forth, almost incomprehensible in its depth. The pressure increased until Duncan felt the joint give. He flinched. The bai dropped the hand at once.

And the bai turned ponderously and levered himself back into his sled, settled. It whined, backing, and turned and retreated.

Duncan stood and stared after it, after the others, who withdrew almost as quickly. A sound came from Stavros.

"Sir?" he asked at once, trying to keep his voice natural. He turned and saw Stavros beckon toward the table. Stavros' notes were there. He gathered them up and offered them, but Stavros with his right hand fumbled after the tablet only. Duncan understood and found the pen to give him. He knelt down and braced the tablet as Stavros wrote, heavily, with childlike awkwardness.

Regul not upset, he read. *Process with them natural to age. Mobility may return. No reason for panic.* The awkward, slanted writing reached the accessible limits of the page. Duncan reversed the tablet, braced it higher.

Humans due soon, Stavros resumed. *Disaster at port— truth. Regul evacuation schedule hampered; Hazan damaged. Regul much concerned. Mri—need to find out what mri doing. This most urgent. Listen to regul talk, learn of mri, don't provoke.*

"Even leaving the Nom if I have to?"

SurTac—now become diplomat. Careful. Take my instruc-

tions. Regul kill younglings here—many. Consult first on everything. Move me. Now. Console.

He did not want to move him; but Stavros cursed at him thickly and ordered him aloud, and evidently was determined. Duncan carefully, tenderly gathered up the old man and placed him within the sled console in the corner, supported him, adjusted the form-fitting cushions to hold him securely. Stavros' right hand sought after controls, made further adjustments. The sled console turned. The screen turned independently. A message, hand-keyed, crawled across the small screen.

Can learn even this.

"Yes, sir," Duncan said with a tightness in his throat. He was suddenly concerned for this man, for Stavros personally.

The message-crawl resumed. *Order food for you. Rest.*

"And for yourself, sir?"

Stavros turned the sled, jerkily maneuvered it next to the bed. He operated the console arm to dim the lights. *I wait,* the screen said. *No needs.*

Chapter Ten

———◆—◆—◆———

"TRUEBROTHER."

On the step beside the dus, Niun looked over his shoulder.
It was seldom now that he met his sister informally, brother
and sister, daithen and daithe, as they had been before. She
surprised him with the dus. He was embarrassed to be found
at this charity: there had been a distance between them,
though they had been much together in the she'pan's hall. He
did not like to be with her, alone, not any longer. It was
painful, that the closeness between them was gone.

He continued a moment, trying to tempt the dus with a
scrap of food, for until she had come, he had deceived himself that there was the slightest flicker of interest in the dark
eyes of the dus. Now it would not come. But he had so deceived himself many a time since its coming to the edun. He
shrugged and casually tossed the prize to the dus, letting it
land between its massively clawed forepaws. Sometimes,
eventually, it would eat. It accepted just enough to stay alive;
and sometimes he would see the scrap shrivelled and neglected
that evening, and the dus moved slightly elsewhere until it
was taken away; for the dus was very proud, and did not
really want to eat.

Someone else saw that the waterbowl by the step was constantly full. This was great extravagance on Kesrith. Ordinarily a sick dus simply complained when thirsty and received
what it needed; and a healthy one derived all its moisture re-
quirement from food it ate. Niun suspected kel Pasev of this
wasteful charity. She had her own dus, but she was capable
of such feelings toward a good animal. He was not himself so
deft in his offerings as was Pasev. Doubtless everyone in the
edun knew how desperately he tried to feed the creature, and
claim it, and how it stubbornly refused him.

Doubtless another kel'en would be feeding it if he did not. The dus shamed them all in its loyal grief. It found not one of them worthy to take it; and rarely would they transfer affection, but he still hoped, desperately, for the life of this one.

"Sometimes," said Melein, "they simply cannot be saved."

She sat down on the dusty step with him, heedless of her robes of caste: but the granular sand of the edun grounds did not cling so much as white lowlands powder. She wore the light veil over her silken mane in the out-of-doors, for the Sen disdained to cover.

The body of a kel'en is itself a Mystery of the People, the teachings held, *and therefore the Kel veils; the body of a sen'en is a veil to that within, which is a Mystery of the People, and therefore the Sen veils not.*

Save to the unacceptable.

The weather was fair after the storm of days past, in which wrack and disaster had blown down the passes and dealt havoc in the regul town. The smoke of the destruction in the lowlands had been visible even through the rain, and when the worst of the storm was done, the kel'ein had looked out from the summit of the Sen-tower with a new and bitter satisfaction.

"Ah," Eddan had said, when they noted the smoke and the fire, "Kesrith has her way with the masters even yet."

It was likely that many regul had perished in the conflagration. Such satisfaction was a thing that once no mri would have thought or felt. But that was before the death of a kel'en unaccounted for on a regul ship, and before it was clear that humans would possess the world.

Now the stars of evening began to show in a clear sky, and there was no wind to stir the sand and make the *mez* advisable. Such crystal evenings were frequent after the greatest storms, as if the very world lay exhausted after the recent violence.

He dropped his own veil and looped it under his chin, refastening it. There was no likelihood of tsi'mri here, and he did not need it.

"Shall we walk?" Melein suggested.

He had no such thing in mind; but rarely did Melein ask anything of him any longer. He arose and offered her his hand to help her up. Thereafter they walked, side by side in the direction Melein chose, on the small trail that led from the corner of the edun to the rocks at the top of the causeway. He found himself remembering the times that they had run that distance, they three, agile as the dusty lizards, children without the veil, small slim-limbed boys and smaller girl, racing illicitly for the vantage point from which they could see the ships at the port come and go.

They had been ships with magical names then, mri ships, regul ships: *Mlereinei, Kamrive, Horagh-no,* that came from distant stars and the glory of battles. As children they had played at war and duel, and imagined themselves great kel'ein, glittering with honors like the far-travelled kel'ein that visited from the ships and departed their own ways again—like their truemother and their father that left separately with the ships and never visited homeworld again.

Tonight they walked, he of the Kel, she of the Sen, weighted with their robes of caste and their separate laws. When they reached the rock that overlooked the valley, he leaped up first and pulled her up after with a single tug— there was still the girl Melein within the golden robes, agile and quick as a kel'e'en, unbecoming the gravity of her caste.

They sat together while the red sun vanished, and watched the whole of the valley, and the glow of lights where the port was, and the wound the storm had made there, a darkness amid the lights near *Hazan.*

"Why did you ask me here?" he asked of her at last.

"To talk with you."

He did not like this manner in her. The last light touched her face. It was that of a stranger for a moment, someone he should remember, and did not, quite. It was not Melein as he knew her, but a sen'e'en that contained quiet, secret thoughts. He suddenly wished she would not pursue the opening he had given her. He foreknew that she might rob him of his peace; and he could not stop her from doing it.

"You do not smile anymore," she said. "You do not even look up when you are named."

"I am not a child."

"You do not love the she'pan."

"I came. I sit. I wait. This seems to be all she wants of me. It is her right."

"You do not much go out of the edun."

"I have given up, Melein. That is all."

She looked up, where the stars glittered. Her arm resting on her raised knee pointed toward Elag's star, that shone and danced above the hills. "There are humans now," she said. "But this is different, here—Kesrith. This is homeworld. Sanctuary for the People. The Holy."

He looked at her, sullen, frightened. "Remember that I am kel'en."

"The Kel must remain unlearned because the Kel ventures where our enemies are, and where knowledge that cannot serve the Kel cannot be permitted. For all traditions, however minor, there are reasons. You are a kel'en of homeworld, and you will hear what it would not be good for a kel'en elsewhere to hear."

He rose and set his back against the rock, leaning there with his arms folded and the rising breeze touching him with more chill than was comfortable. It was night now, the last of the sun slipped from view. He did not know why she had wished to come out here. The hills were full of menace. The ha-dusei, wild relatives of the tame companions of the kel'ein, were not to be trusted. There were windflowers and burrowers, and serpents that hid in the rocks. He owed a sen'e'en his protection; and it was arrant stupidity to be out here with Melein in his charge after dark. Her value to the edun was incalculably above his.

"We can talk elsewhere, later," he said. "I do not think we should have come here at this hour."

"Listen to me!"

Her voice was edged, cruel, a blow that stunned. Melein was his little sister. She had never used that tone with him.

"Today," she said, "the she'pan called me in private. Today she gave me rank with Sathell. And you understand this."

She'pan's successor, her Chosen.

In the nethermost parts of his mind he had known it would come, this the only reasonable purpose behind Intel's snatching Melein out of Kel and into Sen.

Not to bear children, but to learn the Pana, the Mysteries; not to continue the People, but to rule them.

And Intel had taken him likewise, to defend challenge to herself, to guard her—to kill, if need be, any overanxious successor, and the kel'en that supported her challenger's cause.

He gave a single bitter curse, understanding; and saw the hurt leap into Melein's eyes.

"I am sorry that you take it so," she said.

"Why must she have kept me by her and not Medai?"

"She trusted you, and never Medai."

He considered that, and its reasons. "She trusted you," he said softly, "while I guard her sleep. While she could set me against you."

The hurt became shock. The thought seemed to startle her. "No," she said. "I am not apt to challenge her."

"Not so long as you have regard for me," he answered. "She feels her mortality on her or she would not have named you yet. And some kel'en will guard her tomb."

"She would not take you. Eddan—Sirain—they would seek the honor. But not you.

"Maybe with the humans at hand the question is pointless. I am thinking ahead of the hour, and that is beyond my caste. You will have to think that through, truesister. I am far from knowing the future. I can only speak for what is true now."

"She is not preparing to cede homeworld quietly. Niun, I am young, I am nothing compared to Intel's experience. Other she'panei would hesitate to challenge her: she knows too much. Killing her would rob the People of so much, you do not know how much. It would be an act of—I do not know, Niun, I do not know. If I should succeed her as she'pan of homeworld, here am I—young, inexperienced. I know that some older she'pan will come then and challenge, and it will be my place to die. I want her to live, I desperately want her to live, and she is dying, Niun."

He found himself trembling, hurting to reassure her; and there was no comfort. She spoke of things beyond his caste; and yet he thought that she had laid out all the truth for him, and stole what remained of his peace and hope. He had always thought that she would survive him.

"We were unlucky," she said, "in being last-born of the People: not alone of Kesrith, Niun, but of all the People. We were without choice because we were simply the last. I wish it were different."

What she said struck at other confidences. He looked at her with the wind whipping at them and chilling to the skin and ceased even to shiver. "Of all the People?"

"Edunei have fallen," she said, "and children have died; and kel'e'ein are occupied with war, and nothing else. I should not have answered," she added. "But of our generation, there is little left. Those older—they will get other children. It is not too late."

She tried to comfort him. He reassured himself that she had faith in their future, and this was enough. "But then," he said, catching up a thought, "then Intel will not plan to lose you. You might be after all the ablest after her; and if she bequeaths my service to you—if you should challenge or return challenge, Melein, I can defend you. I am not unable to defend you: I am skilled in the yin'ein. Nine years they have kept me in training. I must be capable of something."

She was silent a long time. Finally she arose. "Come," she said. "Let us return to the edun. I am cold."

And she was silent as they climbed down to the trail and walked back; she wept. He saw it in the starlight, and took off his own veil and offered it to her, a gesture of profound tenderness.

"No," she said fiercely. He nodded, and flung the *mez* over his shoulder, walking beside her. "You are right," she said finally. "I will not surrender the office and die without challenge if it comes to me. I will kill to hold it."

"It is a great honor for you," he said, because he thought that he should have said something of the kind when she first told him.

She let go her breath, a slow hiss. "What honor—to go into some strange edun, and into a strange Kel, and kill some woman who never did me hurt? I do not want that honor."

"But Intel will arm you for this," he said. "She will make you able. She has surely planned for this for many years."

She looked up at him, her shadowed face set and calm. "I think you are not far wrong," she said, "that she wanted you by her because she knows I could make trouble in the House. She trusts you. She does not trust me."

He shivered, hearing in her voice the bitterness he had always suspected was there, and shadows tore away between himself and the Sen-tower and the she'pan. He remembered Melein preparing the cup each evening, the cup that helped she'pan sleep; and each evening, the she'pan drinking, nothing questioning. He suspected what ungentle things might run in

Intel's drug-hazed mind—a she'pan foreseeing her own death and mistrusting her successor with good reason.

Intel had wanted Melein disarmed: had sent Medai into service, had kept her brother close by. Some kel'en would guard Intel's tomb: normally it would be one of her Husbands, not a son. But there might be one instruction if she passed of age, and another if by Melein's hand.

And Melein would have to challenge against him to challenge Intel: he would die before Intel would; but Melein would have to find a kel'en to champion her—and there was none who would agree to that.

Intel had done well to banish Medai.

But Melein was not capable of the things of which Intel suspected her; he insisted on believing that she was not. Caste and teaching and the bitterness of her imprisonment could not have changed his truesister to that extent. He would not believe that Intel's fears were justified.

I want her to live, I desperately want her to live, Melein had said.

"How much," he asked finally, "did she bid you tell me?"

"Less," she said, "than I told you."

"Yes," he said, "I had thought so."

They came back to the edun, she drawing ahead of him as they entered. He looked aside at the dus that turned its head from him. When he looked up, she had gone on into the shadows, toward the stairs of her own tower.

She did not look back.

He went toward the she'pan's tower, to take up his duty, where he belonged.

Chapter Eleven

THERE WAS quiet over Kesrith. After so many hazards, after
two days stalled with the port in chaos from the storm, that
last shuttle had lifted with its cargo of refugees, to the station
where the freighter *Restrivi* was forming the last regular civil-
ian list that would leave the world. Hereafter there was time,
necessary time, for setting final matters in order. Against the
ruddy sun of Kesrith there was only *Hazan* remaining—
armed and, when her minor repairs were completed, star-
capable; she waited with her crew constantly within her. She
carried in her tapes the way to Nurag, to regul homeworld, to
safety and civilization for the few hundred left on Kesrith.

A ten of times each passing day bai Hulagh Alagn-ni,
working in his heated offices in the Nom complex, looked up
at the windows and concerned himself with the condition of
Hazan. The dual-capable ship, strong enough behind her
screens for combat, was yet a perilously fragile structure
when grounded. He had hesitated to take her down in the
first place; he had suffered agonies of mind in the hours of
the storm's approach, had decided against lofting her to sta-
tionside.

And then—then, to have a witless aircraft pilot attempt to
outrun the storm and risk the crosswinds, a known peril at
Kesrith's field—on such an occurrence the whole mission was
almost lost. Hulagh cursed each time he thought of it, the
youngling pilot and passengers, of course, beyond retribution.
He was relieved that, at the least, damage had been confined
to the tower and loading facilities, and that to *Hazan's* structure was minimal. Luck had been with him. *Hazan* was in his
trust over the objections of powerful influences back on
homeworld. He had risked everything in securing for himself

and his interests this post, replacing old Gruran and Solgah Holn-ni—an assignment for which his personal age and erudition had qualified him, and thereby won doch Alagn the status it was long overdue.

But as with landing the ship, as in other decisions he had made along the way, it was necessary to risk in order to gain. It was necessary to demonstrate to homeworld his claimed ability and that of doch Alagn in order to obtain the influence permanently.

He could do so by salvaging the most possible benefit of Kesrith, after its loss by Gruran Holn-ni and his get; and Solgah Holn-ni—he thought with disgust and contempt of the prolific female who had ruled Holn's establishment of Kesrith, and lorded it so thoroughly over the zone and over the war that was her creation—Solgah was on her way to homeworld in utter confusion, stripped of her command, most of her younglings left behind, their ranks decimated by Holagh's own orders, survivors parcelled out to many different colonies, the doch in complete disorganization. She would be lucky if her influences on homeworld enabled her to escape sifting and the execution of her younglings. At the least, Holn was due for some years of obscurity.

The memory still pleased him, how Solgah had received the shock of *Hazan's* unscheduled and unauthorized landing: how she had fluttered and blustered with prohibitions and objections, until he had made known to her his homeworld-granted authority to assume control.

Now it was his office to complete the evacuation Solgah had begun, to save as much as possible from the concessions her weak kinsman Gruran Holn-ni had granted in negotiations at Elag, trying to save the inner portions of the vast Holn empire. It was his task to prepare Kesrith to receive human occupation, and to remove regul properties as much as could be saved, and regul personnel, as many as could be saved; and to ensure that humans drew the least possible benefit from what they had won in war and in negotiations.

Hulagh had dealt with humans indirectly for three homeworld years, and met with a few after replacing Gruran, and knew them—including the two that had come in on *Hazan*—with a quiet but mild distaste, less distaste, in fact, than he had ever felt for mri, who served regul. The human war, of course, had been a complete mistake, an error in calculations, and not one attributable to doch Alagn. It had been abundantly clear to wiser regul minds for the better part of five years that the companies of Holn doch had involved themselves in an utter fiasco, from which the mri were unable to rescue them, and that error would have been corrected then, if it had been possible to restrain the obstinacies and military power of such as Holn, whose employ of mercenary kel'ein and whose obvious self-interest in retaining the disputed territories had stalled off any change in policy.

Now, at last, after the consequences of the original error were multiplied to great cost, after regul lives and properties and home territory itself had been lost, the Holn empire tottering on the brink, now the military Holn handed the tangled and dangerous situation—reluctantly even so—over to older, wiser minds on Nurag.

And politics, in a turn of events unforeseen by the Holn, had served to turn the Holn authority finally into the hands of Alagn, and to elevate Alagn to a status in which Alagn, with the right Alagn in command, could utterly ruin doch Holn.

Holn had left a tangle behind them. Bai Hulagh was far from satisfied with the treaty terms within which he must operate, but they were Holn's legacy, sealed, legal, recorded and beyond his power to adjust. Yet if the cession of three colonial systems, costly as that was, had created a permanent and reliable boundary between human and regul claims, it could turn out to be one of the wiser things doch Holn had done in its administration. Doubtless, Hulagh felt, the humans now clearly knew that they had made all the cheap gain they could reasonably expect in this adventure, and that hereafter regul would resist with more vigor. The humans were apparently perplexed and disturbed by this sudden change of authority on the frontier, and yet they seemed anxious to honor the treaty. Kesrith was a likely and sensible boundary: the dead space of the Deep discouraged exploration regulward without considerable routing round by Hesoghan, an old and firmly regul holding; and the lure of the Haze-stars would lead humans from Kesrith rimward in due time. So Hulagh planned in his strategies, mapping what he considered might be new directions in regul policy. The humans would be attracted by the wealth toward which Kesrith had been reaching; but likewise the regul stars had mineral wealth sufficient to sustain industries without the convenient luxury of doch Holn's outermost colonies. Economic effects would be felt, but only in small degree on homeworld; and so long as the elders of homeworld were well-supplied in their needs, the Alagn operation would be favorably judged.

And afterward, it was only one arm of regul expansion that had been cut off. Two others remained. One of them was the presently meager holding of doch Alagn.

To direct, to shape, to rule, to settle himself eternally into the memory not alone of doch Alagn, but of the center of Nurag—this was the dream Hulagh savored. In his vast age he had outlived his rivals, had seen them dust; and he remembered, and planned long. He had obliterated the younglings of his chiefest enemies. He risked everything now in assuming personal command of Kesrith: if matters went amiss, it would be remembered that Hulagh of Alagn was in charge when they did so; but here on Kesrith also lay wealth he desperately needed.

The terms of the human/regul treaty surrendered only the bare earth of the ceded worlds. There was no specified claim of valuable hardware, cities, resources. Bare earth was all the encroaching humans need find when they arrived; and redeveloping the stubborn wilderness of Kesrith would occupy them long enough to give regul-kind a breathing space—while the plunder of Kesrith would go into the stores of Alagn doch, legitimate salvage on which Holn had no claim.

And all this under the very eyes of the human envoys.

This satisfied Hulagh no less, to discredit the human who had been sent to oversee the transition of power. The sudden illness of the human elder and the natural timidity of its single youngling were a convenience beyond measure. A regul elder would have demanded constant and detailed reports of actions by his hosts; a competent one would have demanded them in such volume and at such a pace that nothing escaped his notice; a resourceful one would have used his youngling's eyes to see what he was not meant to see. But none of this had the human envoy managed on any great scale. The human concentrated on the wrong materials, learned the language assiduously and reheard reports which he had already been given in his own language, going over old information as if he suspected he could learn something new from it, as if there were discrepancies or untruths in plain statements. Such deceptions might be the human practice; they were not regul. What was happening was as wide as the port and as plain as the ships that daily lifted, and when humans arrived some few days hence they would find a stripped and ruined possession and their delegate in command of a barren wilderness incapable of sustaining life on any large scale.

This was itself a coup that the council on Nurag would savor when it heard.

Hulagh had been perplexed originally that the two humans had contrived no means of circumventing the onerous restrictions placed on them. Only once had they broken quarantine, a quarantine no regul would have accepted in principle in the first place; and that one success seemed without forethought and was embarrassedly, tacitly ignored by the envoy. It had succeeded only because it had been uncharacteristic of the humans, a minor victory in the sense of its unhappy result, but actually of no possible benefit to them. In the end only the kel'en had suffered for it, and that needlessly, as impractical as all his kind. The mri had been a man of importance among their bloody, stubborn species. He had promised perhaps to be valuable; but he had been ruined. The humans remained ignorant even of this small revenge they had inflicted on their old enemies. They sat, helpless, obedient.

And hereafter there remained nothing much on Kesrith but what waited loading, now that work crews were free to clear the debris at the docks. There were charges to be set, a few small installations to be stripped, mines to be closed, but the most valuable cargo waited at the dock already.

Of personnel there remained only the lowest priority evacuees, who would leave with him on *Hazan.*

Records bequeathed him from doch Holn indicated that there had been some eighteen million regul adults on Kesrith at the beginning of the evacuation procedure, a colony once exceedingly prosperous and supporting a university and a few first-rate elder minds (excluding the Holn, whom he despised as overvalued). He knew the exact number, and the disposition Holn had made, and the disposition he himself had made of the remaining citizens and properties from the instant he had taken charge, and what goods he had placed on the evacuation ships to be consumed enroute, and what to be allotted as personal baggage, and what he was sal vaging to take himself, down to fractional weight and space requirements for shipping. He had absorbed all this data in minute detail. He made occasional written records, against the event of his sudden death and the passing of Alagn doch to his immediate heirs—he did not entirely trust humans—or his sudden incapacity; but these were only for such an event. In the ordinary course of transactions he did not consult written records at all. It was physically impossible for a sane and healthy regul to forget anything he had ever determined to remember, and it was also quite likely that he would remember what he heard only casually. Hulagh believed implicitly in the accuracy of the record he had obtained from Solgah Holn-ni, his enemy, as he believed implicitly in her sanity. It was inconceivable that Solgah, however lacking in astuteness and over-impressed with her own ability as an administrator, would not have at least recalled accurately what was the number of regul on her world, and what their resources, and how disposed.

He knew therefore that 327 regul young remained with him outside the ship, the barest minimum necessary to carry out the dismantling operation, and three of those were almost adult. The majority were younglings below the age of twenty-five, as yet undetermined in sex—this would manifest itself at about thirty—and far more mobile than would be possible for them as they began to attain their adult weight. They were of use to him when it came to errands or heavy labor, for the observations of the evacuation that later would be gleaned from their memories by expert scholars on Nurag. Their memories, presently, save in their most recent unique experiences and knowledge of the events passing around them, had not yet acquired any data that would make them intrinsically valuable to any elder, simply because they had not lived long enough or travelled far enough to have rivalled the experience or comparative observatory powers of an elder. They belonged only to the doch of their birth, and had not seen what they might yet accomplish, and since they would not sex and reproduce for another several years, they were not distracted by these considerations.

Only those fully mature and those protected by adult choice of a doch (even Holn) had been lifted off to safety in the main evacuation—they and such infants as could be contained in their mothers' pouches for the duration of the voy-

ages, life-supported without undue expenditure of resources
by the crowded rescue ships.

These last younglings, more fortunate than the masses of
Holn that had not fitted into either category, knew that they
were still expendable, and why, and they were accordingly
nervous about the coming of humans and petulant about
their personal losses—and, which was the common quality of
the young—abysmally stupid in their anxieties, believing, for
so their limited experience misled them, that they were the
first and most important younglings in the history of the race
to suffer such things.

One fretted outside now and craved admittance for the
fifth time, urgent with some message doubtless protesting the
conditions under which they were confined in the Nom and
forbidden to wander the square during off-hours, or protesting the long hours that they had been required to work since
the crisis at the port, or their increasing fear of the coming
humans and the fact that they were not yet on board the
safety of *Hazan*, which was at the root of everything. Hulagh
had answered enough such requests for attention, both from
regul younglings and from dull-witted humans. He was busy.
The youngling in question was not assigned anywhere near
the human delegate, so it could not be an emergency in that
quarter, which was all that would have truly interested him
within the Nom. He dealt with the destructions of the storm
as best he could, covering the one error he had committed, in
failing to ask of Solgah concerning the behaviors of the sea-
sons and the climate of Kesrith. He had little time for petulant and frightened assistants.

The youngling persisted. Hulagh sighed at last and pressed
a button and admitted the youngling, whose agitation was extreme.

"Be gracious, bai." It was the one named Suth Hara-ri,
bred of the university bai-dach. It gave a polite suck of
breath.

Hulagh reciprocated. There was at least some grace in
Suth, who had been unmannered and fearful to a degree unbecoming any age when it began service. This former grace-
lessness on the part of Kesrith's younglings in general was
surely due to the years of war which had encompassed
the younglings' entire experience. The Kesrithi younglings left
in Hulagh's charge were acquiring some graces. Hulagh con-

tinually took care to reprimand them, so that they would not arrive ashamed and misfit in the inner worlds: this also he took for part of his duty in salvaging what he could of Kesrith—and also anticipated winning the best of them to Alagn's enlistment as adults, hand-trained, augmenting his private staff to that of a colonial governor.

He reached a place where stopping would not overmuch inconvenience him, but he let the youngling wait with the petition awhile more, while he enjoyed a cup of soi, and midway through it saw fit to gesture his willingness to listen.

"Be gracious," Suth breathed, then blurted in desperate haste: "Bai, the station reports a mri vessel incoming."

This struck through all courtesies and lack of them, commanding Hulagh's attention. Hulagh leaned back, the cup forgotten on the console, and looked at the youngling in unconcealed dismay.

The mercenary Kel—in this situation with humans but a few days removed from Kesrith. Hulagh's hearts became at once agitated and anger heated his face. It was like the mri to be inconvenient.

To arrive always in the moment other elements had reached their maximum vulnerability.

"They have given notice of their intentions?" Hulagh asked of Suth.

"They say that they will land. We urged them to make use of the station facilities. They did not respond to this. They said that they have come for their people onworld and that they intend to land."

"Mri never lie," said Hulagh, for the youngling's reference, if it had never dealt face-to-face with the mercenaries. "Neither do they always tell the truth. In that, they resemble regul."

Suth blinked and sucked air. Subtleties were wasted on this one. Hulagh frowned and blew heated air through his nostrils.

"Are they to have their permission to land?" asked Suth. "Bai, what shall we say?"

"Tell me this, youngling: Where are our station ships?"

"Why, gone, gracious lord, all but the freighter and the shuttles, with the evacuation."

"Then we cannot very well enforce our instruction not to land, can we? You are dismissed, youngling."

"Favor," Suth murmured and withdrew, hasty and graceless in departure. Hulagh, already deep in thought, failed to rise to the provocation.

Mri.

Inconvenient as the stubborn kel'en he had inherited from Gruran. Bloody-handed and impulsive and incapable of coherent argument.

His memory informed him that there were constantly some few mri on Kesrith, and that this was true of no other world since Nisren had fallen to humans forty-three years ago. There were thirteen mri in residence. There was nothing to indicate why Kesrith had been so favored, save that mri had a tendency to choose one or another world as a permanent base, designating it as homeworld, and thereafter behaving as irrationally and emotionally as if this were indeed the true land of their birth. There had been three such homeworlds thus far in the regul-mri association, all within the Holn domain, since the mri had constantly come within Holn jurisdiction and remained unknown in home territories of the regul. This employment of the mercenaries was, curiously, not an arrangement of regul seeking, but an arrangement which the mri had offered the regul 2,202 years ago—for no apparent reason, for no apparent compulsion, save that this arrangement seemed to satisfy some profound emotional need of the mri. Regul had inquired into this mri peculiarity, but remained unsatisfied. There was a regul joke about mri, that mri had made records about their home and origin, but had forgotten where they had left them: hence their nomadic condition. The fact that mri had no memories was a laughable matter to one who had not dealt personally with the intractable mri.

One could not argue with them, could not reason, could not persuade them from old loyalties, and could not—above all could not tamper with their sense of proprieties. He remembered Medai's suicide with a shudder; stubborn and without memory and prone to violence. It was like the mri to prefer bloodshed to reason, even when it was one's own blood that was shed. Medai, Kesrith-born, would not compromise: the mri treaty held only so long as regul maintained a homeworld for mri, so long as that homeworld was inviolate from invasion. Medai had seen what he had seen, and could not reason otherwise; and therefore he had chosen to set himself against his lawful employers.

His suicide was supposed, Hulagh recalled, to put some burden of shame or social stigma on the man who had offended against the mri in question. This self-destruction was an act of reproach or of complete repudiation supposed to have devastating effect on the emotions of his superior.

A mri kel'en would do such a thing, even knowing that regul were not impressed, casting away his precious life rather than compromise on a small point of duty that could make no ultimate difference to him personally. Mri doubtless imagined that it made a difference.

It was that mri ferocity that had originally appealed to the regul, an amazement that this savage, fearsome species had come peacefully to the regul docha and tendered their services—services without which the colonizing of the humanward worlds and the rise of the Holn might never had occurred, not in the manner in which Holn had created monopoly. And this very ferocity ought by rights to have warned sensible regul of the nature of mri. Mercenaries by breeding and choice, their strict, dull-witted codes made them in the beginning utterly dependable as guards in commerce of the outworld docha. They did not change allegiance in mid-service; it was impossible to bribe them; it was impossible even to discharge them save by the completion of a service or by suicide. They had not sense enough to retreat; they had no strong instincts of self-preservation, a fact which balanced their prolific breeding, in which all males of the Kel were free to mate with the low-caste females, besides the mates of their own caste: they therefore tended in the years of peace to multiply at an alarming rate, if it were not for the attrition worked on them by their way of life, their rejection of medical science, and their constant passion for duelling. How these fierce warriors had supported themselves before they found the regul to hire them was another mystery to regul, which the mri had never chosen to reveal. Mri would not do manual labor, not even sufficient to provide themselves food. A mri would starve rather than bear burdens or work the earth for another. They broke this rule only for the building and maintenance of their towers and the managing of the few ships they were allotted personally; but beyond those two exceptions, they would not turn a hand if there were regul available to take over the menial tasks. Once in Hulagh's recall a certain ship with a kel'en aboard had met a difficulty other than human, a navigational malfunction that had the crew in a panic; they had summoned the ship's kel'en—an old kel'e'en it was—who had leisurely come to see the difficulty, sat down at the console, and made the appropriate adjustments; then, with consummate arrogance, the kel'e'en had retired to the solitude of her own quarters, neither speaking nor offering courtesies nor accepting thanks.

Yet this kel'e'en could not read a simple sign to direct herself to the messhall on station liberty, but had to be directed by her regul employers.

There was nothing to match either the arrogance or the ignorance of the mri Kel: touchy, suiciding when offended by regul, fighting when offended by other mri—there was no knowing what truly motivated the species. Hulagh himself reckoned that he knew humans better than he knew mri, although he had dealt with humans for three years and his ancestors had dealt with mri for 2,202 years. Humans were simply territorial like regul, and while they were creatures of brief memory and small brain like the mri, they did have the industry to work, and to mend the deficiencies of their talents with an admirable technology.

It was a curious thing that in the forty-three-year war, the regul had come to trust humans far more than they did the mri; they had come to fear humans far less than they feared mri. Constantly regul had to command the mri to observe the decencies of restraint, actually had to intervene to prevent the mri escalating the war out of the territorial zone of conflict and into reaches far beyond regul limits, into a scale in which regul technology was inadequate to maintain defenses around vital homeworlds. The mri, who were specialists in war, yet had not been able to perceive this; even the Holn had done so, and had put restraints to the war, or there would have been incredible devastation and economic collapse. Mri might lose one homeworld after another and move on, but they were nomadic—perhaps, Hulagh estimated, the source of their contempt for national boundaries. Regul could not contemplate the loss of even one world of home space, with artwork, technology, trade routes: they did not intend at any time to enter war with the all-out dedication of mri.

The most serious losses were, at the end of matters, to the

mri themselves. Mri had begun the war with one million, nine hundred fifty and seven kel'ein according to regul census; and this small figure was still a great increase over their former numbers, reflecting the prosperity that had been theirs in regul service over the span of 2,202 years. Only a hundred thousand had they numbered when their leaders had first approached the regul and begged to be allowed to take service with the regul species. But now most recent records indicated that there were but 533 mri of all castes surviving in known space.

It was impossible, considering that small number and the mri's unrestrainably fierce inclinations, that the species could survive at this low ebb—ironically—without regul protection during their recovery. An era had ended, with the passing of the basis of Holn power, with the passing of the kel'ein. A few could be preserved by Alagn, if the mri would in extremity permit themselves to see reason: and Hulagh could see use for them, if only in the regul awe of the ferocity of the Kel. But they must be removed from the path of the human advance or the mri would continue like automatons to dash themselves to death against the inevitable.

And in the midst of other confusions, one mri must suicide and now a mri ship must come interfering in the evacuation of the mri homeworld. It would be an armed ship. Mri vessels, at least vessels totally mri, were small, but mri did not go anywhere unarmed.

The humans who were coming to take possession of Kesrith would likewise be armed.

Hulagh considered for one wild moment making a graceless withdrawal from his duty on Kesrith, bundling surviving younglings and himself aboard *Hazan* tonight and leaving the mri and the humans to each others' mercies.

But *Hazan* was not ready, not fully repaired, her important cargo impossible to load until the dock machinery had been repaired.

And he would not retreat in such fashion, which would be told on homeworld to his discredit; in that much he understood the mri compulsion to stand fast when pushed.

He reached to his left and pressed a button, contacting the youngling Hada Surag-gi, kosaj of the Nom, who served him personally for sufficiently important errands: a twenty year old, Hada, extraordinarily competent in its advanced post. "Hada," he said, "send the records of mri settlement on Kesrith."

"Be gracious," replied Hada's voice. "Such records go back 2,202 years. Kesrith was among the first worlds possessed by the mri and it is locally believed that they were here before first contact. What information does the bai wish in particular? I may perhaps recall what is of help."

This was utter impudence, that such a youngling supposed its own personal knowledge sufficient to remedy the desire of an elder.

"O young ignorance," said Hulagh peevishly, remembering that he was the only elder presently on Kesrith and that the youngling, though impudent and self-important, was probably offering with the best of intentions, to save him valuable time and effort. This was not, after all, Nurag; there was a limit on everyone's time and patience, most particularly his own. "Hada, what do you suppose would bring a mri ship now to Kesrith?"

"This is," said Hada, "the present mri homeworld. Perhaps they mean to defend it. They are not accustomed to retreat."

It was not a comforting conjecture, and precisely the one that Hulagh had made for himself. Yet the mri had accepted the treaty that regul had made with humans; mri had been advised at every step of the negotiations that they might not carry on further war with humans.

"Hada, what is the present number of mri on Kesrith?"

"Bai, there are thirteen, mostly elders of the edun and entirely unfit for war."

He was surprised by this. He had not been interested in the small edun, since it had not intruded into his notice; he had known the number accurately but not the incapacity of its members.

"Send the records anyway, whatever you possess on the leaders personally and on the history of the species here." *Perdition*, thought Hulagh miserably, *mri have been on Kesrith for far too many years that I can sift through such as this. There is no time. The records will be mountainous.* "Hada."

"Favor?"

"Contact their kel'anth. Tell him I want him to report to this office immediately."

There was a very long pause. "Be gracious, bai," ventured Hada at last. "The Kesrithi edun is headed by a she'pan, one Intel. Onworld, a kel'anth must defer to a she'pan. He is not the leader of the mri on Kesrith."

Hulagh's oath cut short the youngling. There was silence in the chatter for a moment, welcome silence. He absorbed the new information, embarrassed by his reliance on a youngling's knowledge, aware that, where mri were concerned, no one actually knew what the chain of command was within their community. Hada claimed to possess this knowledge. Perhaps Hada had acquired it from elders of Holn doch, who had commanded mri for generations. *Plague and perdition,* thought Hulagh, *there is no time, there is no time. Confound all mri to perdition.* But neither did one summon a she'pan: he knew that much. None but Kel caste would respond to a summons to leave their community and meet with outsiders. There was the necessity to brave the process of records search, or the necessity to ignore the incoming ship, with all its ugly possibilities.

Or there was the necessity to leave his desk and his work and his important duties to the incompetent mercies of youngling assistants at such a crisis, while he paid slow courtesies to a mri religious leader, whose memory was fallible and whose graces were probably lacking, who trammelled up the cleanly relations between regul doch and mri kel'anth. He and the war leader of the Kel might have settled things with a simple exchange; with one of the ceremonial leaders of the mri involved, whose power was nebulous and whose authorities and compulsions were somehow linked to the mri regligion, whatever it was—a regul petitioner must suffer tedious and pointless discussion that might only perhaps produce what he wanted.

"Hada," said Hulagh, surrendering, "fetch me my car and the most reliable driver, a youngling who does not flinch from mri."

Many humiliations had he accepted in dealing with the invading humans, in negotiations concerning arrangements, in accepting two inconvenient observers whose presence, if known, could cause impossible complications with the mri treaty. He had succeeded in handling the humans, which was thought to have been the most difficult matter; he had outmaneuvered them in a way that would bring him prestige.

And now it came to this, that he must interrupt the saving of regul lives and regul properties to counsel with mri hirelings, to rescue an ungrateful people who most likely would not treat with him courteously for his efforts.

A thought struck him. "Hada," he said.

"Favor?"

"Is it or is it not possible that the mri would know that one of their ships is coming?"

"That information has not been released by this office," said Hada. Then: "Be gracious, bai; mri have learned things before this that have not been released by this office. They have their own communications."

"Doubtless," said Hulagh, and broke the connection and went about the laborious and painful business of rising. He was 290 years removed from the class of younglings. His legs were proportionately shorter, his senses duller, his body many times heavier. His rugose skin was prone to cracking and developing sores when directly exposed to the dry cold of Kesrith's air. His double hearts labored under the exertion of lifting his adult bulk, and his muscles trembled with the unaccustomed strain. As an elder of the regul, his principal business was of the mind and the intellect.

And he was reduced to this, to visit mri.

Chapter Twelve

THE MRI EDUN hove into view, a set of truncated, common-based cones ominously alien—and located, inevitably, in the most inconvenient and inaccessible place available. Hulagh settled uneasily into his cushions in the rear of the landsled and saw it grow nearer: built of the soil of the mineral flats, cemented and dull-surfaced, it was of a color with the earth, but startling to the eye and forbiddingly sterile in its outlines. It wasted space with its slanting walls—but then, mri never did anything the simple way. It was, he reflected, indicative of the mri mind, nonutilitarian, alien in its patterns, deliberately isolate. The sled labored in the climb up the causeway, which the rains, that other of Kesrith's terrestrial nuisances, had left in ill-repair, dissolving the salts that lay in thick deposits thereabouts and creating alarming channels in the earth and rock of the causeway. On either side lay a fatal plunge to the thin crusts of the flats, volcanic and constantly steaming at one or another vent. Hulagh tried not to think of what depths lay beside the treads of the sled as it ground its way over a series of ruts that had almost eaten the road away.

Mri did not choose to repair it. Old they might be, but even if they had been physically capable, they would have disdained to do it, not as long as there remained onworld a single regul on whom to cast the responsibility. The road would wash away before mri would stir to mend it, and there was no intention in Hulagh's mind to do so for human benefit.

He only hoped it would suffice to carry him to and from, and that once only.

The car jolted up the last few feet of incline and came to the main entry of the edun. The structure itself was in similar

120

disrepair, already yielding to the rains that would claim it in
the end, that would reduce it to the white earth again. The
slanted walls bore dim traces of colors that must once have
made it bright.

He had seen pictures of edunei, but he had never seen one
in reality, and never seen one in such a state. This was surely
an ancient structure, and declined sadly. Mri were usually
more proud. Even the front walk was guttered with erosion
channels, and with the sled grinding to a halt, bai Hulagh
looked on that irregular surface with dread. It was a long
walk, a difficult walk on soft ground. And there was a dus
guarding the entry, a massive brown lump, all wrinkles and
folds of flesh, rising to a hump at the shoulders and descending at either end. It seemed to be asleep, resting with its back
a quarter as high as the door—higher by more should it stir,
which Hulagh fervently hoped it would not do. Dusei were
wherever mri travelled, but on ship they kept entirely to the
kel'en's cabin and were not allowed to range the premises. He
had never encountered one at close range, had let his younglings tend to that unpleasantness. He knew only what he had
heard: that while mri were legally class-two sapients on a
scale which rated regul as one, dusei were tentatively classed
at ten, although many who had dealt with the frustrating
creatures reckoned that dusei should be considerably higher
or lower. They were Kesrith's native dominant species; he
knew this too, although they ran wild wherever mri had been
for long, which was every world where mri had ever been
permitted—none, happily, in the inner territories of regul
space—this was their origin. They were a plague in the wilds
of whatever world they adopted, and they were dangerous.
There were surely wild ones prolific in the hills and plains—
slow, patient omnivores, a gift such as regul gladly bestowed
on the humans. Mri purchased with their service food to feed
their dusei, which accordingly haunted their dwellings and ac-
companied them into space; but dusei did nothing, contributed nothing, did not fight unless cornered, and were
never eaten. Their only visible benefit was that to keep them
nearby pleasured the mri, who apparently derived some social
status among their own kind for the keeping and support of
such useless and expensive creatures. Hulagh himself collect-
ed gems, stones, geological curiosities. He attempted to com-

prehend the mentality of the mri, who treasured such live and dangerous specimens.

This one in particular looked diseased. Its hide was patched and his attitude was more sluggish than was natural even for a dus. It had not even lifted its head as the car drew up at the walk.

The sight of the ugly creature did more than the decay of the edun itself to distress Hulagh's aesthetic sense. He looked at it and did not wish to look, as he forced his own considerable bulk from the confines of the sled and waited for his driver, one Chul Nag-gi, to assist him up the walk. Chul also seemed to regard the dus with distaste, and as they walked together toward the step, Chul dutifully walked on the side nearest the creature and kept a constant eye on it. The dus lifted its head to investigate them as they came to the doorway. Its eyes were running and unhealthy.

Perdition, thought Hulagh uneasily, *the thing is dying of disease on their doorsill, and will they not destroy it?—for the sake of hygiene, if not mercy.*

The dus investigated them, snuffling wetly, emitted a strange sound, a low rumbling and whuffing that was not pleasure and not quite menace. "Away!" Chul exclaimed, in a voice edged with panic. Hulagh edged past with all possible speed, while Chul fended the creature away with a violent kick. Chul overtook him just inside the dark door, and offered an arm once more, whereupon they began the long walk together.

A mri saw them and vanished, a black shadow among shadows, and none offered to guide them. Hulagh needed no guidance. He had been acquainted before they left the Nom with the plan of edunei, which was universal. He knew the general design of the ground level, and where the fourth cone of the she'pan ought to sit, and to this cone he walked slowly, panting, struggling as the approach offered, `to his horror, stairs, winding up and up toward the crest.

A shout echoed above. Yet he saw no one and came at his own agonized pace, step by step, past mud-plastered walls cheaply decorated with rough designs or symbols, so irregularly and stylistically painted that they seemed impossible of decipherment even if one knew the mri system. Designs in black and gold and blue serpentined round the windings of the corridor upon walls and ceilings. They might be religious in nature: it was another thing the mri had never revealed—to avert evils or call them down on intruders; or perhaps they simply thought it beautiful. It was difficult to reconcile this with the modern lighting and the other evidences of mri sophistication with regul machinery—a people that could handle starflight and yet lived in this primitive manner. The doors that shielded the hall where the she'pan would hold state, most of the doors in the edun, in fact, were steel, of regul manufacture, and steel likely reinforced the mud-and-binder architecture.

"They do not mind furnishing their mud hovels with good regul metal," Chul said, an undertone, but the youngling saved its comments for itself when Hulagh gave it a hard look, for the acuteness of mri hearing was legendary.

"Open the door," said Hulagh.

And when Chul had done so, the youngling gave a sharp intake of breath, for there was a mri directly confronting them, a black-veiled kel'en, a mere youngling himself; Hulagh reckoned so, at least, by the unmarred brow and clear golden skin. He was grim, impudent, barbarous, a golden man bedecked in black and weaponry, warlike gear that even included the archaism of a long knife at his belt. Hulagh was minded instantly and painfully of Medai, who had been such as this. It was like meeting a ghost.

Youngling fronted youngling, and it was the regul that backed a pace, a weakness that sent a wave of angry heat to Hulagh's head.

"Where is the she'pan?" Hulagh asked sharply, embarrassed by his driver's discomfiture and seeking to recover regul dignity. "Young mri, get out of the door and call someone of authority. You were advised that I would call on the she'pan."

The mri turned neatly on his heel and walked away, silent, graceful, disrespectful. Mri warrior. Hulagh hated the whole breed. They were utterly unmannered as a nation, and encouraged it in their younglings. The youth, like the whole edun, stank of incense. It lingered in the air, and Hulagh fought a tendency to sneeze, to clear his violated air passages. His legs were shuddering from the long walk upstairs. He walked in and bent his knees and lowered his heavy body the necessary small degree to sit on the carpets. Mri furniture, of which there was only the she'pan's chair of honor and two benches near the entry, was too high and too fragile for an adult regul, nor could a regul stand and bear his own weight for any length of time.

In proper courtesy the youngling should have summoned some of his kind to bring furniture apt to him; but this was a very poor edun by all evidences, and perhaps unused to regul callers at all. The carpets were at least clean.

Shouting echoed in the depths of the hall beyond the partition that screened the privacies of the central chamber. Hulagh mentally winced at the unseemliness of this behavior, and Chul stirred uneasily. In a moment more the room began to admit other warriors, likewise veiled and armed.

"Bai," said Chul. There was fear in that tone. Hulagh dealt with it with a foul look: ignorant, this youngling. The mri, while graceless and arrogant, were still subjects of the regul, and they were subjects by choice, not compulsion. Mri were many things, and they were unpleasant, but they were not dangerous, at least in the personal sense—not to regul.

Several dusei wandered in, heavy-boned heads held low to the carpet, looking as if they had lost something and forgotten just what it was. They settled their great bulks into the corner and lowered their heads between their paws and watched, their tiny, almost invisible eyes glittering. One rumbled an ominous sound, quieted as a kel'en settled against him, using his broad shoulder for a backrest.

The sneeze came, unexpected and violent. Hulagh contained it as best he could. None of the mri affected to notice this terrible breach of etiquette. He counted those present. There were eleven, and nine of these were veiled, males and perhaps a female of the Kel; one young female was unveiled, robed in gold; and with her was one of the oldest, a presumed male of the gold-robed caste. They were the only mri whose faces he had ever seen. He could not help staring, amazed at the graceful delicacy of the young female.

Odd, Hulagh reflected, that this backward species sexed when young and aged into sameness. He stored that thought away for further pondering, did mri chance to survive this era and remain relevant to the living.

And with a soft rustling, the she'pan herself arrived, leaning on the arm of the young kel'en; she settled among them, in her chair, veilless. She was also very, very old, and, Hulagh thought, although he was not sure, that she had been disfigured on one side of her face. Young mri were smooth-skinned and slim; and the young woman's hair shone in the light like textured bronze, but the she'pan's was faded and brittle, and on the side with the apparent injury it was dark at the temple. The young warrior knelt at her side, golden eyes darting mistrust and hostility at the visitors. The she'pan's look contained the placidity of age and long, long experience, qualities which Hulagh valued, and he suddenly revised his opinion and reckoned that it might be better after all to deal with this aged female than with an intractable war-leader, if she could indeed guide her people in areas other than in the obscure mri religion.

She had no great awe of regul, this was plain enough; but neither was she hostile or slow-witted. Her eyes were quick and appraising. There was the look of higher sentience there.

"She'pan," said Hulagh, recognizing age's right to dignity, even if she were mri.

"Hulagh," she said, stripping him of titles.

His nostrils snapped shut, blew air in irritation. He remembered the presence of the youngling Chul at his elbow, Chul, whose witness he did not particularly want at this moment, and the heat of anger seethed in him as it had not in many sheltered years.

"She'pan," said Hulagh, persistent in proprieties, "we have made room for your people on our ship." This was, basically, the truth: he had allotted space, which he had hoped would not have to be too extensive, and he had hoped for young-lings, who could be civilized and moulded anew under Alagn guidance; but he saw only two. He revised opinions quickly. These elders, it might be, could control young mri loose elsewhere, render them tractable, perhaps—gather a colony of mri in Alagn territory. He thought again of the young kel'en who had suicided, and thought perhaps that that would not have happened if there had been an elder mri to provide that youngling with a proper perspective on his act.

If there were not that restraint and sense even in elders like this, and they would not have dissuaded him, then the whole of mri civilization had failed, and there was no rescuing it from itself.

"We would desire," he told the she'pan, "for you to board within the coming night."

The she'pan stared at him, neither joyed nor dismayed by that short time. "Indeed, bai?"

"As soon as possible. We are at that stage of our loading."

The she'pan stared at him and considered that in silence. "And our dusei?" she asked.

"And the dusei, one for each," Hulagh painfully conceded, mentally deducting two times the resources that would have been necessary to accommodate the mri; he had hoped to take no dusei at all; but when he considered the matter, he reflected that the unpleasant beasts might keep the mri content, representing their wealth, and it was very desirable that the mri remain content.

"We will consult upon the matter," said the she'pan, her hand on the shoulder of the young warrior who sat beside her, and at her other side, silent, settled the gold-robed young female.

"There is no time for lengthy consultations," Hulagh objected.

"Ah," said the she'pan, "then you have heard about the ship."

Blood drained from Hulagh's face, slowly resumed its proper circulation. He did not look at the youngling, hoping for once its wits would prevent its repeating this insult and humiliation elsewhere, among its youngling fellows. He had scant hope that this would be the case.

"Yes," said Hulagh, "we have naturally heard. Nevertheless we are anxious to speed our departure. We are not familiar with this incoming ship, but doubtless—" he stammered over the not-truth, compelled to lie, for the first time in his life, for the sake of regul, for the welfare of the younglings in his protection, and most of all for his own ambitions and for the survival of his knowledge; but he felt foul and soiled in the doing. "Doubtless after you are aboard, we may intercept this ship of yours and divert it also toward the safety of our inner zones."

"Would you permit that?" The dry old voice, heavy with accent, was careful, devoid of inflections that could have betrayed emotion and concealed meanings. "Shall mri go to the regul homeworld at long last? You have never permitted us knowledge of its location, bai."

"Nevertheless—" He could not build upon the lie. He was not able to consummate this, the supreme immorality—to falsify, to lend untruth to memory, which could not be unlearned. He had learned this practice of aliens. He had watched them do it, amazed and horrified; he had learned that humans lied as a regular practice. He felt his own skin crawl at the enormity of it, his throat contract when he tried to shape more to his fiction, and knew that if he refused to build upon it, it would not be believed at all; and then he would be caught, lose credibility, with fatal consequences for the mri, with unfortunate result for the regul under his command, and for his own future.

If it were known on Nurag—

But they were only mri, lesser folk; they had no memories such as regul had; and with them the lie could not live as it would among regul. Perhaps therein lay at least a lesser immorality.

"Nevertheless, she'pan," he said, controlling his voice carefully, "this is so. Matters are different now. We will not delay here as long as we had planned. We will board with all possible speed."

"Do you fear lest the humans should gain us?"

This came too near the mark. Hulagh sat still, looking at the she'pan and suspecting deeper things within her words. Mri were, like regul, truthful. He had this on the tradition of all his predecessors who had made the records which he had learned, and an ancestry that made records on the truth of which all the past and therefore all the future depended.

Had the ancestors also been tempted to lie, to play small games with truth and reality?

Had they in fact done so? The very doubting increased the pace of Hulagh's overtaxed hearts, pulled the foundations from beneath his firmest beliefs and left everything in uncertainty. Yet in spite of this tradition of the ancestors, a bai now lied, to save lives, for a good cause and the welfare of two species: but the truth had been altered, all the same, and now the lie shaped truth to cover it.

"We are anxious," said Hulagh, wading deeper into this alien element, "that you be safe from humans. We are anxious to speed our own departure, for our safety's sake, and for yours. Our own younglings are at stake, and myself, and my reputation, and I am extremely valuable in the eyes of my people, so you may know that we will take unusual care to ensure the safety of this particular ship. If you wish to go with us, and I advise it, she'pan, I strongly advise it, then prepare your people to embark at once."

"We have served regul," said the she'pan, "for 2,000 years. This is a very long service. And scant have been the rewards of it."

"We have offered you what you ask and more: we have offered you technicians who would give you all the benefits of our experience; we have offered you our records, our histories, our technology."

"We do not," said the she'pan, "desire this knowledge of yours."

"It is your own misfortune then," said the bai. He had met this stupidity in mri before, in Medai. "She'pan, you keep to your own dwellings and to ships, but they are regul-built ships; even your weapons are regul-made. Your food is produced by regul. Without us you would starve to death. And yet you still affect to despise our knowledge."

"We do not despise your knowledge," said the she'pan. "We simply do not desire it."

Hulagh's eyes strayed past her shoulder to the chamber itself, a gesture of contempt for the conditions in which the she'pan held state, in rooms barely sanitary, in halls innocent of amenities, decorated with that frighteningly crude and powerful art of symbols, the meaning of which he doubted even the mri remembered. They were superstitious folk. If ill or injured, mri would turn from regul help and die rather than admit weakness, desiring only the presence of other mri or the presence of a dus. This was their religion at work.

Usually they died, all the same. *We are warriors,* regul had heard often enough, *not carriers of burdens, sellers of goods, practitioners of arts, whatever the offered opportunity or benefit.* Medicine, engineering, literature, agriculture, physical labor of any sort as long as there was a single regul to do it for them—all these things the mri despised.

Animals, Hulagh thought, *plague and pestilence—they are nothing but animals. They enjoy war. They have deliberately prolonged this one in their stupidity. We ought never to have unleashed them in war. They like it too well.*

And to the youth, the arrogant young kel'en who sat by the she'pan's knee, he asked, "Youngling, would you not wish to learn? Would you not wish to have the things that regul enjoy, to know the past and the future and how to build in metals?"

The golden eyes nictitated, a sign of startlement in a mri. "I am of the Kel," said the young warrior. "And education is not appropriate for my caste. Ask the Sen."

The young woman in gold looked on him in her turn, her unveiled face a perfect mask, infuriating, expressionless. "The Sen is headed by the she'pan. Ask the she'pan, bai, whether she desires your knowledge. If she bids me learn, then I will learn what you have to teach."

They played with him, games of ignorance, mri humor. Hulagh saw it in the eyes of the she'pan, who remained motionless through this circular exchange.

"We know," said the she'pan finally, "that these things have always been available to us. But the rewards of service that we desired were other than what you offer; and of late they have been scant."

Enigmas. The mri cherished their obscurities, their abstruseness. There was no helping such people. "If one of you," Hulagh said with deliberate patience, "had ever deigned to specify what reward you sought, then we might have found the means to give it to you."

But the she'pan said nothing to this, as the mri had always said nothing on this score: *We serve for pay,* some had said scornfully, similarly questioned, but they offered nothing of the truth of the whole; and this she'pan like her ancestors said nothing at all.

"It would be a comfort to my people," said Hulagh, trying that ancient ploy, the appeal to legalities of oath and to mri conscience, and it was partly truth at least. "We are accustomed to the protection of mri with us. We are not fighters. Even if one or two mri should be on the ship as we leave, we would feel safer in our journey."

"If you demand a mri for your protection," said the she'pan, "I must send one."

"She'pan," said Hulagh, trying again to reach some point of reason, forgetful of his dignity and the watching eyes of Chul. "Would you then send one, alone, without his people, to travel so far as we are going, and without the likelihood of return? This would be hard. And what is there possibly in these regions to detain you once we have gone?"

"Why should we not," asked the she'pan, "bring our own

ship in your wake—to Nurag? Why are you so anxious to
have us aboard your own, bai Hulagh?"

"We have laws," Hulagh said, his hearts pounding. "Surely
you realize we must observe cautions. But it will be safer for
you than here."

"There will be humans here," said the she'pan. "Have you
not arranged it so?"

Hulagh found nothing in his vast memory with which to
understand that answer. It crawled uneasily through his
thoughts, rousing ugly suspicions.

"Would you," Hulagh asked, compelled to directness,
"change your allegiance and serve humans?"

The she'pan made a faint gesture, meaningless to a regul.
"I will consult with my Husbands," she said. "If it pleases
you, I will send one of my people with you if you demand it.
We are in service to the regul. It would not be seemly or lawful for me to refuse to send one of us with you in your need,
o Hulagh, bai of Kesrith."

Now, now came courtesy; he did not trust this late turn of
manners, though mri could not lie; neither had he thought that
he could lie, before this conference and his moment of necessity, which had been spent all in vain. Mri might indeed not lie;
but neither was it likely that the she'pan was without certain
subtleties, and possibly she was laughing within this appearance of courtesy. And the Kel was veiled and inscrutable.

"She'pan," he said, "what of this ship that is coming?"

"What of it?" echoed the she'pan.

"Who are these mri that are coming? Of what kindred?
Are they of this edun?"

Again the curious gesture of the hand that returned to
stroke the head of the young female who leaned against her
knee.

"The name of the ship, bai, is *Ahanal*. And do you make
formal request that one of us accompany you?"

"I will tell you this when you have consulted with your
Husbands and given me the answer to other questions," said
Hulagh, marking how she had turned aside his own question.
He smoldered with growing anger.

These were mri. They were a little above the animals. They
knew nothing and remembered less, and dared play games
with regul.

He was also within their territory, and of law on this forsaken world, he was the sole representative.

For the first time he looked upon the mri not as a comfort, not as interestingly quaint, nor even as a nuisance, but as a force like the dusei, dull-wittedly ominous. He looked at the dark-robed warriors, this stolid indifference to the regul authority that had always commanded them.

For mri to challenge the will of the regul—this had never happened, not directly, not so long as mri served the varied regul docha and authorities; Hulagh sorted through his memory and found no record of what the mri had done when it was not a question of traditional obedience. This was that most distasteful of all possible situations, one never before experienced by any regul on record, one in which his own vast memory was as helpless as that of a youngling, blank of helpful data.

Regul in the throes of complete senility sometimes claimed sights of memories that were yet in the future, saw things that had not yet been and on which there could not possibly be data. Sometimes these elders were remarkably accurate in their earliest estimations, an accuracy which disturbed and defied analysis. But the process then accelerated and muddled all their memories, true and not-yet-true and never-true, and they went mad beyond recall. Of a sudden Hulagh suffered something of the sort, projected the potentials of this situation and derived an insane foreboding of these warlike creatures turning on him and destroying him and Chul at once, rising against the regul docha in bloody frenzy. His two hearts labored with the horror not only of this image, but of the fact that he had perceived it at all. He was 310 years of age. He was bordering on decline of faculties, although he was now at the peak of his abilities and looked to be for decades more. He was terrified lest decline have begun, here, under the strain of so much strangeness. It was not good for an old regul to absorb so much strangeness at once.

"She'pan," he said, trying the last, the very last assault upon her adamancy. "You are aware that your ill-advised delay may make it impossible in the end to take any of your people aboard to safety."

"We will consult," she said, which was neither aye nor nay, but he took it for absolute refusal, judging that he would never in this world hear from the she'pan, not until that ship had come.

There was something astir among mri, something that involved Kesrith and did not admit regul to the secret; and he remembered the young kel'en who had suicided when he was denied permission to leave—who would have borne the news of human presence to the she'pan already if he had been allowed off that ship; and there was that perversity in mri, that, deprived of their war, they might be capable of committing racial suicide, a last defense against humans, who came to claim this world—and when humans met this, they would never believe that the mri were acting alone. They would finish the mri and move against regul: another foresight, of horrid aspect.

Mri would retreat only under direct order, and if they slipped control, they would not retreat at all. Of a sudden he cursed the regul inclined to believe the mri acquiescent in this matter—Gruran, who had passed him this information and caused him to believe in it.

He cursed himself, who had confirmed the data, who had not considered mri as a priority, who had been overwhelmingly concerned with loading the world's valuables aboard *Hazan*, and with managing the humans.

Hulagh heaved himself up, found his muscles still too fatigued from his first climb to manage his weight easily, and was not spared the humiliation of having to be rescued from relapse by the youngling Chul, who flung an arm about him and braced him with all its might.

The she'pan snapped her fingers and the arrogant young kel'en at her knee rose up easily and added his support to Hulagh's right side.

"This is very strenuous for the bai," Chul said, and Hulagh mentally cursed the youngling. "He is very old, she'pan, and this long trip has tired him, and the air is not good for him."

"Niun," said the she'pan to her kel'en, "escort the bai down to his vehicle." And the she'pan rose unaided, and observed with bland face and innocent eyes while Hulagh wheezed with effort in putting one foot in front of the other. Hulagh had never missed his lost youth and its easy mobility; age was its own reward, with its vast memory and the honors of it, with its freedom from fear and with the services and respects accorded by younglings; but this was not so among mri.

He realized with burning indignation that the she'pan sought this comparison between them in their age, furnishing her people with the spectacle of the helplessness of a regul elder without his sleds and his chairs.

Among mri, light and quick, and mobile even in extreme age, this weakness must be a curiosity. Hulagh wondered if mri made jest of regul weakness in this regard as regul did of mri intelligence. No one had ever seen a mri laugh outright, not in 2,202 years. He feared there was laughter now on their veiled faces.

He looked on the face of Chul, seeking whether Chul understood. The youngling looked only bewildered, frightened; it panted and wheezed with the burden of its own and another's weight. The young mri at the other side did not look directly at either of them, but kept his eyes respectfully averted, a model of decorum, and his veiled face could not be read.

They left the steel doors and entered the dizzying windings of the painted halls, down and down agonizingly painful steps. For Hulagh it was a blur of misery, of colors and cloying air and the possibility of a fatal fall, and when they finally reached level ground it was blessed relief. He lingered there a moment, panting, then began to walk again, leaning on them, step by step. They passed the doors, and the stinging, pungent air outside came welcome, like the hostile sun. His senses cleared. He stopped again, and blinked in the ruddy light, and caught his breath, leaning on them both.

"Niun," he said, remembering the kel'en's name.

"Lord?" responded the young mri.

"How if I should choose you to go on the ship with me?"

The golden eyes lifted to his, wide and, it seemed, frightened. He had never seen this much evidence of emotion in a mri. It startled him. "Lord," said the young mri, "I am duty-bound to the she'pan. I am her son. I cannot leave."

"Are you not all her sons?"

"No, lord. They are mostly her Husbands. I am her son."

"But not of her body, all the same."

The mri looked as if he had been struck, shocked and offended at once. "No, lord. My truemother is not here anymore."

"Would you go on the ship *Hazan*?"

"If the she'pan sent me, lord."

This one was young, without the duplicities, the complexities of the she'pan; young, arrogant, yes, but such as Niun could be shaped and taught. Hulagh gazed at the young face, veiled to the eyes, finding it more vulnerable than was the wont of mri—rudeness to stare, but Hulagh took the liberty of the very old among regul, who were accustomed to be harsh and abrupt with younglings. "And if I should tell you now, this moment, get into the sled and come with me?"

For a moment the young mri did not seem to know how to answer; or perhaps he was gathering that reserve so important to a mri warrior. The eyes above the veil were frankly terrified, agonized.

"You might be assured," Hulagh said, "of safety."

"Only the she'pan could send me," said the young kel'en. "And I know that she will not."

"She had promised me one mri."

"It has always been the privilege of the edun to choose which is to go and which to stay. I tell you that she will not let me go with you, lord."

That was plainly spoken, and the obtaining of permission through argument would doubtless mean another walk to the crest of the structure, and agony; and another debate with the she'pan, protracted and infuriating and doubtful of issue. Hulagh actually considered it and rejected it, and looked on the young face, trying to fix in mind what details made this mri different from other mri.

"What is your name, your full name, kel'en?"

"Niun s'Intel Zain-Abrin, lord."

"Set me in my car, Niun."

The mri looked uncertainly relieved, as if he understood that this was all Hulagh was going to ask. He applied his strength to the task with Chul's considerable help, and slowly, carefully, with great gentleness, lowered Hulagh's weight into the cushion. Hulagh breathed a long sigh of exhaustion and his sight went dim for a moment, the blood rushing in his head. Then he dismissed the mri with an impatient gesture and watched him walk back to the doorway, over the eroded walk. The dus by the door lifted his head to investigate, then suddenly curled in the other direction and settled, head between its forelegs. Its breath puffed at the dust. The young mri, who had paused, vanished into the interior of the edun.

"Go," said Hulagh to Chul, who turned on the vehicle and

set it moving in a lumbering turn. And again: "Youngling, contact my office and see if there are any new developments."

He thought uneasily of the incoming ship, distant as it surely was, and of everything which had seemed so simple and settled this morning. He drew a breath of the comfortably filtered and heated air within the vehicle and tried to compose his thoughts. The situation was impossible. Humans were about to arrive; and if humans perceived mri near Kesrith and suspected treachery or ambush, humans could arrive sooner. They could arrive very much sooner.

Without a doubt there would be confrontation, mir and human, unless he could rid Kesrith and Kesrith's environs of mri, by one method or another; and of a sudden reckoning she'pan Intel into matters, Hulagh found himself unable to decide how things were aligned with mri and regul.

Or with mri and humans.

"Bai," came Hada Surag-gi's voice over the radio. "Be gracious. We have contacted the incoming mri ship directly. They are *Ahanal*."

"Tell me something I do not already know, youngling."

There was a moment's silence. Hulagh regretted his temper in the interval, for Hada had tried to do well, and Hada's position was not enviable, a youngling trying to treat with mri arrogance and a bai's impatience.

"Bai," said Hada timidly, "this ship is not based on this world, but they are intending to land. They say—bai—"

"Out with it, youngling."

"—that they will be here by sunfall over Kesrith's city tomorrow. They have arrived close—dangerously close, bai. Our station was monitoring the regular approaches, the lanes—but they ignored them."

Hulagh blew his breath out softly, and refrained from swearing.

"Be gracious," said Hada.

"Youngling, what else?"

"They rejected outright our suggestion to dock at the station. They want to land at the port. We disputed their right to do so under the treaty, and explained that our facilities were damaged by the weather. They would not hear. They say that they have need of provisioning. We protested they could obtain this at the station. They would not hear. They

demand complete re-provisioning and re-equipage of a class-
one vessel with armaments as on war status. We protested
that we could not do these things. But they demand these
things, bai, and they claim—they claim that they number in
excess of 400 mri on that ship."

A chill flowed over Hulagh's thick skin.

"Youngling," said Hulagh, "in all known space there are
only 533 of the species known to survive, and thirteen of
these are presently on Kesrith and another is recently de-
ceased."

"Be gracious," pleaded Hada. "Bai, I am very sure I heard
accurately. I asked them to repeat the figure.—It is possible,"
Hada added in a voice trembling and wheezing with distress,
"that these are all the mri surviving anywhere in the universe."

"Plague and perdition," said Hulagh softly and reached
forward to prod Chul in the shoulder. "The port."

"Bai?" asked Chul, blinking.

"The port," Hulagh repeated. "O young ignorance, the
port. Make for it."

The car veered off left, corrected, followed the causeway
the necessary distance, then left along the passable margin of
the city, bouncing over scrub, presenting occasionally a view
of the pinkish sky and the distant mountains, Kesrith's highlands, then of white barren sands and the slim twisting trunks
of scrub luin.

To this the humans fell heir.

Good riddance to them.

He began to think again of the mri that had suicided, and
with repeated chill, of the remaining mri that had by that
time already tended toward Kesrith—all the mri that survived
anywhere, coming to their homeworld, which was to go to
the control of humans.

To die?

He wished he could trust it were so simply final. To stop
the humans; to breathe life into the war again; to ruin the
peace and the regul at once, and then, being few, to die
themselves, and leave the regul species at the mercy of
outraged humans: this was like the mri.

He began to think, his double hearts laboring with fear,
what choice he had in dealing with the mercenaries; and as
he had never lied before he dealt with mri, so he had never

contemplated violence with his own hands, without mri hired as intermediaries.

The sled made a rough turn toward the port gate, bouncing painfully over ruts. The disrepair was even here.

He saw with utter apprehension that clouds had gathered again over the hills beyond the city.

Chapter Thirteen

———•——•—•———

THE RAIN CAME, a gentle enemy, against the walls of the edun. The winds rushed down, but the mountain barrier and the high rocks broke their force and sent them skirling down slopes toward the regul town and port instead. No strong wind had ever touched the edun, not in 2,000 years.

It was comfortable on such a night to take the common-meal, all castes together in the she'pan's tower. All evening long there had been a curious sensitivity in the air, a sense of violent pleasure, of satisfaction as strong as the storm winds. The dusei, mood-sensitive, had grown so restive that they had been turned out of the edun altogether, to roam where they pleased this night. They disappeared into the dark, all but the *miuk'ko* at the gate, finding no discomfort at all in the world's distempers.

And the spirits of the kel'ein were high. Old eyes glittered. There was no mention of the ship that was coming, but it was at the center of everything.

Niun likewise, among the kel'ein, felt the surge of hope at the arrival of *Ahanal*. Of a sudden, dizzying views opened before his feet. Others. Brothers. Rivals. Challenge and hope of living.

And himself, even unfledged, even without experience in war, hitherto no person of consequence: but this was home-world, and he of homeworld's Kel; and he was, above all, the she'pan's kel'en. It was a heady, unaccustomed feeling, that of being no longer the least, but one among the first.

"We have been in contact with a mri ship," was all the word the she'pan had given them that morning, before the arrival of the regul bai; and that, outside its name, was all that they knew. The Lady Mother had gathered them together in

138

the dawning, and spoken to them quietly and soberly, and it was an effort for her, for she lay insensible so much of the time. But for a moment, a brief moment, there had been an Intel Niun had never seen: it awed him, that soft-voiced, clear-headed stranger who spoke knowledgeably about lanes and routings around Kesrith that were little-monitored by regul—in riddles she spoke at times, but not now: "Soon," she had said, "Very soon. Keep your eyes on the regul, kel'ein."

And quickly then, more quickly than they had anticipated, the regul bai had come making them offers.

The regul were concerned. They were presented something that had never happened before, and they were concerned and confused.

"Intel," said Eddan, her eldest Husband, when dinner was done and Niun had returned from carrying the utensils to the scullery—that and the storerooms the only part of the Kath-tower that remained open. "Intel, may the Kel ask permission to ask a question?"

Niun settled among the kel'ein quickly, anxious and at once grateful that Eddan had waited until his return; and he looked at Intel's face, seeking some hope that she would not deny them.

She frowned. "Is the Kel going to ask about the ship?"

"Yes," said Eddan, "or anything else worth the knowing."

The she'pan unfolded her hands, permission given.

"When it comes," asked Eddan, "do we go or do we stay?"

"Kel'ein, I will tell you this: that I have seen that Kesrith's use is near its end. Go, yes; and I will tell you something more: that I owe the regul bai one kel'en, but no more. And I do much doubt that he will come back to collect that promise of me."

Old Liran, veilless as they all were veilless in the intimacy of the common-meal, grinned and made a move with his scarred hand. "Well, she'pan, Little Mother, if he does come back, send me. I would like to see whether Nurag is all it is claimed to be, and I would be of scant use in the building of another edun. This one, all cracks as it is, is home; and if I am not to stay with this one, why, I might as well take service again."

"Would a service among the People not do as well, Liran?"

"Yes, Little Mother, well enough," Liran answered, and his

old eyes flickered with interest, a darted glance at Eddan—an appeal: *ask questions, eldest.* The whole Kel sat utterly still. But the she'pan had turned their question aside. Eddan did not ask again.

"Sathell," said Intel.

"She'pan?"

"Cite for the Kel the terms of the treaty that bind us to the service of regul."

Sathell bowed his head and lifted it again. "The words of the treaty between doch Holn and mri are the treaty that keeps us in service to the regul. The pertinent area: *So long as regul and mri alone occupy the homeworld, whereon the edun of the People rests . . . or until regul depart the homeworld, whereon the edun of the People rests . . .* This long we are bound to accept service with regul when called upon. And I hold, she'pan, that in spirit if not in letter, regul have already failed in the terms of that treaty."

"Surely," said the she'pan, "we are not far from that point. We contracted with doch Holn. Doch Holn might have known how to deal with us; but this bai Hulagh is apparently of Nurag itself, and I do not think he knows the People. He erred seriously when he did not take urgent care to see to our evacuation long before now."

"Holn knew better," said Sathell.

"But Holn neglected to pass on to her successor all that she might have told him. The old bai Solgah kept her silence. Neither do regul tend to consult written records. The regulkind do not make good fighters, but they are, in their own way, very clever at revenge."

And Intel smiled, a tired smile that held a certain satisfaction.

"May the Kel," asked Eddan, "ask permission to ask a question?"

"Ask."

"Do you think the Holn deliberately excluded us from the assets she turned over to this bai Hulagh?"

"I believe the Holn will consider this a stroke of revenge, a salve to their pride, yes. Bai Hulagh has lost the mri. In such manner regul fight against regul. What is that to us? But I am sure of this," she said in a hard tone, "that Medai was the last of my children to leave on a regul ship, the last of my children to die for regul causes. And hereafter, hereafter,

kel'ein, do not plan that mri should fight mri again: no. We
do not fight."

There was palpable dismay in the whole Kel.

"May the Kel ask?—" Eddan began, unshakably formal.

"No," she said. "The Kel may not ask. But I will tell you
what is good for you to know. The People are dangerously
declined in numbers. Time was when such fighting served the
People; but no longer, no longer, kel'ein. I will tell you a
thing you did not ask: the ship *Ahanal* bears what remains of
all the People; and we are the rest. There are no more."

There was cold in the room, and no one moved. Niun
locked his arms tightly about his knees, trying to absorb personally what the Mother said, hoping that it was allegory, as
she often spoke in riddles: but there was no way to believe it
a figure of speech.

"At Elag," said Intel in a thin hard voice, "while regul
evacuated their own kind, they threw the kel'ein that served
them against humans again and again and again, and summoned the kel'ein of Mlassul and Seleth edunei, and lost
them as well. But this mattered little to regul, to this new bai,
Hulagh—to this new master sent out from Nurag."

There was a sudden sound, an impact of fist on flesh; and
Eddan, who did not swear, swore. "She'pan," he said then.
"May the Kel ask—"

"There is nothing more to ask, Eddan," said Intel. "That is
the thing that happened: that cost 10,000 mri lives, and
ships—ships of which I do not know the tally; many, many
of the ships were regul, without regul personnel aboard, because the regul feared to stay. They killed 10,000 mri. And I
curse the she'panei who lent their children to such as that."

A fine sweat beaded Intel's face, and pallor underlay her
skin. The sound of her breathing was audible, a hoarseness,
above the sound of the rain outside. Never had the gentle
Mother cursed anyone; and the enormity of cursing she'panei
chilled the heart; but neither was there repentance on her
face. Niun drew his breaths carefully, sucking in air as if he
drew it off the noon-heated sands. His muscles began to
tremble, and he clenched his hands the harder lest someone
notice it, if anyone could notice anything but his own heart-
beat in that terrible silence.

"Little Mother," Sathell pleaded. "Enough, Enough."

"The Kel," she said, "finds it necessary to ask questions.

They are due their answer." And she paused a moment, drawing great breaths, as if she intended next something necessary, something urgent. "Kel'ein," she said, "chant me the *Shon'jir*."

There was a stirring among the kel'ein, outright panic and dismay. *She is dying,* was Niun's first thought, and: *O gods, what an ill omen of things!* And he could not say the words she asked of them.

"Are you children," she asked of her Husbands, "to believe any longer in luck either good or bad? Chant me the Passing ritual."

They looked at Eddan, who inclined his head in a gesture of surrender, and began, softly. Niun joined them, uncertain in this insanity in which they were bidden join.

> *From Dark beginning*
> *To Dark at ending,*
> *Between them a Sun,*
> *But after comes Dark,*
> *And in that Dark*
>   *One ending.*

> *From Dark to Dark*
> *Is one voyage.*
> *From Dark to Dark*
> *Is our voyage.*
>   *And after the Dark,*
>   *O brothers, o sisters,*
>   *Come we home.*

Intel listened with her eyes closed, and afterward there was a long silence; and her eyes opened, and she looked on all of them as from a far place.

"I give you," she said, "a knowledge which Kel'ein knew long ago, but which passed from the Kel-lore. Remember it again. I make it lawful. Kesrith is only a between, and Arain only one of many suns, and we are near an ending. In the People's history, kel'ein, are many such Darks; and the regul have afforded us only the latest of our many homes. For this reason we call it *Shon'jir*, and in the low language, the Passing ritual. For this reason we say it at the beginning of each life of the People and at each life's ending; and at the beginning of each era and at its ending. Until another she'pan shall bid your children's children, Niun, forget what I have told you, the Kel may remember."

"Mother," he said, raising hand to her in entreaty, "Mother, is it the moving of homeworld you mean?"

Too long she had been mother to him, and he realized after he had spoken his question that she was due more courtesy; he sat with his heart pounding and waited to hear her coldly rebuff him by asking Eddan if the Kel had a question to pose.

But she neither frowned nor refused his question. "Niun, I give you more truth to ponder. The regul call themselves old; but the People are older. The 2,000 years of which you know are only an interlude. We are nomads. I say that the Kel shall not fight; but the Kel has other purposes. Last of my sons, the Kel of the Darks is a different Kel from the Kel of the Between. Last of my daughters, the she'panate of the Darks is a duty I do not envy you."

Upon an instant the whole Kel was torn from one to the other of them, a fearful, astonished attention.

The succession was passed, not in fact, but in intent; and Niun looked at his onetime brothers, and saw their dismay; and looked at Melein and saw her pale and shaken. She veiled herself and turned away from them; and of a sudden he felt himself utterly alone, even amid the Kel. He bowed his head and stayed so while the voice of Eddan, subdued, begged leave to question, which the she'pan refused.

"The Sen asks," said Sathell's voice then, and by that, posed a question that could not be refused. "She'pan, we cannot make these plans without consulting together."

"Is that a question, Sen?" the she'pan asked dryly, and in the shock of that collision of wills, there was silence. Niun looked at them, from one to the other, appalled that those who ruled his life did not agree.

"It is a question," said Sathell.

The she'pan bit at her lip and nodded. "Yet," she said, "we have made these plans without consulting. I did not consult when I made sure that *Ahanal* was reserved from the madness of Elag. I did not consult when I maintained our base on Kesrith against the urging of some to leave. I have made these plans without consulting—and I have left the People no other choice."

"To the death of our Kath and most of our Kel, when we might have had Lushain for homeworld instead, where there is water and gentle climate, where we might have had a rich world, she'pan."

"That old quarrel," she said in a still voice. "But I had my way, Sathell, because the she'pan, not the sen'anth, leads the People. Remember it."

"The Sen asks," said Sathell in a trembling voice, *"why. Why* must it have been Kesrith?"

"Is your knowledge adequate? Do you know the last Mysteries, sen'anth?"

"No," Sathell acknowledged, an answer wrung from him.

"Kesrith was the best choice."

"I do not believe it."

"I said at the time," said Intel softly, "that I decided as I saw fit. That is still true. I do not require your belief."

"This I know," said Sathell.

"Kesrith is hard. It kills the weak. It performed its function."

"This forge of the People, as you called it, performed its function too well. We are too few. And Elag has left us with nothing."

"Elag has left us with a remnant like the remnant of Kesrith," said Intel. "With what has been through fire."

"A handful."

"We have given the People," she said, "a place to stand, and stand we shall until humans stand on Kesrith. And then the Dark. And then a decision that will belong to others than you and me, Sathell."

There was silence. Sathell rose suddenly and caught at the wall for support, his weakness betraying him. "To others then," he said, "let it pass now."

And he walked out. His footsteps descended the tower.

Eddan bowed himself, came to Intel and took her hand. "Little Mother," he said gently, "the Kel approves you."

"The Kel knows little," she said, "even now."

"The Kel knows the she'pan," he said in a faint voice. And then he looked about him at the others, at Melein last of all. "Sen Melein—make the cup for her."

"I will not drink it tonight, Eddan," Intel said.

But Eddan's look said otherwise, and Melein nodded, silent conspiracy against Intel's will, and rose and poured water and *komal* into a cup, preparing the draught that would give Intel ease.

"Go," said Eddan to the Kel.

"Niun will stay," said Intel, and Niun, who had risen with the others, stopped.

And downstairs the main door opened and closed, a hollow crash.

"Gods," Pasev breathed, and cast a look at Intel. "He is leaving the edun."

"Let him go," said Intel.

"She'pan," said Melein's voice, a clear note of anguish. "He cannot stay the night out there in the weather."

"I will go after him," said Debas.

"No," said the she'pan. "Let him go."

And after a moment it was clear that there was no changing her mind. There was nothing to be done. Melein settled at Intel's side, still veiled, her eyes averted.

"The Kel is dismissed," said Intel, "except Niun. Sleep well, kel'ein."

Eddan did not wish to be dismissed. He stayed last of all; but Intel gestured him away. "Go," she said. "There is nothing more I can tell you tonight, Eddan. But in the morning, set one of the kel'ein to watch the port from the high rocks. Sleep now. This storm will keep the regul inactive, but tomorrow is another matter."

"No," said Eddan. "I am going after my brother."

"Without my blessing."

"All the same," said Eddan, and turned to go.

"Eddan," she said.

He looked back at her, "We are getting too few," he said, "to make too many journeys to Sil'athen. Sathell would not willingly have left Nisren. Neither would I. Now we will not leave Kesrith. We will walk toward Sil'athen, he and I. We will be content."

"I give my blessing," she said after a moment.

"Thank you," he said, "she'pan."

And that was all. He left; and Niun stared after him into the dark of the hall and trembled in every muscle.

They were as dead, Eddan and Sathell. They had chosen, Sathell after the fashion of his kind, and Eddan, untypical for his caste, to go the long walk with him. And he had seen Eddan's face, and there was no heaviness in it. He heard the kel'anth's steps going down the spiral, a quick and easy stride, and the door closed behind him too; and it was certain that the edun was less by two lives, and they had been great ones.

"Sit by me," Intel bade them.

"She'pan," said Melein in a thin, strained voice, "I have made your cup. Please drink it."

She offered it, and the tray shook in her two hands. Intel took the cup from her and drank, then gave it back, leaning back as Niun settled, kneeling, on her left hand, and Melein on her right.

So they had spent many of the nights since Medai's death, for Intel's sleep was not easy and she would not sleep without someone in the room.

This night, Niun envied her the draught of *komal;* and he would not look at her while she waited for the draught to have effect, but bowed his head and stared at his hands in his lap, shaken and shattered to his inmost heart.

Eddan, Eddan and Sathell, that had been a part of all his life. He wept, naked-faced, and the tears splashed onto his hands, and he was ashamed to lift a hand to wipe them away, for the Kel did not weep.

"Sathell is very ill," said Intel softly, "and he knew well what he did. Do not think that we parted hatefully. Melein knows. Eddan knows. Sathell was a good man: our old, old quarrel—he never agreed with me, and yet for forty-three years he has given me his good offices. I do not grudge that he simply stated his opinion at the last. We were friends. And do not feel badly for Eddan. If he did otherwise, I would have been surprised."

"You are hard," said Niun.

"Yes," she said. And her slight touch descended on his shoulder, brushed aside the *zaidhe.* He slipped it off, wadded his cloth in his clenched fists, head still bowed, for his eyes were wet. "Last son of mine," she said then, "do you love me?"

The question, so nakedly posed, struck him like a hammer blow; and in this moment he could not say smoothly, yes, Mother. He could not summon it.

"Mother," he said painfully, of her many titles, the best and dearest to the Kel.

"Do you love me, Niun?" Her soft fingers brushed past his mane, touched the sensitivity of his ear, teasing the downy tufts at its crest, an intimacy for kinswomen and lovers: *Here is a secret,* the touch said, *a hidden thing: be attentive.*

He was not strong enough for secrets now, for any added burden; he looked up at her, trying to answer. The calm face looked down on him with curious longing. "I know," she said. "You are here. You pay me duty. That is still a good and pious act, child of mine. And I know that I have robbed you and denied you and compelled everything that you have done and will ever do."

"I know that your reasons are good ones."

"No," she said. "You are kel'en. You do not know; you believe. But you are proper to say so. And you are right. Tomorrow—tomorrow you will see it, when you see *Ahanal. Melein—*"

"She'pan."

"Do you mourn Sathell?"

"Yes, she'pan."

"Do you dispute me?"

"No, she'pan."

"There will be a she'pan on *Ahanal,*" said Intel. "That she'pan is not fit as I have made you fit."

"I am twenty-two years old," protested Melein. "She'pan, you could take command of *Ahanal,* but if they challenge, if they should challenge—"

"Niun would defend me, defend me well. And he will defend you in your hour."

"Do you pass his duty to me?" Melein asked.

"In time," she said, "I will do this. In your time."

"I do not know all that I need to know, she'pan."

"You will kill," said Intel, "any who tries to take the Pana from you. I am the oldest of all she'panei, and I have prepared my successor in my own way."

"In conscience—" Melein protested.

"In conscience," said the she'pan, "obey me and do not question."

And the drug began to come over her and her eyes dimmed and she sank into her cushions and was still.

In time she slept soundly.

It was said, in a tale told in the Kel, that at the fall of Nisren, humans had actually breached the edun, ignoring mri attempts to challenge to *a'ani:* this the first and bitterest error the mri had made with humans. A human force had swept through the halls while the Kath in terror tried to escape: and Intel had put herself between humans and the Kath, and fired the hall with her own hand. Whether it was Intel or the fire, those humans had not come against her. She had held long enough for some of the Kath to escape, until the embattled Kel could reach that hall and get her to safety, to the regul ship.

That aspect of gentle Intel had always been incredible to Niun, until this night.

Chapter Fourteen

———◆◆◆———

DUNCAN HEARD the hum of machinery. It wakened him, advising him at once that Stavros had need of something. He pulled himself off the couch and gathered his fatigue-dulled senses. He had not undressed. He had not put Stavros to bed. Storm alarms had made most of the night chaotic. There was a time that constant storm advisories were coming over communications.

He heard the storm shields in Stavros' quarters go back. He wandered in to see that the alarms were past, that the screens showed clear. The dawn came up ruddy and murky, flooding a peculiar light through the glass.

Stavros was in the center of that glow, a curious figure in his mobile sled. He whipped it about to face Duncan with a jaunty expertise. The communication screen lighted.

Look outside.

Duncan stepped up to the rain-spattered window and looked, scanning the desolate expanse of sand and rock, toward the sea and the towers of the water-recovery system. There was something wrong, a gap in the silhouette, a vacancy where yesterday towers had stood.

There was a particularly dark area of cloud over the seacoast, flattened by the winds, torn and streamered out to sea.

Stavros' screen activated.

Advisory just given: water use confined to drinking and food preparation only. 'Minor repairs at plant.' They ask we remain patient.

"We've got people coming down here," Duncan protested.

Suspect further damage at port. Regul much disturbed. Bai 'not available.'

The rain slacked off considerably, leaving only a few spatters on the windows. The murky light grew for a moment red like that from fire, only Arain through thick cloud.

And on the long ridge that lay beyond the town there was a shadow that moved. Duncan's eyes jerked back to it, strained upon that one spot. There was nothing.

"I saw something out there," he said.

Yes, the screen advised him when he looked. *Many. Many. Maybe flood drove beasts from holes.*

In a moment another shadow appeared atop the ridge. He watched, as yet another and another and another appeared. His eyes swept the whole circuit of the hills. Against the sullen light there was a gathering row of black shapes, that moved and milled aimlessly.

Mri, he had feared.

But not mri. Beasts. He thought of the great unpleasant beasts that had been found with dead mri, ursine creatures that could be as dangerous as their size warned.

"They're mri-beasts," he said to Stavros. "They've got the whole area ringed."

Regul call them dusei. They are native to Kesrith. Read your briefings.

"They go with mri. How many mri are supposed to be here? I thought it was only a handful."

So the bai assures us—a token presence—to be removed.

He looked at the horizon. The clouds stretched unbroken.

And the dusei were a solid line across the whole ridge, encompassing the visible circuit of the sea to the town.

Duncan turned from the sight of it, shivered, looked back again. He considered the rain, and the land—worked his sweating hands and looked at Stavros. "Sir, I'd like to go out there."

"No," Stavros murmured.

"Listen to me." Duncan found it awkward to talk at such an angle, dropped to one knee so that he could meet the old man eye to eye, set a hand on the cold metal of the sled. "We've got only regul word for it that the regul don't lie; we've got mri out there; we've got a colony mission coming in here in a matter of days. You took me along. I assume you had some feeling then you might need me. I can get out there and take a look and get back without anyone the wiser. You can cover for me that long. Who cares about a youngling more or less? They won't see me. Let me go out there and see what kind of situation we're facing with those ships coming in. We don't know how bad it is with the water; we don't know what shape the port is in. Are you that confident we're always told all the truth?"

Weather hazardous. And incident with regul likely.

"That's something I can avoid. It's my job. It's what I know how to do."

Argument persuasive. Can you guarantee no incident?

"On my life."

Estimate correct. If incident occurs, then regul law prevails out there. You understand. Survey facilities, plant, port, return. Can cover you till dark.

"Yes, sir." He was relieved in some part; he did not look forward to it: he knew the hazard better perhaps than Stavros did. But for once he and the honorable Stavros were of one mind. Hunting out the hazards was more comfortable than ignoring them.

He rose, looked outside, found the dusei's dark line vanished in that brief interval. He blinked, tried to see through the haze of rain, made out little in the distance.

"Sir," he murmured to Stavros by way of farewell; Stavros inclined his head, dismissing him. The screen stayed dark.

He went quickly to his own quarters and changed uniforms, to khaki weatherproofs and sealed boots, still common enough in appearance that he did not think regul would notice the difference. He put into the several pockets a tight roll of cord, a knife, a packet of concentrates, a penlight, whatever would fit without obvious outlines. He flipped the hood into the collar and zipped the closures.

Then he strolled out into the hall on a pattern he had followed several times a day since he had studied the layout of the building, down the hall to the left and out toward the observation deck window. No one was in the hall there. He opened the door and went out into the rain-chilled air, walked the circuit of the low-walled observation deck, looked over his shoulder to see that the hall beyond the doors was still clear.

It was.

He quite simply sat down on the edge of the wall, held with his hands as he dropped, and let go. The regul stories were short by human standards. He landed on cement at the bottom, but it was not a hard drop at all, only a flex of the knees; and the cement showed no tracks. By the time that he reached the edge of the concrete and disappeared into the gentle rolls of the landscape, he was confident that he was unobserved.

He walked toward the water plant, turning up the hood of his uniform as he went, for he knew the warnings about the mineral-laden rains and cared to expose as little of his skin as possible. Now off the pavements of the city he left tracks as plain as wet sand could show them, but he did not reckon to be tracked at all. He felt rather self-pleased in this, which he had thought about for days, idle exercise of his professional mind during the long inactivity in the Nom: the fact was that no regul could have possibly done what he had just done, and therefore the regul had not taken precautions against it. Such a drop would have been impossible to their heavy, short-legged bodies, and likewise there was no regul that could come tracking him crosslands.

That would take a mri.

And that was the only possibility that made him a little less self-pleased than he might have been under the circumstances. He had wanted arms at the outset of the voyage, but the diplomats had denied them to him: unnecessary and provocative, they had reasoned. Now he was unarmed but for the kit-knife in his pocket, and a mri warrior could carve him in small portions before he could come close enough to make use of that for defense.

The fact was plainly that if regul would set a mri on his trail, he was dead; but then, he reasoned, if regul would dare do that, then the treaty was worth nothing, and that fact had as well be known early.

There was also the possibility that the mri were out in force, and that they were not under regul control; and that most of all needed to be known.

For that reason he exercised more caution in his walking than he would have shown if he feared only regul: he watched the ridges and the shadows of gullies, and took care to look behind him, remembering the dark shapes that had moved upon the hills, the dusei that were out somewhere: he crossed dus-tracks, long-clawed, ominous reminders that there were hunters aprowl other than regul or mri.

Briefings said that the beasts did not approach regul dwellings.

Briefings also said that crossing the flats off the roads was not recommended.

The jetting steam of geysers, the crunch of thin crusts underfoot, warned him that there was reason for this. He had to draw a weaving course around hot zones, approaching the lowest part of the flats, that near the seashore and the water plant.

There was a road of sorts, badly washed, along the seacoast. Parts of it were underwater. A regul landsled was down in a trench where it had run off the edge.

Duncan sat down, winded in the thin, cold air, his head and gut aching, and watched from a distance as a regul crew tried to extricate it. He could see the water plant clearly from this vantage point. There was chaos there too, beyond its protective fences. The towers extended far out into the white-capped water, and several of those towers were in ruins.

From what he could see there was no possibility those towers could even be cleared for repair in the few days before human ships would arrive, certainly not with prevailing weather. What was more, he could not see any evidence of heavy machinery available to do repairs.

Realistically estimating, it was not going to be done at all. A large human occupation force was going to land, having to depend totally on ships' recycling: irritating, but possible—if there was a place to land.

He looked to the right along the shoreline, toward the city and beyond, where he could see the low shape of the Nom— no building high enough to obstruct his view of the port. He recognized *Hazan*, saw its alien shape surrounded by gantries, a web of metal.

There was no way to set a ship down on the volcanic crusts that overlay most of the lowlands. If the port was in the same condition as the water plant, then there was going to be merry chaos when the human forces tried to land.

And the regul had not been forward to inform them of the extent of damages to the facilities at the plant: they had not lied, but neither had they volunteered all the truth.

He drew a breath of tainted air and looked behind him suddenly, chilled to realize that he had been thinking about something other than his personal safety for a few seconds.

The horizon was clear. There were only the clouds. A man did not always find himself that fortunate in his lapses.

He let go that breath slowly and gathered himself up, conscious of the pounding of his head and the pounding of his heart in the thin air. He saw a way to work around some low rocks and a sandy shelf and so cross between the city and the sea, working toward the port. Regul were reputed to have dim eyesight—to be dull, as it happened, in all sensory capacities. He hoped that this was so.

Stavros, sitting back in the embrace of his regul machine, had said that he could cover his absence. He reckoned that Stavros might be good at that, being skilled at argument and misleadings.

Out here, he knew his own job—knew with a surety that the instinct that had drawn Stavros to choose a SurTac for Kesrith had been a true one. Stavros had not ordered him, had only relied on him, quietly—had waited for him to move of his own accord, sensing, perhaps, that a man trained in the taking of alien terrain would know his own moment.

He could not afford a mistake. He was afraid, with a different sort of fear than he had ever known in a mission. He had operated alone before, had destroyed, had escaped—his own life or death on his head. He was not accustomed to work with the life or death of others weighing on his shoulders, with the weight of decision, to say that an area was safe or not safe for the landing of a mission involving hundreds of lives and policies reaching far beyond Kesrith.

He did not like it; he far from liked it. He would have cast it on any higher authority available; but Stavros, bound to his machine, had to believe either the regul or his own aide, and he desperately wanted to be right.

Chapter Fifteen

———— •=•=• ————

THE EDUN woke quietly; the People moved quietly about the daily routine. Niun went back to the Kel, which was now empty-seeming; and the Kel sat in mourning. Eddan did not return.

And Pasev's eyes bore that bruised look that told of little sleep; but she sat unveiled, in command of her emotions. Niun brought her a special portion at breakfast, and it tore his heart that she would not eat.

After breakfast the brothers Liran and Debas spoke together and rose up and put on the belts with all their honors, and *mez'ein* and *zaidh'ein,* and gave their farewells.

"Will you all leave?" asked Niun, out of turn and out of place and terrified. And he looked then at Pasev, who had most reason to go, and did not.

"You might be needed," said Pasev to the brothers.

"We will walk and enjoy the morning," said Liran. "Perhaps we will find Eddan and Sathell."

"Then tell Eddan," she said softly, "that I will be coming after him when I have finished my own duties, which he left to me. Goodbye, brothers."

"Goodbye," they said together, and all the remaining Kel echoed, "Goodbye," and they walked down from the tower and out across the road.

Niun stood in the doorway to watch them go, a deep melancholy upon him; and a knot settling in his throat to consider their absence hereafter. They continued to the horizon, two shapes of black; and the sky was shadowed and threatening, and they had not so much as the comfort of their dusei in their journey, for none of the beasts had come home. The *miuk'ko* from the door had disappeared also, dead, perhaps,

155

in the storm: dusei went away to die, alone, like kel'ein that found no further hope in their lives.

Loyal to Intel, he thought, and loyal to Kesrith, and foreseeing the end of both; they could not help now, and so they departed, with their honors on them, not seeking burial of a young kel'en too overburdened with duties to see to them.

They had chanted the rites last night. It was ill-omened; they all knew it. It was as if they had chanted them over Kesrith itself, and he suddenly foresaw that few of the old ones at all would board the ship.

They did not want Intel's dream. She had shown them the truth of the rites and they had not wanted it; they had seen only the old, familiar ways.

She had promised them change, and they would have none of it.

He was otherwise shaped, formed by Intel's hands and Intel's wishes, and loyalty to Melein would hold him bound to Intel's dream. He looked on the place in the rocks where the brothers had disappeared and could have wept aloud at what he then realized of them and him, for Pasev would follow, rather than take ship into uncertainties for which she had no longing; and after her would go the others. He would never be one with the like of them: black-robe, plain-robe, honorless and untested, shaped for different ways. *The Kel of the Darks*, she had said, *is a different Kel*.

It was he who already stood in the Dark; and they had walked away from the shadow, into what they knew.

He turned, to seek the edun, the Shrine's comfort for his mood; and his heart chilled at what he saw along the lower ridges, with row upon row of shadows moving there.

Dusei.

They ringed the regul town in every place that offered solid ground. Ha-dusei, wild ones, and dangerous.

The dusei of the edun had not returned.

And there were far too many of the ha-dusei, far too many.

The sky roiled overhead, stained with red and sullen grey: stormfriends, the dusei, weather-knowing. In the days before the edun stood, they had watered here below: the Dus plain, the lowland flats were called. They came as if they sensed change in the winds, they came as if waiting the regul departure, which would give the Dus plain back to the dusei.

Waiting.

It was told of regul stubbornness that the first mri had warned the regul earnestly that they should build their city elsewhere, as the edun itself had been carefully positioned off the plain, in respect to the bond between mri and dusei; but regul had wanted rock for their ships to land on, and they had sounded the area thereabouts and found only on the Dus plain rock suitable for a port near the sea. Therefore regul had built there, and there had grown a city, and the ha-dusei had gone.

But dusei returned now, with the unseasonal rains and the destroying winds. They sat and waited.

And the dusei had left even the mri.

He shrugged, half a shiver, and walked inside and stopped, not wishing to bear that news to the Kel or to the she'pan. The Kel was in mourning, the she'pan still lost in dreams; and Melein, her Chosen, had veiled herself and sealed herself alone in the Sen-tower.

He cast a yearning thought skyward, through the spiral corridors that massed over him, that *Ahanal* hasten its coming, for he did not think that he could bear the endless hours until the evening.

And each thing that he thought of doing this day was pointless, for it was a house to which they would never return; and outside, the weather threatened and the lightning flashed in the clouds and the thunder rumbled.

So he sat down in the doorway, watching all the flats below, the geysers' plumes, predictable as the hours, their clouds torn and thrown by gale-force winds. It was a cold day, as few days on Kesrith were chill. He shivered, and watched the heavy drops pock the puddles that reflected a sky like fire-on-pewter.

A heavy body trod the wet sand: a whuff of breath, and a great dus lumbered round the corner, head hanging. Others followed. He scrambled up in terror, not sure of their mood; but wet and muddy-pawed, they came, and nosed their way past him into the edun, rumbling that hunger sound that betokened a dus with a considerable impatience. He counted them in: one, two, three, four, five, six. And last came the *miuk'ko*, the seventh, bedraggled and angular, to cast itself down in the puddle at the base of the slanted walls, drinking with great laps of its grey tongue at the water between its massive paws.

Three did not come. Niun waited, a relief and a disquiet growing in him at the same time—relief because a bereaved dus was dangerous and pitiable; and disquiet because he did not know how they had known. Perhaps the three that were missing had encountered their kel'ein.

Or perhaps, with that curious sense of dusei, they had known and sought them.

Perhaps they were far along the trail to Sil'athen. He earnestly hoped so. It would be best for both men and dusei.

He went to the storerooms in the cellar of Kath. The dusei must have care.

And first of all of them, he waited on the *miuk'ko*, that had left its post of mourning for the first time and then returned. He hoped it would be in a different mind.

But it would not eat. Perhaps, he thought, it had fed during its hours of wandering. But he did not believe it. He left the food on the dry edge of the step and went to carry portions to the others.

Save for the insistence and irreverence of the dusei, save for Melein, who grieved in her tower, the edun had become a place of dreams, and a sense of finality hung over everything: the dus by the gate, the old men and the old women. He crept about his tasks with the utmost quiet, as if he, living, walked in the caves at Sil'athen.

And in the evening the ship came.

The she'pan was asleep when they heard it descending; and they that were left of the Kel hurried out to the road to see it, and on tired faces there were smiles, and in Niun's heart there was misgiving. Dahacha took his arm on impulse and pressed it, and he looked at the sun-wrinkled eyes and felt an unspoken blessing pass between them.

"Dahacha," he whispered. "Will you come, at least?"

"We that have not walked will come," said the old man. "We will not send you alone, Niun Zain-Abrin. We have made our reckoning. If we would not, we would have gone with Eddan, like Liran and Debas."

"Yes," said Palazi at his other side. "We will reason with the kel'anth."

And it struck him like a blow upon a wound, that this now referred to Pasev.

The commotion of the ship's landing was visible in lights, in flares of regul headlights that crawled serpent-wise toward that far side of the field, half-glow in the red twilight: regul eyes were not adapted to the night.

"Come," said Pasev, and they followed her into the halls and to the she'pan's tower.

Melein was there, beside Intel, and she touched the she'pan's hand and tried to wake her, but it was Pasev who laid a firm grip on the she'pan's arm and shook her from her dreams.

"She'pan," said Pasev, "she'pan, the ship has come."

"And the regul?" In the she'pan's golden eyes the dream finished and that keenness returned, focused and struggling for control. "How do the regul bear it?"

"We do not know that yet," said Pasev. "They are all astir, that is all we saw."

Intel nodded. "No contact by radio. Regul will be monitoring; *Ahanal* will observe that caution also." She struggled with the cushions, a small moue of pain upon her face, and Melein adjusted them for her. She sighed and breathed easily a moment.

"Shall we," asked Dahacha, "Little Mother, carry you to the ship? We can bear you."

"No," she said with a sad smile. "A she'pan is guardian of the Pana: there is no ship-going for me until that care of mine is finally discharged."

"At least," said Dahacha then, "let us take you down to the road, so that you can see toward the port."

"No," said Intel, firmly. And then she touched Dahacha's hand upon the arm of her chair and smiled. "Do not fear: I am in possession of my faculties and in possession of this edun and this world, and so I will remain until I am sure that it is my time; and yours will not be until mine is. Do you hear me?"

"Aye," said Pasev.

Intel met the eyes of the kel'anth and nodded, satisfied; but then her glance strayed about the room, perhaps counted faces, and her eyes clouded.

"Liran and Debas left some time ago," said Pasev. "We gave them farewell."

"My blessing," she murmured dutifully.

Pasev bowed her head in acknowledgement. "Until the she'pan dismisses me," she said, "I serve you, and there are still enough of us to do what needs doing."

"We will not be long about it," said Intel. "Niun, child," she said, and held out her hand.

He knelt at her knee and took her hand in his, bowed his bared head to her touch, felt her fingers slip from his and give that gesture of blessing.

"Go crosslands," she said. "Go to the ship and talk with the visitors face to face, and hear what they have to say. Answer wisely. You may have to take decisions on yourself, young kel'en. And do not go carelessly. We have almost ceased to serve regul."

Something passed his bowed head: he felt weight settle on his neck, and caught at it, and his fingers closed on cold metal. When he turned it and looked at the amulet on the chain he saw the open hand emblem of Kesrithun edun, and Intel's silken fingers touched his chin and lifted his face to meet her eyes.

"Only one *j'tal*," she said softly. "But a master-one. Do you recognize it, my last son?"

"It is an honor," he said, "of a she'pan's kel'en."

"Bear yourself well," she said. "And make speed. Time is important now."

And she pushed at him with her fingers and he rose, almost fearing the eyes of the others, the kel'ein who might have been honored with such a *j'tal;* and he the youngest and least. But there was no envy there, only gladness, as if this were something in which they were all agreed.

He took off his houserobe, and there in the she'pan's chamber, they all took hand in preparing him for the journey, hastening to bring him the *siga* that he should wear in walking the dusty lands, and *zaidhe* and *mez;* and they gave him their own weapons, both yin'ein and zahen'ein, finer than his own; and with a smile, a laugh that deprecated superstition older than memory among the People, Palazi unclipped a luck amulet from his own belts and gave it him, a maiden warrior, giving him of his luck.

"Years and honors," said Palazi.

He hugged the old man, and others, and returned to the she'pan for a last hasty bow at her feet, his heart pounding

with excitement. But as he received her kiss upon his brow
she did not let him go at once, but stared into his face in
such a way that it chilled all the blood in him.

"You are beautiful," the she'pan said to him, her golden
eyes brimming with tears. "I have a great fear. Be careful,
youngest son."

The People no longer believed in presciences with any
great fervor, no more than he really trusted Palazi's luck-
wish; but he shivered. There was mri-reason and regul-reason,
and always to believe only what could be demonstrated by
experience was the regul way, not the mri.

One who had lived so many years as Intel might have reasons he did not understand. His whole life had been spent in
the presence of the forbidden and the incomprehensible; and
she'pan Intel had been involved in most: she'pan—keeper of
mysteries.

"I shall be careful," he said, and she let him go then; he
avoided the eyes of Melein when he rose, for if she'pan and
Chosen shared anything concerning him, he did not want to
carry it with him on this mission.

"Do not trust any regul," said the kel'anth. "See all that
you look upon."

"Yes," he agreed earnestly, and took Pasev's hands and
pressed them gently by way of farewell to the brothers and
sister of his caste.

He turned away quickly and left, long strides carrying him
hurriedly down the spiraling stairs, past the written names of
the history and heroes of the People and the truth of all the
things that Intel had hinted at, that he could not read. He felt
their meaning this day, the remembrance of his ancestors.

All, all that Intel had desired had come down to him; and
she had been able, at the last, to let him go, to cast him like
the as'ei in shon'ai. And she had not lost him. There was too
much of love poured into him by these old ones that he could
fail the wishes of Eddan, of Intel, of Pasev and Debas and
Liran. They had made sure that he would succeed before
they had launched him about the she'pan's mission.

He passed the main doors and closed them against the
night, and saw there the monstrous bulk of the miuk'ko, a
shadow beside the door. The great head lifted and the eyes
stared at him invisibly in the dark.

Perhaps, he thought, optimism uncrushed in a hundred repetitions of this coming and going, *perhaps this time. It would be good if it were this time at last, who needs me, who need him.*

But it murmured and turned its face and laid its massive head in the mud. Male, female, or neither; no one had ever ascertained the sex of a dus, nor reckoned why they came to one mri or why they refused to come to another; whether this one had yet comprehended that Medai would never return, whether it grieved, or whether it starved out of simple stupidity, waiting for Medai to feed it, Niun could not fathom.

With a sad shrug he went his way, hardly having paused that half-step; but in this passing there was a difference, for things the dus did not understand had changed, were changing, were about to change. And it was doomed, having rejected him.

Likely the humans would destroy the dusei. Regul would have done so gladly, if not for mri protection. The size and the slow-moving power of dusei was very like that of regul, but regul instinctively hated the dusei. Regul could not, as mri could, become immune to the poison of the claws; they could not, as mri could, abandon themselves to the simplicity of the beasts. Therefore regul fled them.

And the unease the contact of the dus had left in him stayed the while he walked down toward the flats, toward the ghostly plumes of geysers under the windtorn clouds. He smelled the wind, felt the familiar force of it, like some living thing.

He found himself looking at the familiar places that he had seen and known all his life, and thinking of each: *this is almost the last time.* There was excitement in his heart and an uncertainty in his stomach that was far from heroic and cheerful. His senses were alive to the whole world, the scents of the earth, acrid and wet, the feel of the damp hot breath of the geysers, that each had their name and manner.

His world.

Homeworld.

Impermanent as the wind, the Kel, but capable of loving the earth. It struck him that they did not know where they were going, that Intel spoke of the Dark as if it were a place, as if it had dimension and depth and duration like the world itself. It came to him that after leaving Kesrith he might never feel earth under his feet again: a Dark with promise, the she'pan had insisted; but he could not imagine what it promised.

And hereafter to deal with kel'ein who were not old, long-thinking men—kel'ein who knew only war and were touchy of their pride and their prerogatives of caste, in a way that the gentle Kel of Kesrith had never been.

To live among the Kel of strangers, where there were kath'ein, who would be his for the asking, and the chance to get children, and to see his private immortality. He would be son to one she'pan, truebrother to another, honored next whatever fen'ein, Husbands, she would choose to sire her children on the kel'e'ein and the kath'ein of the edun, if first he survived the combat of succession.

Choices spread before him in dazzling array, in dizzying profusion, a future full of things neither stale nor predictable nor sure.

He walked swiftly, where reeking sulphur and steam obscured his way, where water dripped from recently sprayed rocks and the heat underground prepared further eruptions. He knew his timing to a nicety. The thin crusts on the right—boiling water and mud underlay much of that ground. The edge that he trod would bear a mri's weight, but not that of a dus or a regul. Regul had learned bitter lessons about Kesrith's flatlands; they did not stray now from the safety of their vehicles and aircraft and carefully chosen roads and landing sites. It would take a long time for humans to learn the land, if they would ever dare leave the security of the regul city.

Some would surely die learning it. A few mri had done so.

He could cease to care what humans did. They would gather up the People and go, all of them, Dahacha and Palazi and the others; and Intel too—they would persuade her too, though she was old and very tired of struggles; she could at least begin their journey.

And then they could leave without even wanting to look back.

He gazed at last from the long white ridge that was above the port and saw the shape of the regul ship *Hazan* and opposite it, the new one of *Ahanal*.

Ahanal—the Swift.

He slid down the moonlit ridge in a white powdering of dust, and crossed the long slope to the lower ground.

And a shadow flowed among the rocks, large and menacing. He turned, hand on his pistol, and looked up at the hulking form that had mounted a ridge.

Ha-dus. For a moment he did not breathe, did not move. Three others showed. Silent, the great beasts could be, when they stalked; but they did not stalk him. He had only disturbed their vigil.

He remained still, respectful of their right to be here, and they snuffed the air and regarded him with their small eyes, and finally gave that explosive question sound that indicated the fighting mood was not on them.

Pardon, brothers, he wished them in his mind, which was the best way to deal with a strange and skittish dus, and backed a few paces before he edged on toward his former course: language the dus understood, a matter of movements that one made and did not make.

His hand shifted from the pistol to the amulet at his breast. Not the moment to risk his life with the ha-dusei, far from it; he walked more slowly, more cautiously, remembering Pasev's admonishment to use his eyes and his wits.

They let him go, and when he looked back they were no longer there.

He walked from the white dust to the artificial surface that covered the firm rock of the north rim area; and there was a fence, a laughable affair of wire screen that could stop nothing that was truly determined, not on Kesrith. He burned it, made himself a door in it, with fine disregard for regul obstructions on the free land. Any mri would do the like rather than walk round a fence, and regul met the like with outrage; but it was the mri way, and in this mri would not oblige the masters.

Bloody-handed savages, he had heard one of the regul younglings call him in the town.

But regul built fences and made machines that scarred the earth, and tried to divide up space itself into territories and limits and parcels to be traded like foodstuffs and metals and bolts of cloth. It was ludicrous in his eyes.

He walked amid the great tangle of abandoned equipage and skeletal braces and vehicles—as he had foreseen, a vast graveyard of vehicles and machines, a clot of metal so tightly jammed together that he had to detour round the whole of it, a heap of vehicles and sleds and aircraft indiscriminately mixed as if some giant hand had piled them there, the vehicles that had brought out the inhabitants of all the settlements the regul had ruled. And there, there a great burned area, a tower in charred and jagged outline against the port lights, an angular tangle of braces and more goods that the regul had cast aside as waste. Storm-shattered, burned: the damage at the port had then been very extensive. He looked about him as he walked, taking inventory of things he had once seen whole and what he saw now damaged, and he began to see reason for the regul's distressed behaviors.

Hazan stood in a vast assemblage of gantries and hoses and fragile extensions, and about that ship too he saw evident damage. She was aglow with lights, acrawl with black figures that labored on her like carrion insects; and a steady line of vehicles crawled toward her, bearing goods, no doubt, for loading and for repairs.

He passed this area, careful of being seen, and rounded the shape of *Hazan*. There, a tower before him, stood *Ahanal* once more, looming against the sky with only one light brought to bear upon her hull.

He drew near and saw that she was old, her metal pitted as with acids, her markings seared almost beyond recognition. Long scars marked where shields must have failed.

He voice-hailed them, conscious of the nearness of regul sentries; of a sled that had already started his way.

"*Ahanal!*" he cried. "Open your hatch!"

But either they were not prepared to hear or they had reason to be uneasy of the regul; and there was no response from *Ahanal*. He saw the sled veer sharply, coming to a halt near him, and a youngling regul opened the sidescreen to speak to him.

"Mri," said the regul, "you are not permitted."

"Is this the order of the bai?" he asked.

"Go away," the regul insisted. "Kesrithi mri, go away."

There was a crash of metal: the hatch had opened. He ignored the regul to glance upward at the ship, from which a ramp began to extend. He walked toward it, simply ignoring the regul.

The sled hummed behind him. He moved, narrowly missed: its fender clipped the side of his leg, and the sled circled in front of him, blocking his path.

The window was still open. The youngling regul was

breathing hard, his great nostrils opening and shutting in extreme agitation.

"Go back," it hissed.

He began to step round the sled; it lurched forward and he rolled on his shoulder across its low nose, landed on the other side and ran, shamed and frightened: mri were watching from the ramp, doubtless outraged at his discomfiture. His legs were weak under him with terror for what he had done, a thing which no mri had ever done: he had defied the masters directly; but he was the she'pan's messenger, and if he delayed to argue with the youngling there would be regul authority involved, with orders to obey or disobey, with a crisis for the she'pan that a mere kel'en could not resolve without direct violence.

He ran, hit the echoing solidity of the ramp and raced up it as quickly as he could to meet the mri of the ship, but they were already fading back into the ship and did not stay for him. He heard and felt the ramp taking up behind him, shortening its length as he overtook the last of them. Lights came on, blinding; doors shut, sealing them safely inside.

Ten kel'ein: Husbands, by their age and dignity. There was cold light and air piercing in its sterility after the air of Kesrith. The final seal of the lock closed between them and the outside, the ramp in place. There was silence.

"Sirs," he remembered to say, and stopped looking at them, with their many *j'tai* and their grim, stranger's manner, long enough to touch his brow and pay proper respect. He looked up again and unveiled, a courtesy which they grudgingly returned.

"I am Niun s'Intel Zain-Abrin," he said in the high language, as all mri used in formalities. "I bear service to Intel, she'pan of Edun Kesrithun."

"I am Sune s'Hara Sune-Lir," said the eldest of them, an old man whose mane greyed at the temples and who looked to be of the age of Pasev or Eddan; but his fellows were younger, more powerful-looking men. "Does the she'pan Intel fare well?"

"The edun is safe."

"Does the she'pan intend to come in person?"

"As to that, sir, not until I return wth the word of your she'pan."

He understood somewhat their attitude, that of men who

loved and defended their own, who must yield to she'pan Intel, who must yield them too. It was natural that they look on Intel's messenger with resentment.

"We will take you to her," said Sune s'Hara, with formal grace. "Come." And with better courtesy: "You are not injured?"

"No, sir," he said, and remembered with a sudden flush that it was not proper for him to defer to this man, that he was a messenger, and more than that; he betrayed himself for a very young kel'en and inexperienced in his authority. "Regul and mri are not at ease in Kesrith," he added, covering his confusion. "There have been words passed."

"We were met with weapons," Sune said. "But there were no casualties."

He walked with them, through corridors of metal, in halls designed for regul. He saw kel'ein and he saw kel'e'ein, veiled and youthful as he; and his pulse quickened—he thought them glorious and beautiful, and tried not to stare, though he knew that their eyes were taking close account of him, a stranger among them. Some unveiled in brotherly welcome when he met them, and a great company of them went through the corridors to the mainroom, to that center of the ship that was now the hall of a she'pan.

She was middle-aged. He came and bowed his head under her hands, and looked up at her, vaguely disturbed to be greeted by a she'pan not in the familiar earthen closeness of a tower but in this metal place, and to a greeting a she'pan who was not kin, whose emblem on her white, blue-edged robes was that of a star, not the hand emblem of Edun Kesrithun.

She was a stranger who must die, who must choose to die or whose champion he must defeat, if she challenged; and he prayed silently all the gods that this one would be brave and gracious and forego challenge.

Her eyes were hard and she existed in light harsh enough to hurt; and the world that surrounded her was cold and metal. Many, many of the ship-folk surrounded them now, their she'pan, their beloved Mother, and not his: he an intruder, a threat to her life.

They saw a she'pan's messenger, but one innocent of *j'tai* won in battles—a youth unscarred, untried, and vulnerable to challenge.

He felt her eyes go up and down him, reckoning this, reckoning his world and those who sent him. And beyond her, about her, he saw gold-robed sen'ein; and black-robed kel'ein; and shyly observing from the recesses of the further hall, he saw kath'ein, blue-robes, veilless and gentle and frightened.

And about them, within the other corridors, row on row of hammocks slung like the nestings of Kesrith's spiders, threads of white and webbings that laced the room and the sides of the corridors. He was overwhelmed by the number of those that crowded close: and yet it struck him suddenly that here was his whole species, all reduced to this little ship, and under the present command of this woman.

"Messenger," she said, "I am Esain of Edun Elagun. How fares Intel?"

Her voice was kinder than her face, and shot through him like sun after night. His heart melted toward her, that she could speak kindly toward him and toward Intel.

"She'pan," he said, "Intel is well enough."

He put kindness in his voice, and yet she understood, for a shadow passed through her eyes, and fear; but she was a great lady, and did not flinch.

"What does Intel wish to tell me?" asked Esain.

"She'pan," he said, "she gave me welcome for you; and sent me to listen to you first of all."

She nodded slightly, and with a move of her hand bade council attend her: kel'anth and sen'anth and kath'anth came and sat by her; and the fen'ein, her Husbands of the Kel; and the body of the Sen; and while these took their places the others withdrew, and doors were closed.

He remained kneeling before her, and carefully removed his *zaidhe* and laid that before him; and on it he laid the *avkel*, the Kel-sword that was Sirain's lending, sheathed before him, hilt toward her, a token of peace. His hands he folded in his lap. Her kel'ein did the same, hilts toward him, the stranger in their midst, the visitor admitted to council.

"We send greetings to Intel," said Esain quietly. "Of her wisdom long ago was *Ahanal* reserved for the People, and of her wisdom was *Ahanal* freed to come. She placed such a burden on the Kel, refusing regul assistance, that there was no honorable choice. Honor outweighed honor. This was wisely done. All aboard understand and are grateful that it was done in time, for nothing else could have compelled us from the front. Is it true as we guess, that she intends to leave regul service?"

"Her words: We have almost left regul service. Your fen'ein and the kel'anth saw the result of it when I came toward the ship."

She looked at the kel'anth. He gave agreement with a gesture.

"I have seen a thing I have never seen," the old man said. "A regul attacked this messenger—not with hands, to be sure; but with his machine. These regul are desperate."

"And the edun?" the she'pan asked, her brow crossed with a frown. "How fares the Edun of the People, with the regul in such a mood?"

"Presently secure," he said, and, for he saw the real question burning in her, that she would hesitate to ask a mere kel'en: "She'pan, the Forbidden is in her keeping; and the regul are busy with the damage the weather has done them. Humans are close, and the regul fear delays that could hold them grounded. I think what happened out there was the act of a youngling without clear orders."

"Yet," said the she'pan, "what if we were to leave the ship in a body?"

"We are mri," said Niun with supreme confidence, "and regul would give way before us, and they would dare do nothing."

"Did you so judge," asked the she'pan, "of that youngling that attempted your life?"

Heat mounted in his face. "She'pan," he said, made aware of his youth and his inexperience. "I do not think that was a serious threat."

She thought, and looked at the Sen and the others, and finally sighed and frowned. "I bear too great a charge here to risk it. We will wait until Intel has made her decision. We have force here at her call; I will send it or reserve it as she says. And, messenger, assure her that I will respect her claim on the People."

He was shocked and relieved at once, and he bowed very low to her, hearing the murmur of grief run the length and breadth of the room. He could hardly bear to meet her eyes again, but found them gentle and unaccusing.

"I will tell her," he said, recovering the courtesies trained into him, part of blood and flesh and bone, "that the she'pan of Edun Elagun is a grand and brave lady, and that she has earned great honor of all the People."

"Tell her," she said softly, "that I wish her well with my children."

Many veiled themselves, hearing her, and he found his own eyes stinging.

"I will tell her," he said.

"Will you, messenger, stay the night with us?"

He thought of it, for it was a walk of the rest of the night to come again to the edun, and likely a great deal of sleep lost thereafter, once Intel had begun to give orders; but he thought of the regul that had crossed his path, and the weather, and the uncertainties that hemmed him about.

"She'pan," he said, "my duty is to go back now—best now, before the regul have time to take long consultations."

"Yes," she said, "that would be the wisest thing. Go, then."

And she, when he had gathered up the *av-kel* and replaced the *zaidhe*, and come to touch her hand and do her heartfelt courtesy, gave into his hand a ring of true gold, at which his heart clenched in pain; for it was a gracious, brave thing to do, to give a service-gift as if he had well-pleased her. Off her own finger she drew it, and pressed it into his hand, and he bowed and kissed her fingers, before he stood and took his leave. He laced the ring into one of the thongs of his honors, to braid it in properly later, and bowed her farewell.

"Safe passage, kel'en," she said.

He should wish her long life, and he could not; he thought instead of that parting of kel'ein: "Honors and good attend," he said, and she accepted that courtesy with grace.

The Kel veiled, and he did so likewise, grateful for that privacy as they led him back to the doors, to let him out into the dark.

He heard the mournful protest of a confined dus, attuned to the mood of the Kel it served; and with that he entered the lock, and the lights were extinguished, to make them less a target.

For a moment the darkness was complete. Then the opening ramp and the double doors let the light in, the floodlights on the field, and the acrid wet wind touched them.

They did not speak as he left. There had not been a word passed. It was due to their Lady Mother's courage that he and one of hers would not shed blood in the passing of power; but it was settled.

When there was only one she'pan on Kesrith, then there would be time for courtesies, for welcome among them.

He did not look back as he started down the ramp.

Chapter Sixteen

NIUN HAD expected trouble at the bottom of the ramp: there was nothing, neither regul guard nor the assistance that guard might have summoned. He questioned nothing of his good fortune, but ducked his head and ran, soft-soled boots keeping his steps as quiet as possible across the pad.

He threaded again the maze of machinery, and there, there were the regul he had feared, a flare of headlights beyond the fence. He caught his breath and paused half a step to survey the situation, slipped to the shadows and changed course, reckoning that there was no need to use the same access twice. He burned through the wire fence and kicked the wire aside, and ran for it, his lungs hurting in the thin air. Somewhere a dus keened, over the rumble of machinery that prowled the dark.

He reached the edge of the apron and bolted for the sand, startled and shocked as a beam hit the sand across his path. He gasped for air and changed directions, darted round the bending of a dune and ran with all the strength he had remaining.

After a moment he reckoned himself relatively safe, enough to catch his breath again. Regul could not outrace him and the noisy machines could not surprise him. He smothered a cough, natural result of his rash burst of speed, and began uneasily to take account of this new state of affairs, that regul had premeditatedly sought not to catch him, but to kill him.

He lay against the side of the dune, his hand pressed to his aching side, trying to keep his breathing normal, and heard something stir——dus, he thought, for he knew that the hills were full of them this night, and did regul come out very far into the wild after him, they would meet a welcome they would not like. The dusei of the edun would do no harm to regul; but these were not tame ones, and the regul might not reckon that difference until it was too late to matter.

He gathered himself up and started to move, hearing at the same time a rapid sound of footsteps, mri-light and mri-quick, and following his track through the dunes. He reckoned it for one of Esain's kel'ein, on some desperate second thought; and for that reason he froze, hissed at the shadow a warning as it fronted him, respectful of it, another kel'en.

But no kel'en.

Half a breath they faced each other, human and mri; and in that half-breath Niun whipped up his pistol and the human dived desperately to retreat, vain hope in that narrow, dune-constricted area.

And in the next instant another thought flashed into Niun's mind—that a dead human could provide little answer to questions. He did not fire. He followed; and when he overtook the human he motioned with his hand, come, come. The human, casting desperate looks behind and at him, was a fair target if he fired.

And the human chose regul and whirled and ran.

A creature that had no business on Kesrith.

Niun thumbed the safety on, holstered the pistol and chose a new direction, a direction the regul could not, up over the arm of a dune; and cast himself flat, scanning the scene to know what manner of ambush he had sprung. Indeed the human had run directly into regul hands, in the person of one daring youngling who had him cornered against a ridge the human could easily climb if he had the wit to think of it; and the human did think of it and scrambled for his life, fighting to gain the top. But the regul laid hold on his ankle, and dragged him back again, inexorably.

They noticed nothing else. Niun retreated behind the ridge, raced a distance, came over and down in a plummeting slide, hit the solid mass of the regul and staggered it; and when it rounded on him clumsily, making the mistake of aiming a weapon at a kel'en, it was the youngling's final mistake. Niun did not think about the flash of the as'ei that left his hand and buried themselves in the youngling's throat and chest: they were sped before the thought had time to become purpose.

And the human, scrambling to reach the regul's gun—Niun hit him body to body, and if there had been a knife in Niun's intentions, the human would have been dead in the same instant.

No mean adversary, the human: Niun found himself countered, barehanded, in his attempt to seize hold of him; but the human was already done, bleeding from the nostrils, his bubbling breath hoarse in Niun's ear. He broke the human's hold: his arm found the human's throat and snapped his head back with a crack of meeting teeth.

Not yet did the human fall, but a quick blow to the belly and a second snap to the head toppled him writhing to the sands; and Niun hit him yet another time, ending his struggles.

A strip from his belt secured the human; and he recovered his *as'ei* and sheathed them quickly, hearing the slow grinding of machinery advancing on this place, and both of them having made tracks even the night-blind regul could read.

The human was showing signs of consciousness; he gave him a jerk by the elbow and dragged him until the man tried to respond to the discomfort. Then he gave him slack to drag his legs under him and try to stand.

"Quiet," Niun hissed at him.

And if the human thought to cry out, he thought better of it with the edge of the *av-tlen* near his face; he struggled up to his knees and, with Niun's help, to his feet, and went silently where he was compelled to go. He coughed and tried to smother even that sound. His face was a mask of blood and sand in the dim light that shone from the field, and he walked as if his knees were about to fail him.

Onto the edge of the flats they went, and slow, ominous shadows of dusei stood watching them from the dunes, but gave them no threat. There was no sound of pursuit behind them. Perhaps the regul were still in shock, that a kel'en had raised hand against the masters.

Niun knew the enormity of what he had done, had time to realize it clearly; he knew the regul, that they would take time to consult with authority, and beyond that he could not calculate. No mri had ever raised hand to his sworn authority. No regul had ever had to deal with a mri who had done so.

He seized the human's elbow and hurried him, though he

stumbled at times, though he misstepped and cried out in shock when a crust broke with him and he hit boiling water. They went well onto the flats, where neither regul nor regul vehicles could go, into the sulphuric steam of geysers that veiled them from sight. By now the human coughed and spat, bleeding in his upper air passages if not in his lungs, Niun reckoned.

In consideration of that he found a place and thrust the human down against the shoulder of a clay bank, and let him catch his breath, himself glad enough of a chance to do the same.

For a moment the human lay face down, body heaving with the effort not to cough, correctly reckoning that this would not be tolerated. Then the spasms eased and he lay still on his side, exhausted, staring at him.

Unarmed. Niun took that curious fact into account, wondering what possessed the humans; or what had befallen this one, that he had lost his weapons. The human simply stared at him, eyes running tears through sand: no emotion, no other expression than one of exhaustion and misery. Unprotected he had come into Kesrith's unfriendly environment; unwisely he had run, risking damage to his tissues.

And he had run from regul, with whom his people had made a treaty.

"I am Sten Duncan," the human whispered at last in his own tongue. "I am with the human envoy. Kel'en, we are here under agreement."

Niun considered that volunteered information: human envoy, human envoy—the words rolled around in his mind with the ominous tone of betrayal.

"I am kel Niun," he said, because this being had offered him a name.

"Are you from the edun?"

Niun did not answer, there seeming no need.

"That is where you're taking me, isn't it?" And when again the human had no answer of him, he seemed disquieted. "I'll go there of my own accord. You don't need to use force."

Niun considered this offer. Humans lied. He knew this. He had not had experience to be able to judge this one.

"I will not set you free," he said.

It was not the custom of humans to veil themselves; but Niun was sorry, all the same, that he had so dealt with a human kel'en, taking dignity from him—if he was kel'en. Niun judged that he was: he had handled himself well.

"We will go to the edun," he said to Duncan. He stood up and drew Duncan to his feet—did not help him overmuch, for this was not a brother; but he waited until he was sure he had his balance. The man was hurt. He marked that the human's steps were uneven and uncertain; and that he walked without knowledge of the land, blind to its dangers.

And deaf.

Niun heard the aircraft lift from the port, heard it turn in their direction; and the human had not even looked until he jerked him about to see it—stood stupidly gazing toward the port, malicious or dull-witted, Niun did not pause to know. He seized the human and pulled him toward the boiling waters of Jieca, that curled steam into the night; and by a clay ridge, their lungs choked with sulphur, they took hiding.

Regul engines passed. Lights swept the flats and lit plumes of steam, fruitlessly seeking movement. Heat sensors were of limited usefulness here on the volcanic flats. The boiling springs and seething mud made regul science of little value in tracking them.

"Kel'en," Duncan said. "Which one are they looking for? Me or you?"

"How have you offended the regul?" Niun asked, reckoning it of no profit to give information, but of some to gain it; and all the while the beams of light swept the flats, lighting one plume and another. "Were you a prisoner?"

"Assistant to the human envoy, to come—" A burst of fire lit their faces and spattered them with boiling water. They made a single mass against it, and as the firing continued and the water kept splashing, a rumble began in the earth and a jet of steam broke near them, enveloping them, uncomfortably hot but not beyond bearing.

"Tsi'mri," Niun cursed under his breath, forgetting with what he shared shelter; and as the barrage kept up he felt the human begin trembling, long, sickly shudders of a being whose strength was nearly spent.

"—to come ahead of the mission," the human resumed doggedly, still shaking. "To see that everything is as we were promised. And I don't think it—"

A near burst threw water and mud on them. The human cried out, smothered it.

"How many of you are there?" Niun asked.

"Myself—and the envoy. Two. We came on *Hazan*—back there."

Niun grasped Duncan's collar and turned his face to the light that glared from the searching beams. He saw nothing to tell him whether this was truth or lie. This was a young man, he saw, now that the face was washed clear by the moisture that enveloped both of them—a kel'en of the humans: he shrank from applying that honorable title to aliens, but he knew no other that applied to this one.

"There was a kel'en on *Hazan*," said Niun, "who died there."

For the first time something seemed to strike through to the human: there was a hesitancy to answer. "I saw him. Once. I didn't know he was dead."

Niun thrust him back, for the moment blind with anger. Tsi'mri, he reminded himself, and enemy, but less so now than the regul. *I saw him. I didn't know he was dead.*

He turned his face aside and stared bleakly at the rolling steam and the lights that crisscrossed the flats, searching.

Forgive us, Medai, he thought. *Our perceptions were too dull, our minds too accustomed to serving regul or we could have understood the message you tried to send us.*

He made himself look at the hateful human face that had not the decency of concealment—at the nakedness of this being that had, unknowingly perhaps, destroyed a kel'en of the People. *Animal,* he thought; *tsi'mri animal.* The regul-mri treaty was broken, from the moment this creature set foot on Kesrith; and that had been many, many days ago. For this long the People had been free and had not known it.

"There is no more war," Duncan protested, and Niun's arm tensed, and he would have hit him; but it was not honorable.

"Why do you suppose that the regul are hunting us?" he asked of Duncan, casting back his own question. "Do you not understand, human, that you have made a great mistake in leaving *Hazan?*"

"I am going with you," the human said, with the first semblance of dignity he had shown, "to talk to your elders, to make them understand that I had better be returned to my people."

"Ah," said Niun, almost moved to scornful mirth. "But we

are mri, not regul. We care nothing for your bargains with the regul, much good they have done you."

The human stayed still and reckoned that, and there was no yielding at the implied threat. "I see," he said. And a moment later, in a quiet, restrained tone: "I left the envoy down there in town—an old man, alone with regul, with this going on. I have to get back to him."

Niun conšidered this, understanding. It was loyalty to this sen'anth for which he endured this patiently. He gave respect to the human for that, touched his heart in token of it.

"I will deliver you alive to the edun," he said, and felt compelled to add: "It is not our habit to take prisoners."

"We have learned that," Duncan said.

Therefore they understood each other as much as might be. Niun considered the flats before them, reckoning already what might have been done to familiar ground by the bombardment: what obstacles might have been created on the unstable land, where they might next find securest shelter if the regul swept back sooner than anticipated.

It was well that he and the human had come to an understanding, that Duncan considered his best chance and most honorable course was to cooperate for the moment. A man unburdened could make the journey by morning, all things in his favor; but not with regul blasting away the route about them; and day would show them up clearly, making it next evening before they could reach the edun if things kept on as they were.

A sick dread gathered in Niun's stomach: for very little even so, he would have killed the human and run for the edun at all speed.

He cursed himself for his softness, which had put him to such a choice between butchery and stupidity, and gripped the human's arm.

"Listen to me. If you do not keep my pace, I cannot keep you; and if I cannot keep you, I will kill you. It is also," he added, "very likely that the regul will kill you to keep you from your superior."

He slipped from cover then, and drew the human with him by the arm, and Duncan came without resisting.

But the regul craft, lacing the area, swept back, and they made only a few strides before it was necessary to hurl themselves into other cover.

The barrage began again, deafening, spattering them with boiling water and gouts of mud.

The edun would be aware of this. They were doubtless doing something; perhaps—Niun thought—Duncan's sen'anth likewise knew and was doing something; and there was also *Ahanal*, independent of Intel.

He understood the human's helpless terror. Of all who had power on Kesrith, they two had least; and the regul, who did not fight, had taken up arms, impelled by malice or fear or whatever driving motive could span the gap between cowardice and self-interest.

Chapter Seventeen

THERE WAS firing, a sound unmistakable to a man who had lived a great part of his life in war.

Stavros turned his sled to view the window and saw the lights of aircraft circling under the clouds. His fingers sought the console keyboard, adjusted screens with what had grown to be some expertise: simple controls, a phenomenal series of coded signals, each memorized. The regul had provided him the codings with an attitude of smug contempt: learn it, they challenged him with that look of theirs that rated beings of short memory with sub-sapients.

Stavros was not typical in this regard, had never been typical, not from his boyhood on remote Kiluwa, to his attachment to the Xen-Bureau to his directorate on Halley during first contact. He found nothing difficult in languages, nor in alien customs, nor in recognizing provincial shortsightedness, whether offered by humans or by others.

He was Kiluwan by allegiance, a distinction the regul and most humans did not appreciate: remote, first-stage colony, populated by religious traditionalists, among whom writing was a sin and education an obsession. He had been born there a century ago, before peaceful, eccentric Kiluwa became a casualty of the mri wars.

A number of Kiluwans had distinguished themselves in Service; they were gone now, among casualties forty years ago, retaliation for Nisren. Stavros survived. It was characteristic of his Kiluwan upbringing that he should be driven to understand the species that had ordered Kiluwa obliterated. Regul had done this, not mri. Therefore he studied the phenomenon of regul—minds much like the perfection Kiluwa had sought; and they had destroyed all that Kiluwa had built. There was, as the university masters had once said, a 'rhythm of justice' in this, a joining of cancelling forces. Now a Kiluwan came to displace regul, and the rhythm continued, binding them both.

He learned regul ways, looking for resolution to this; he observed meanness and coldness and self-seeking ambition, as well as reverence for mind. He had come from fear of regul to a yearning over them—not a little of sorrow for Kiluwa, whose dream in the flesh had come to this flawed reality; and there were truths beyond what he had been able to grasp, vices and virtues inherent in the biology of regul. He saw these, began to understand, at least, constraints of species perpetuation and population control—division into hive structures, breeding-elders and younglings, the docha that answered roughly to nations: he acquired suspicions about the value of treaties, which bound and yet did not bind docha which had not been party to the agreement.

They had contracted with Holn and suddenly found themselves dealing instead with Alagn; and Alagn honored the agreement.

Outwardly.

It had come to the point of truth. He had sat the long hours through the day and into dark and covered for Duncan's absence and committed every deception but the outright lie which the regul would not forgive. In the hours' passage he had grown more and more certain, first that Duncan had found something amiss or he would have returned quickly, certainly by the time dark gave him concealment—and when the fall of night did not bring him back, he became well sure that something amiss had found Duncan.

The pretenses with the regul became charade bitterly difficult to maintain. They could murder the SurTac and blandly fail to mention it with the morning's reports. And there was not a human going to land on Kesrith without Stavros' clearance: not in peace, at least, not without removing all possible resistance.

The regul surely understood this.

He sat and listened to the firing, knowing while it continued that Duncan was likely still alive.

He had been a shaper of policy in his days, had settled a new world and founded a university; had plotted strategies of diplomacy and war, had disposed of lives in numbers in which ships and crews were reckoned expendable, in which the likes of Sten Duncan perished in their hundreds.

But he heard the firing, and clenched his right hand and agonized in a desperate attempt to move his unwilling left with any strength at all. He was held to the sled. He was constrained to be patient.

There was new catastrophe at the port. There were hints in regul communications, into which he had intruded, that a ship had come down, that it was not friendly to regul.

Human, rival regul, or mri. He could guess well enough what had drawn Duncan to overstay his leave. Create no incident, he had told the lad, knowing then that there was little Duncan could do to create anything: it waited to happen, all about them. He had felt it increasingly, in the silences of the regul, the tension in the atmosphere of the Nom.

The regul were trying something illicit. Human interests were endangered. And there was no word of approval going from him to the human mission when it arrived, no matter what the coercion.

If that was not what had already happened.

Stavros was not a man of precipitate action: he thought; and when he had concluded chances were even, he was capable of rashness. He found no need to cooperate further with hosts that would either kill them or not dare to kill them: it was time to call their bluff.

He fingered the console, whipped the sled about and opened doors. He guided it through Duncan's apartment and with a smooth, well-practiced series of commands, and a turn to the right, locked it into the tracking that ran the corridors.

Youngling regul saw him and gaped, jabbering protests which he ignored. He knew his commands, calculated the appropriate moves, and locked into a turn, whisked into the side of the building that faced the port. There he stopped and keyed into the window controls, brightening windows, commanding storm shields withdrawn.

A new ship, indeed.

And lights glared over the countryside, flaring garishly in the haze of smoke and steam, aircraft lacing the ground with their beams.

Ah, Duncan, he thought with great regret.

A youngling puffed up to him. "Elder human," it said. "We regret, but—"

Bai Hulagh. Where? he demanded via the screen, which took the youngling considerably aback. *Youngling, find me the bai.*

It fled, at least with what dispatch a regul could manage, and Stavros whipped the sled about and took it to the left, engaged a track and shot down the ramp, whipped round the corner and entered the first level of the Nom, from which they had been carefully excluded.

Here he disengaged and went on manual, edging through the gabbling crowd of younglings. *Mri,* he heard, and: *mri ship;* and: *alert.*

And they made way for him until one noticed that the sled, the symbol to them of adult authority, contained a human.

"Go back," they wished him. "Go back, elder."

Bai Hulagh. Now, he insisted, and would not move, and there was nothing they dared do about it. When they began to murmur together in great confusion, he directed the sled through them and toured the ground floor in leisurely fashion, with the air vibrating with the attack out on the flats and the building vibrating to the shocks. Mentally he noted where doors were located, and where accesses were, and where it was possible to come and go with the sled.

A message flashed on his receiver.

It was Hulagh's sigil. Hulagh's face followed. "Esteemed elder human," Hulagh said. "Please return at once to your quarters."

I am unable to believe that they are secure, Stavros spelled out patiently. *Where is my assistant?*

"He has disregarded our advice and is now involved in a situation," said Hulagh with remarkable candor, such that Stavros' hopes abruptly lifted. "Mri have landed, I regret to admit, honorable representative. These mri are outlaws, bent on making trouble. Your youngling is somewhere in the midst of things, quite contrary to our warnings. Please make our task easier by returning to the safety of your quarters."

I refuse. Stavros keyed a window clear. *I will observe from the windows here.*

Hulagh's nostrils snapped shut and flared again. "This lack of cooperation is reprehensible. We are still in authority here. We do not lose this authority until the arrival of your mission. You are here only as an observer, on our agreement."

Therefore I shall observe.

Again the flare of anger. "Do so, then, at your own hazard. I shall inform your youngling if he is found that you miss his services and he would be well advised to return to you."

I should be grateful, Stavros spelled out with deliberation. *I shall inform my people when they come that you are not responsible for any delay in withdrawal—if it should happen that my aide is recovered safely and there is no damage to our chosen landing site, or to necessary facilities, such as this building or the water or power plant. However, if these things do occur, other conclusions may be drawn.*

There was silence, bai Hulagh still on the screen, while the bai reflected on this statement of intent. Stavros had expected anger, threat, bluster. Instead some quieter emotion passed within the bony mask of a face, betrayed only by the rapid flare of nostrils.

"If the human envoy will assure us that this is indeed the case and accommodation may be made, then we will make every effort to preserve these facilities and to accomplish the recovery of your youngling alive. It will, however, be necessary to warn the human envoy that there will be necessary operations at the port and, for the security of the Nom and all within, it will be preferable for the honorable human elder to observe through remote channels and not through the windows. Your consideration, favor, sir."

I understand. Favor, sir. I am presently satisfied that you are doing your utmost. He would not, voluntarily, have surrendered his view through the windows, not trusting the limited view provided by regul services; but the barrage was intense and the windows rattled ominously, and he began to believe the bai's warning. The regul building was undergoing repeated shocks. He knew the bai's warning for an honest one.

It only remained to question what was happening to occasion the firing. The regul, he reminded himself, closing the storm shield, did not lie.

Therefore it was true that mri had landed and that Sten Duncan was somewhere out on the flats, but one never assumed anything with the regul.

Then the floor shook, and sirens wailed throughout the building.

Stavros locked the sled onto a track and whisked himself back to the main lobby, where a group of younglings frantically waved at him, trying to offer him instructions all at once.

"Shelter, reverence, shelter!" they said, pointing at another hall, a ramp leading down. He considered and thought that it might at the moment be wise to listen.

Chapter Eighteen

DUNCAN WAS SPENT, a burden, a hazard. Niun set hands on him and pushed him downslope, to shelter under an overhang by a boiling pool, forcing him farther under as he wedged his own body after.

It was scantly in time. A near burst of fire hissed across the water and crumbled rock near them: blind fire, not aimed. The searching beams continued, lacing the area. Niun saw the face of Duncan in the reflected light, haggard and swollen-eyed—unprotected by the membrane that hazed Niun's own vision when the smoke grew thick. Duncan's upper lip showed a black trail that was blood in the dim light. It poured steadily, a nuisance that had become more than nuisance. The human heaved with a bubbling cough and tried to stifle it. The reek in the air from the firing and from the natural steam and sulphur was thick and choking. Niun twisted in the narrow confines, fastidious about touching the bleeding and sweating human, and at last, exhausted, abandoned niceties in such close quarters. They lay in a space likely to become their tomb should another shot crumble the ledge over them; mri and human bones commingled for future possessors of Kesrith to wonder at.

This was delirium. The mind could not function under such pounding shocks as bracketed them constantly. Niun found the regul amazing in their ineptness. They two should have been dead over and over, had the regul had any knowledge of the land; but the regul had not, were firing blind at a landscape as unknown and alien to them as the bottom of the sea. The world was lit in constant flares of white and red, swirled in mists and steam and smoke and clouds of dust, like the

Hell that humans swore by—that of mri was an unending
Dark.

The water splashed, singing and bubbling; Niun lowered
the visor of the *zaidhe*, he the outermost, shielding the human
with his own body: ironic arrangement, chance-chosen, one
he would have reversed at the moment if it were possible.

An explosion heaved the earth, numbed the senses, drove
their numbed bodies into a fresh convulsion of terror.

And hard upon that a white light lit the rocks, grew, ate
them, devoured all the world; and a pressure unbearable; and
Niun knew that they were hit, and tried to move to roll out
into the open before the ledge came down. The pressure burst
over him, and it was red . . .

. . . wind, wind in great force, skirling away the smoke
and mist, making the red swirl before his membraned, visored
eyes. Niun moved, became aware that he moved, and that he
lived.

And all about them was light, sullen and ugly red.

He gathered himself up, the light at his back, and turned
to the light, and saw the port.

There was nothing.

He stood—legs shuddering under him. He thought that he
cried out, so great was his pain, and shut his eyes, and
opened them, trying to see through the flame, until the tears
poured down his face. But of *Ahanal*, of *Hazan*, there was
nothing to be seen. Within the city itself, fires blazed, sending
smoke boiling aloft.

And even while·he watched, an aircraft lifted from near
the horizon, circled for a distance out to sea, and came back
again, lights blinking lazily.

He followed it with his eyes, the aircraft circling, rounding
over the city, through the smoke—beginning to come about
toward the hills.

Toward the edun.

He wished to turn his face from it, knowing, knowing already the end. He turned with it, watched, a great knot swell-
ing in his throat, and his body cold and numb, and the center
of him utterly alive to what began to happen.

The first tower of the edun, that of the Kel, flared in light
and went, slowly tumbling. The sound reached him, a numbing shock, and after that the wind, as the towers fell, as the

whole structure of the edun hung suspended and crumbled down into ruin.

And the ship circled, light and free, lazily winking in the dark as it rose above the smoke and came, insolently, over their heads.

His pistol was in his hands: he turned and lifted it, and fired one futile burst at those retreating lights, none others in the sky. The lights blurred in his eyes, the betraying membrane, or tears: it flashed and cleared, and he fired again.

And the lights continued on a moment, and a red light blossomed and fragments went spinning in various trajectories, ruin upon ruin, pistol shot or the turbulence that must surround the port.

It healed nothing. He turned, looked again at the edun where not even flames remained, and his stomach spasmed, a wrench that weakened his joints and made him dizzy. In that moment he would have wished to be without senses, to be weak, to fall, to sink down, to do anything but continue to stand, helplessly.

Dead. Dead, all of them.

He stood, not knowing whether to return to the ruin at the port, to go on as he was going, or whether there was reason to go, or to do anything but sit where he was until morning, when the regul would come to finish matters. He found no limit to what senses could absorb. He felt. He was not numb. He only wished to be, battered by the wind that stole the sound from the night, whipping at his robes, a steady snap of cloth that was, here, louder than the silence that had fallen over everything.

The People were dead.

He remained. For survivors there were duties, respects, rites that wanted doing. He was not of Medai's temperament.

He slipped pistol into its holster, and clenched his icy hands under his arms, and began to reckon with the living.

The Hand of the People, a kel'en; and there were his kin to bury, if the regul had not done it in killing them, and after that there was a war the regul perhaps did not look to fight.

And then he looked toward the ledge, and looked on his human prisoner, and met his eyes. Here also was a man that waited to die, that also knew, in small measure, what desolation was.

He could kill, and be alone thereafter, a vast, vast silence;

a tiny act of violence after the forces that had stormed across the skies of Kesrith and ruined the world.

A tiny and miserable act. Vengeance for a world deserved something of equal stature.

"Get up," he said quietly, and Duncan gathered himself up, shoulder to the rock, staring back at him.

"We will go up to the hill," he told Duncan. "The house of my people—I do not think there will be more aircraft."

Duncan turned and looked, and without demur, without question, started walking ahead of him.

The world was changed about them. Landmarks that had been on the Dus plain for eons were gone. The ground was pocked with scars that filled with boiling water. Duncan, leading the way, blind, bound, misstepped and went in up to the knee, with nothing more than a hoarse sob of shock; and Niun seized him and pulled him back, steadying him, while the human stood and gasped for air.

He kept a hand on Duncan's arm thereafter, and guided him, knowing the way; and preserved the human against another time.

The light came, the red light of Arain, foul and murky. Niun looked back toward the port, and saw in the first light the full truth of what he had already known: that nothing survived.

Neither *Ahanal* nor *Hazan*.

And when he looked on the hill where the Edun of the People had stood, it was one with the sand and the rocks—as if nothing built by hands had ever stood there.

He saw also in the light what prize he had taken, an exhausted creature that struggled for every upward step, whose face and mouth and chest were spattered with blood that poured afresh from the nose, injury or atmosphere, it was uncertain. The eyes were almost shut, streaming tears not of seeming emotion but of outraged tissues—a face naked in the sun, and indecent, and more bewildered than evil: he did not know why the human kept walking at such cost, toward such little reward—easier by far the death of the land's violence than what mri and human had exchanged for forty years.

But there was a point past which there was no thinking, only the fact that one lived; and that continued whether one wanted or wished otherwise.

He understood such a mind, that deep shock which admitted no decisions. He had never thought that he would freeze in crisis; yet he had frozen, and the cold of that moment when the People died was still locked round his mind and his heart and seemed never apt to go away, not though he had revenge, not though he killed every regul that breathed and heaped humanity on the desolation as well.

It was a shock in which their two lives were of like value, which was nothing at all.

He pushed the human ahead, neither hating now nor pitying, finding no reason for sparing a human when he had the ruin of the edun to face for himself. He thought perhaps that Duncan sorrowed for his own failed duty, which lay lost in burning Kesrith; that Duncan also mourned failure, as miserable as he.

But Duncan had all the human worlds for kinsmen, knowing that they survived; and it was possible to hate the human when he let himself think on this. He would not return this one to his kind: while he lived, Duncan would live. While he had to face what had become of Kesrith, the man Duncan would do the like.

They came to the edun by full daylight, untroubled by ships or any sign of life from the skies. Down in the city there might be. It did not extend to them. When Niun thought of it, he thought of going down and destroying them—methodically, joylessly: regul, who had no capacity for war.

Who had finally, in one cowardly act, destroyed the People.

There was irony there that was worth bitter laughter. He looked on the mound of rubble that had been the edun and felt moved to that or to tears; and Duncan, no longer forced to walk, simply slumped to his knees and leaned against the shoulder of the causeway. Niun heard his hollow cough and kicked him gently, reached down when that was not enough to rouse him, and caught his arm, pulling him up again.

There was work to be done, at least so far as they could try; and he was loath to have the ruin touched at all by tsi'mri hands, but he had not the strength alone. He drew the *av-tlen* and pried loose the knots at Duncan's wrists with its point, carefully unwound the thongs that were embedded in

Duncan's swollen flesh and looped the recovered leather through its ring on his own belts.

Ducan, trying to work his hands to life, looked at the edun, and looked at him, a question. Niun jerked his head in response and Duncan comprehended and began to walk. They waded through rubble, stepped carefully among chunks of the walls that were cast down and shattered. Here had been simple fire, not the radiation that doubtless bathed the city and made the place uninhabitable. Niun pushed at a heap of rubble that blocked their way, and saw that beneath that pile of heavy stone and fine dust lay at least one of the Kel.

There was no use to move that mass, no hope of moving it entirely. Instead Niun took stones and began to heap them round the visible body like a cairn, and Duncan, seeing what he was about, began to gather up rocks of the proper size and pass them to him.

This offended him bitterly, that the human offered rather than suffered compulsion; but it was needed, and he would not suffer the human to touch the grave itself. And it occurred to him at the same moment that Duncan might well smash his skull with one of those self-same stones the moment he turned his back entirely, and that this might be what the human was preparing, so he kept from turning his head while he worked.

They finished, and from this place they went deeper into the ruin and into places dark and difficult, where heaps of rubble towered overhead and sifted dust and pebbles downslope at them. And the core of all the deepest ruin was the Shrine that he had sought.

It was all too deeply buried.

If it had been possible, he would have sought out whatever relics he could carry and taken them away into the sanctity of Sil'athen, where his kinsmen also would have been buried; but perhaps humans would never be curious enough to desecrate this place with their machines, to sift out the debris and leavings of a species which no longer mattered in the universe.

And here the destruction reached that central citadel of himself that had yet to feel it; and he trembled and his senses almost left him. He reached out and sought support, and touched the wrong stone, bringing a slide that buried the place at their feet and brought a sift of powder down on them. The only thing he saw clearly was Duncan's face, terror in his eyes as for an instant they seemed likely to go under the weight of rubble and earth; and then the sifting stopped and the place grew still.

A stone shifted somewhere, and another; there was another slide, and silence, the fall of a few pebbles.

And in that silence came a thin and distant cry.

Duncan heard it: if not for that confirming glance sideward, Niun would have thought it illusion. But it came from the direction that had been Kath, where the deepest storerooms were.

He turned and began to pick his way through the ruin, careful, careful with his life now, and that of her who had cried aloud, down in the dark.

"Melein!" he cried, and paused and listened, and that same thin sound returned to him.

He reached the place, estimating where it lay, and a wall had fallen there, and finer rubble atop it; but the steel regulmade doors had held.

Too well. They were barred by a weight that could not be moved, that they lacked tools to chip away and machines to lift. Niun tore his hands on it, and his muscles cracked, and Duncan added his force, but it would not slide; and at last they both sat down, gasping for air, coughing. Duncan's nose started pouring blood again. He wiped it in a bloody smear and his hands were shaking uncontrollably.

"Is it," Duncan asked, "ventilated down there?"

It was not. It added a fear atop the others. "Melein," Niun called out. "Melein, do you hear?"

He heard some manner of answer, and it was a woman's voice and a young voice, high and thin and clear: it was Melein. He reckoned it below them, and tried to figure the exact location of it, and marked with a heel a spot on the floor.

Then he wrenched a reinforcing rod from the ruin and began with careful chips to dig—no firing down into that sanctuary, no such recklessness. He dug with that and with his fingers, and Duncan saw what he was doing and helped him, alternating strokes that pounded deeper into the cubit-thick flooring, and now and again they paused to paw away the dust they had made. The sun grew hot, and the only sound now was the steady chink of steel on the cemented earth, and he had heard no word from Melein in a very long time. He was tormented with fear, knowing how small the space below was, how scant the air must be; and fear lest the gap they were making miss the small space where she was sheltered; and fear lest the whole floor give way.

They broke through. Air flooded out of that blackness, stale and depleted and cold.

"Melein," he shouted down, and had no answer.

He began to work yet harder, ramming chips from the edges of the hole, widening it, admitting more and more air, sending a shaft of sunlight down into that place. They exposed steel rods, and worked in the other direction, where they could make a wider hole, and from time to time he would call down to her, and hear nothing.

It was at last a size to admit a body; and he considered it, and the human who would remain above, and how they were to get up again, and thought desperately of killing Duncan; but he could not come up with Melein in his arms, not so easily; and he was not sure whether the cloth of his robes could bear his weight, or what else might avail.

"I will go down," said Duncan, and opened a pocket and took out a length of cord, and from another a small light. He offered these precious things with a naive forthrightness that for a moment disarmed Niun.

"The drop," Niun said, inwardly shuddering at the thought of him near Melein, "is my height and half again." He did not add what revenge he would take if Duncan were careless, if he harmed Melein, if he could not recover her alive: these things were useless. He sat helpless and watched as Duncan worked his body—a little heavier than his—into that gap and dropped, with a heavy sound, into the dark.

Niun listened as he searched below, through things that rattled and moved, through the shifting of rock. He leaned close and tried to see the tiny glow of the light he held.

"I have found her," Duncan's voice floated up out of that cold. And then: "She's alive."

Niun wept, safe, where the human could not see him; and wiped his eyes and sat still, fists clenched on his knees. He knew that the human could claim her for hostage, could harm her, could exact revenge or some terrible oath of him; he had not thought through these things clearly, a measure of his exhaustion and his desperation to reach her in time; but now he thought, and poised himself on the edge of the pit, to go down.

"Mri! Niun!" Duncan stood in the light with a pale burden in his arms, a gold bundle of robes that lay still against him. "Let down the cord. I will try to guide her up."

Even while he watched, Melein stirred, and moved, and her eyes opened on the light in which he above could be only a shadow.

"Melein," he called down. "Melein, we will pull you up. This is a human, Melein, but do not fear him."

She struggled when she heard that, and Duncan set her feet on the floor. Niun saw her look at his face in the dim light and draw back in horror.

But she suffered him then to put his hands on her waist, and to lift her up, by far the easiest and least hurtful way for her: but she could not lift her hands to reach Niun's, and protested pain—she once kel'e'en. "Wait," Niun objected, and with a turn of cord and a knot fashioned a sling and cast it down. He wrapped it about hand and arm and took the weight carefully as she settled in the sling he had made: Duncan helped lift, but for a time the thin, cutting cord and an upward pull bit into Niun's hands. He tried not to rake her against the jagged opening, pulled ever so carefully, and braced his feet and ignored the pain of his hands. She came through and levered herself out onto the sunlit dust, tried to rise: he had her, he had her safe; and he hugged her to her feet and held to her as he had held to no living being since childhood, they both entangled in the cord. He brushed dust and tears from her face, she still gasping in the outside air.

"The ship is destroyed," he said, to have all the cruelty done with while wounds were still numb. "Everyone else is dead, unless there is someone else alive down there."

"No. None. They had no time. They were too old to run—they would not—they sat still, with the she'pan. Then the House—"

She began to shake as if in the grip of a great cold; but she was once of the Kel, and she did not break. She controlled herself, and after a moment began to disentangle them both from the cord.

"None," he, said, to be sure she understood it all, "could have possibly survived on the ship."

She sat down on the edge of the section of wall that

blocked the doors, and smoothed back her mane with one
hand, her head bowed. She found her torn scarf at her shoulder and smoothed it and carefully covered her head with that
light, gauze veil. She was quiet for a time, her head still
turned from him.

At last she straightened her shoulders, and pointed over to
the hole in the rubble, where Duncan waited. "And what is
he?" she asked.

He shrugged. "No matter to us. A human. A regul guest.
They tried to kill him when we met; then——" The surmise
that it was this, partly his own action, which had killed the
People and left them orphan, was too terrible to speak. His
voice trailed off, and Melein arose and walked from him, to
look at the ruin, her back to him, her hands limp at her sides.
The sight of her despair was like a wound to him.

"Melein," he said to her. "Melein, what am I to do?"

She turned to him, gave a tiny, helpless gesture. "I am
nothing."

"What am I to do?" he insisted.

Sen and Kel: Sen must lead; but she had become more
than Sen, and that was the heaviness on her, which he saw
she did not want, which she had to bear. He stood waiting.
At last she shut her eyes and opened them again.

"Enemies will come here," she said, beginning clearly to
function as she had been prepared for years to function, to
command and to plan: she assumed what she must assume,
she'pan of the People, who had no people. "Find us what we
need for the hills; and we will camp there tonight. Give me
tonight, truebrother—I must not call you that; but tonight,
that only, and I will think what is best for us to do."

"Rest," he urged her. "I will do that." And when he had
seen her seated and out of the direct sun, he bent down over
the hole and cast the cord down. "Duncan."

The human's white face appeared in the center of the light,
anxious and frightened. "Lift me up," he said, laying hand on
the cord, which Niun refused to give solidity. "Mri, I have
helped you. Now lift me out of here."

"Search for the things I name and I will draw them up by
the cord. And after that I will draw you up."

Duncan hesitated there, as if he thought that, like humans,
a mri would lie. But he agreed then, and sought with his tiny
light until he had found all the things that Niun then request-

ed of him. He tied each small bundle on the cord for Niun to draw up: food, and water flasks, and cording and four bolts of unsewn black cloth, for they could not reach better without delaying to pierce a new opening, and Duncan avowed he did not think it safe. A last time the cord came up, with a bolt of cloth; and a last time he cast it down, this time for Duncan, and braced it about his body and his arm.

It was not so hard as with Melein's uncooperating weight: he leaned and braced his feet, and Duncan hauled himself up—gained the lip of the hole and heaved himself to safety, panting, bent double, coughing and trying to stop the bleeding. The coughing went on and on, and Melein came from her place of rest to look down on the human in mingled disgust and pity.

"It is the air," Niun said. "He has been running, and he is not acclimated to Kesrith."

"Is he a manner of kel'en?" asked Melein.

"Yes," Niun said. "But he does not offer any threat. The regul hunted him; likely now they would cease to care—unless this man's superior is alive. What shall we do with him?"

Duncan seemed to know they spoke of him; perhaps he knew a few words of the language of the People, but they spoke the High Language, and surely he could not follow that.

Melein shrugged, turned her head from him. "As you please. We will go now."

And she began, slowly, to walk through the ruin, picking her way with care.

"Duncan," said Niun, "pick up the supplies and come."

The human looked outrage at him, as if minded to dispute this as a matter of dignity; and Niun expected it, waited for it. But then Duncan knelt down and made a bundle of the goods with the cord, heaving it to his shoulder as he arose.

Ninun indicated that he should go, and the human carried the burden where Niun aimed him, his footsteps weaving and uncertain in the wake of Melein.

No firing had touched the hills. They came into a sheltered place that was as it had been before the attack, before the discords of regul or mri or humans—a shelter safe from airships, withdrawn as it was beneath a sandstone ledge.

With a great sigh Melein sank down on the sand in that cold shadow, and bent, her head against her knees, as if this had been all that she could do, the last step that she could take. She was hurt. Niun had watched her walk and knew that she was in great pain, that he thought was in her side and not her limbs. When she was content to stop, he took the supplies from Duncan, and made haste to spread a cloth for a groundsheet and a cover for Melein. He gave her drink and a bit of dried meat; and watched, sitting on his heels, as she drank and ate, and leaned against the bare rock to rest.

"May I drink?"

The human's quiet request reminded him he had another charge on him; and he measured out a capful of water and passed it to Duncan's shaking hands.

"Tomorrow maybe," said Niun, "we will tap a luin and have water enough to drink." He considered the human, who drank at the water drop by drop, a haggard and filthy creature who by appearances ought not to have survived so far. It was not likely that he could survive much farther as he was. He stank, sweat and sulphur compounded with human. Niun found himself hardly cleaner.

"Can you—" he said to Melein, almost having fogotten that her personal name was not for him to speak freely now. He offered her his pistol. "Can you stay awake long enough to watch this human a time?"

"I am well enough," she said, and drew up one knee and rested wrist and pistol on it in an attitude more kel'e'en than she'pan. By caste, she should not touch weapons; but many things ought to be different, and could not be.

He left them so, and went out of sight of the ledge, and stripped and bathed, as mri on dry worlds did, in the dry sand, even to his mane, which when he shook the sand out recovered its glossy feel quickly enough. He felt better when he had done this, and he dressed again, and began to retrace his steps toward the cave.

A heavy body moved behind him, an explosive breath and plaintive sound: dus. He turned carefully, for he had left his gun with Melein, and nothing else could give a ha-dus pause.

It was the *miuk'ko*, gaunt, forlorn, scab-hided. But the face was dry and it shambled forward with careless abandon.

His heart beat rapidly, for the situation was a bad one in potential, for all the dusei were unpredictable. But the dus came to him, and lifted its head, thrusting it against his chest, uttering that dus-master sound that begged food, shelter, whatever things mri and dus shared.

He knelt down there, for the moment demanded it, and embraced the scrofulous neck and relaxed against the beast, letting it touch and be touched. A sense of warmth came over him, a feeling deep and almost sensual, the lower beast functions of the dus mind, that could be content with very little.

This it lent him. He looked up, aware of presence, saw two stranger-dusei on the sandstone ridge above; he was not afraid. This dus knew them, and they knew him, and this, like the warmth, came at a level too low for reason. It was fact. It was dependable as the rock on which they stood, mri and dus. It absorbed his pain, and melted it, and fed him back strength as slow and powerful as its own.

And when he came back to the cave, the great beast lumbered after him, a docile companion, a comical and friendly fellow that—beholding the human—was suddenly neither comic nor friendly.

Distrust: that reached Niun's mind through the impulses of the dus; but that subsided as the dus felt the human's outright terror. This one feared. Therefore he was safe. The dus put thought of the human aside and settled down athwart the entrance, radiating impulses of ward and protection.

"He came," said Niun, gathering his pistol from Melein's hand. "There are more out there, but none even vaguely familiar."

"The old pact," she said, "is still valid with us and them."

And he knew that they might have no better guardian; and that he could sleep this night, sure that nothing would pass the dus to harm Melein. He was overwhelmingly grateful for this. The exhaustion he had held back came down like a flood. The dus lifted his head and gave that pleasure moan, a gap-mouthed smile, tongue lolling. It flicked and disappeared into a dusine smugness.

Niun spoke to it, the small nonsense words the dusei loved, and touched its massive head, pleasing it; and then he took its paw and turned it, the size of it more than a man could easily hold in his hands. The claws curled inward, drawing his wrist against the dew-claw: reflex. It broke the skin, admitting the venom. He had sought this. It would not harm him in such small doses; by such degrees he would become im-

mune to this particular dus, and need never fear it. He took
his hand back and caressed the flat skull, bringing a rumbling
sound of contentment from the beast.

Then, because he could not bear the thought of bedding
down with the human's filth, he took up an armload of cloth
and bade the human come with him, and took him out beyond the ledge.

"Bathe," he told Duncan, and, casting down the cloth
when Duncan seemed dismayed, he bent and with a handful
of sand on his own arm, demonstrated how; he sat with arms
folded, eyes generally averted somewhat, while the human
cleansed himself, and the curious ha-dusei watched from the
heights, grouping and circling in alarm at the strange pale-
skinned creature.

Duncan looked somewhat more pleasant when he had
scrubbed the blood from his face and the tear streaks had
been evened out to a dusty sameness. He shook the dust from
his hair and picked up his discarded clothing and started to
dress; but Niun tore a length from the cloth and tore it in
such a way that it could be worn. He thrust it at the human,
who doubtfully put it on, as if this were some intended shame
to him. Then he thought to search the clothing that the human had taken off, and found pockets full of things of which
the human had not spoken.

He opened his hand, demonstrating the knife that he had
found. Duncan shrugged.

Niun gave him credit at least that he had not attempted
any rashness, but bided his time. The human had played the
round well, though he had lost it.

Niun thrust a second wad of black cloth at him. "Veil
yourself," he said. "Your nakedness offends the she'pan and
me."

Duncan settled the veil over his head, ineptly attempting to
make it stay, for he had not the art. Niun showed him how
to twist it to make a band of it, and how to arrange the veil;
and Duncan looked the better for it, decently covered. He
was not robed as kel'en, which would have been improper;
but he was in kel-black and modestly clothed as a man and
not as an animal. Niun looked on him with a nod of approval.

"This is better for you," he said. "It will protect your skin.

Bury your clothing. You will find when we travel in the day
that our way is best."

"Are we moving?"

Niun shrugged. "The she'pan makes that decision. I am
kel'en. I take her orders."

Duncan dropped to his knees and dug a hole, animal fashion, and put his discarded clothing in it. He paused when he
had smoothed it over, and looked up. "And if I could offer
you a safe way off this world—"

"Can you?"

Duncan rose to his feet. He had a new dignity, veiled.
Niun had never noticed the color of his eyes. They were light
brown. Niun had never seen the like. "I could find a way,"
Duncan said, "to contact my people and get a ship down here
for you. I think you have something to lose by not taking
that offer. I think you would like very much to get her out of
this."

Niun moved his hand to his weapons, warning. "Tsi'mri,
you do assume too much. And if you make plans, present
them to her, not to me. I told you: I am only kel'en. If something pleases her, I do it. If something annoys her, I remove
it."

Duncan did not move. Presumably he reconsidered his dis-
respect. "I do not understand," he said finally. "Evidently I
don't understand how things are with you. Is this your wife?"

The obscenity was so naively put, in so puzzled a tone, that
Niun almost laughed in surprise. "No," he said, and to further confound him: "She is my Mother."

And he motioned the human to cease delaying him, for he
grew anxious for Melein, and there were the ha-dusei about
them, that snuffed the air and called soft cries from their
higher perch. One came down as they left the area. Doubtless
the clothes would not stay buried, but neither would there be
much left of them to catch the eye of searchers.

The dus at the entry of their refuge lifted his head and
pricked his tiny ears forward at their approach, radiating
feelings of welcome; and Niun, already feeling the flush of
the poison in him, and knowing he would feel it more in the
hours of the night, offered his fingers to its nose and brushed
past, putting his body between it and Duncan.

Melein took note of the human and nodded in approval
of the change; but no further interest in him did she show

this night. She settled down to rest in peace now that they had returned. And Niun drank a very small ration of water and lay down and watched as the human likewise stretched himself out as far from them and the beast as he might in the little space.

In time Niun let his eyes close, his mind full, so overburdened that at last there was nothing to do but abandon all thought and let go. The dus-fever was in him. He drifted toward low-mind dreams, that were the murky, sometimes frightening impulses of the dus; but he feared no harm from the impulses because it was in the lore of the Kel that no kel'en had ever been harmed by his own dus, it being sane.

And he was owned by this beast, and the beast by him; and he compassed his present world by this and by Melein. He had been utterly desolate in the morning, and at this evening he rested, kel-ignorant, with a dus to guard his sleep and touch his mind, and with once more a she'pan to take up the burden of planning. His heart was pained for Melein's burden, but he did not try to bear it. She would have her honor. He had his, and it was vastly simpler.

To obey the she'pan. To avenge the People.

He stared at the human during his waking intervals and once, in the dark, he knew that the human was awake and looking at him. They did not speak.

Chapter Nineteen

———•◄══►•———

THE DAY came quietly, with only the sounds of the wind and the dus's breathing. Niun looked and found Melein already awake, sitting cross-legged in the doorway, outlined by the dawn. She was composed as if she had sat so for a long time, arranging her thoughts in private in the last hours of the night.

He rose, while Duncan still lay insensible; and came to her and settled on the cold sand, near the fever-warmth of the drowsing dus. His legs were weak with the poison and his arm was stiff and hot to the shoulder, but it would pass. His mind was still calm, with the muddled thoughts of the dus still brushing it; and he was not afraid, even considering their situation. He knew this for dus courage, that would melt when crisis came and a man needed to think; but it was rest, and he was glad of it. He thought perhaps Melein had enjoyed something of the same, for her face was calm, as if she had been meditating on some private dream.

"Did you rest long?" he asked of her.

"So long as I needed. I was shaken yesterday. I think I shall still find a long walk difficult. But we will walk today."

He heard this, and knew that she had come to some ultimate decision, but it would not be respectful to ask, to go on assuming that he was her kinsman, which he could not be any longer.

"We are ready," he said.

"We are going by the way of Sil'athen," she said, "and further into the hills; and we will find a shrine of which the Kel has known nothing in our generation. Before we two were born it was ordered forgotten by the Kel. The Pana, Niun, never rested in the Edun. It was a time of war. The she'pan

202

did not think it good that the Pana be in the edun, and she was right."

He touched his brow in reverence, his skin chilled even to hear the things that she said; but his spirit rose at what she said. It changed nothing, had no bearing on their own bleak chances; but the Holy existed, and even if they went to destroy it with their own hands, it would not have perished by enemies.

The gods' mission, then. That was something worth doing, something he could well comprehend.

"Know this," she said further. "We will recover the Pana for ourselves, and we two will bear it to a place where we can be safe. And we will wait. We will wait, until we can find a way off Kesrith or until we know that there can be none. Does the Kel have an opinion?"

He considered, thought of Duncan's offer, of bringing it to her, and put it away in his thoughts. There would be a moment for that, if they lived to do the one thing. "I think," he judged carefully, "that we will end by killing humans and then by being hunted to our end. But for my part I had as lief go to the human authorities and contract with them against regul. I am this bitter."

She listened to him attentively, her head tilted to one side, and she frowned. "But," she said, "there is peace between regul and humans."

"I do not think it will last. Not forever."

"But would humans not laugh—to consider one kel'en alone, trying to take service against all regul?"

"The regul would not laugh," said Niun grimly, and she nodded, appreciative of that truth.

"But I will not have this," she said. "No. I know what Intel planned: to take us into the Dark again, to take the long voyage and renew the People during that Dark. And I will not sell you into hire for any promises of safety. No. We two go our own way."

"We have neither Kath nor kel'e'ein," he cried, and dropped his voice at once to half-whisper, for he did not want Duncan waking. "For us there are no more generations, no renewing. We will never come out of that Dark."

She looked up tranquilly at the dawning. "If we are the last, then a quiet end; and if we are not the last, then the way to surest extinction for the People is to waste our lives in pursuit of tsi'mri wars and tsi'mri honors and all the things that have occupied the People in this unhappy age."

"What is there else?" he asked; which was a forbidden question, and he knew it when he had spoken it, and cancelled it with a gestured refusal. "No, do as you will."

"We are free," she said. "We are *free*, Niun. And I will commit us to nothing but to find the Pana and to find whether others of our kind survive."

He looked up and met her eyes, and acknowledged her bravery with a nod of his head. "It is not possible that we do this," he said. "The Kel tells you this, she'pan."

"The Kel of the Darks," she said softly, "is not wholly ignorant; and therefore it is a harder service. No, perhaps it is not possible. But I cannot accept any other thing. Do you not believe that the gods still favor the People?"

He shrugged, self-conscious in his ignorance, helpless as a kel'en always was in games of words. He did not know whether she played ironies or not.

"I cast us both," she said then. *"Shon'ai."*

This he understood, a mystery the Kel easily fathomed: he made a fist, a pantomime of the catch of *shon'ai*, and his heart lightened.

"Shon'ai," he echoed. "It is good enough."

"Then we should be moving," she said.

"We are ready," he said. He gathered himself up and went to Duncan and shook at him. "Come," he told Duncan, and while Duncan began to stir about he made a pack of their remaining belongings. The water he meant to carry himself, and a small light flask also he meant for Melein, for it was not wise to make Duncan independent in that regard or to make her dependent, should it come to trouble—though neither he nor she, whole of limb and untroubled by enemies, needed a flask in a land where they knew every plant and stone.

He threw the bundle of supplies at Duncan's feet.

"Where are we going?" Duncan asked, without moving to pick it up. It was a civil question. Niun shrugged, giving him all the answer he meant to give, with the same civility.

"I am not your beast of burden," Duncan said, a thin, under-the-breath piece of rebellion. He kicked at the bundle, spurning it.

Niun looked at it, and looked at him, without haste. "The

she'pan does not work with the hands. Being kel'en, I do not bear burdens, while there are others to bear them. If you were dead, I would carry it. Since you are not, you will carry it."

Duncan seemed to consider how seriously that was meant, and reached the correct conclusion. He picked it up, and slid his arms into the ropes of the pack.

Then Niun did find some pity for him, for the man was a manner of kel'en, and avowed he was not of a lower caste, but he would not fight for it. It was a matter of the yin'ein, a'ani, honorable combat; and he reckoned that with mri weapons the human was as helpless as a kath'en.

Perhaps, he thought, he had been wrong to insist upon this point, and to have taken some small part of the weight for himself would not have overburdened his pride. It was one thing to war against the tsi'mri kel'en's species; it was another to break him under the weight of labor in Kesrith's harsh environment.

He said nothing, all the same. It troubled him, the while they started out together, the three of them, and the dus lumbering along by his side. It was a difficult question, how it was honorable to deal at close quarters with a human.

It had been the death of the People, that humans refused a'ani and preferred mass warfare; and he began to realize now that humans simply could not fight.

Tsi'mri.

He felt fouled, deeply distressed by what he had discovered. He wished to change what he had said, and could not, for his pride's sake. And he began to think over and over again how bitter the war had been, that so many had perished without knowing the nature of the enemy.

But it was not his to change this, even now. He was not a caste that made ultimate decisions. He reminded himself of this, wondering how much Intel had known.

By the Deog'hal slash they ascended into the high hills, not following the usual track to Sil'athen, lest some survivor down in the city find them the more easily and finish what they had begun at the edun. It was a hard climb, and one which took a great deal from Melein, and from Duncan, laboring as he was under his burden.

"I was too long sitting in the she'pan's tower," Melein

breathed when they had come to the crest. She coughed and tried to smother it, while Duncan sank down in a heap, disengaged himself from the ropes and lay upon his pack. Niun poured a little water to ease Melein's throat, and deep in his heart he was afraid for her, for Melein was not wont to be so easily tired; and he marked how she limped, and sometimes held her arm to her side.

"I think that you are hurt," he said softly.

She made a deprecating gesture. "I fell, closing the door to the storeroom. It is nothing."

He hoped that she was right in that. He gave her to drink again, spendthrift with the water, but it was likely that they would come on more soon enough. He drank enough himself to moisten his mouth, and saw the human looking at him with an intent gaze, unwilling to plead.

"For moisture only," he said, giving him half a measure. "Be slow with it."

The human drank as he had drunk, beneath the veil, keeping his face covered, and handed back the cap with a nod that achieved some grace.

"Where are we going?" Duncan asked again, his voice gone hoarse.

"Human," said Melein, startling them both. "Why does it matter to you to know?"

Duncan drew a breath to answer at once; Niun reached out and caught his arm in a hard grip.

"Before you speak," Niun said to him, "understand that she is a she'pan. The Kel deals with outsiders; the she'pan does not. You are honored that she even looks at you. If you speak a word that offends her, I will surely kill you out of hand. So perhaps you will be more comfortable to direct your words to me, so that you will not offend against her."

Duncan looked from one to the other of them, as if he thought they were making mock of him, or threatening him in some way he could not comprehend.

"I am very serious," said Niun. "Direct your answer to me."

"Tell her," said Duncan then, "that I'm more interested in returning to my own people alive. Tell her what I told you last night. That offer still stands. I may be about to get you offworld."

"Duncan," said Melein, "I already know what you would

like to ask, and I will not answer yet. But you may tell us when your people will come. You know that, surely."

Duncan hesitated in evident distress, surely weighing their purposes. "A matter of days," he said in a low voice. "A very few days—maybe sooner than I would figure. And they're going to find ruins at the city; and the regul will be left to tell them whatever story they like about what happened night before last."

"Tsi'mri," said Melein deprecatingly, which Duncan did not understand.

"The she'pan means," Niun answered that look, "that what outsiders do is not our concern. We have no brothers and no masters. We do not serve regul any longer. Perhaps you do not understand, Duncan, that we are the last mri. The ship *Ahanal* contained all the survivors of the war and the edun contained the rest; and the regul know us, that if they do not finish what they began at the port, then we are likely to deal them hurt. Being regul, they will not wish to meet us face to face to do this, and they will probably try to convince your species to do the work for them. You see how it is. You do better not to press us with questions. There are things to be thought of in their time, if this happens or if that happens—but you do well not to ask so that we will not have to think of it."

Duncan absorbed all that answer in silence, and sat with his arms wrapped about his knees, hands clenched until the knuckles went white.

"Duncan," Melein said then, "it is a saying among us that *Said is done.* So we do not say, so that we are not obligated to do. We do not trap with words, like the regul do. Ask no more questions."

And she held out her left hand to Niun, gesturing that she wanted help to rise. It hurt her, though he was very careful.

"There are clouds," she observed, looking toward the east. "May it descend to the regul."

By afternoon the sky was entirely overcast, sparing them the heat of the direct sun, bringing a chill to the air; and it became clear that the clouds were doing as Melein had wished they would do: that upon the ruin of the city and the port would come storm.

Once, that she gazed over her shoulder toward the plain

and looked upon the lightning that flashed in that shadowed
quarter, she held some impulse that made the dus moan in
startlement and shy off from her: it was Melein that had
done it, for Niun knew himself innocent, and the dus sought
his side afterward.

But the clouds shed no water on them, and their flasks
were only a quarter full when they came to the end of the
long upland rise and entered the flat highland. By late afternoon Duncan was staggering with weariness and would gladly
have stopped at any time, but Niun considered the possibility
of aircraft seeking them and was not willing to stop in the
open, not for Duncan's sake.

He looked often at Melein, anxious for her, but she walked
without appearing to suffer overmuch.

And toward sunset there was a luin-cluster on the horizon,
twisted trunks like a mirage against the red sun, bare limbs
tufted with small leaves only at the ends.

"There is water," Niun told Duncan. "Tonight will be an
easy camp and you will have enough to drink."

And Duncan, who had begun to lag, expended a last effort,
and kept the pace they, unburdened, set toward the trees.

And walked among them, careless.

" 'Ware!" Melein cried, seeing it, even as Niun did, the
glassy strands spread in the evening light.

Niun whipped up his pistol and fired before Duncan had
time to know what had befallen him: and the windflower
died, a stench, glassy tendrils blackened. But where it touched
Duncan's flesh, on hands and forehead, the red sprang up at
once, and Duncan, his clothing covered with the tendrils, fell
and writhed on the sand in agony.

"*Ch'au!*" Niun cursed his stupidity. "Still! Lie still!" And
Duncan lay quietly then, shuddering as with the *av-tlen's*
point he lifted the tendrils from Duncan's flesh. He pulled
them from the cloth too, and urged Duncan to his feet, there
to stand while he inspected the black cloth for any
transparent remnant.

Then Duncan went a few feet away and was dryly sick for
some few moments.

Niun cleansed the *av-tlen* in the sand and with it cut the
trunk of a luin that had not been poisoned by the windflower.
He took from his belt a small steel tube and drove it easily

into the soft wood, and the sweet liquid began to flow, pure and clean of Kesrith's dust.

He filled the first flask and gave it to Melein, so that she might indulge her thirst to the full, for there were many luin. He drank the second, rapidly filled from a second tree; and the third he filled he took to Duncan, who had not succeeded in being as sick as he doubtless wished to be after his shock. The human simply lay on the ground and shuddered.

"It is a point worth remembering," Niun echoed Eddan's words to him on a less painful encounter, "that where there is water on Kesrith, there are enemies and predators. The pain is all, and you are lucky. It will pass. If you had been alone, you would have been wholly ensnared and the windflower would have been the end of you."

"I saw nothing," Duncan said, and swallowed a sip of the water, fighting the pain.

"When you walk among luin, walk with the light in your face, so that the strands of windflowers cast across the sun and shine; and mind where you step." He indicated where a little burrower had his lair, a place marked by a flat and a tiny depression. He flung a pebble. The sand erupted, and there was a flash of a pale back, gone again as the little burrower dived and fluttered his mantle, settling sand over himself again.

"They are venomed," said Niun, "and even a little one can make a man very sick. But since they grow large enough to engulf a dus whole, the venom does not matter much to us. Burrowers lair among the luin, and in shadowed places and among rocks where there is sand to cover them. There are not many large ones. The ha-dusei eat them, if they do not eat the dusei, before they grow to great size. There is a very large old one by the way we will pass tomorrow. I think he has been there all my lifetime. Burrowers are like regul: when they grow so big, they do not move much."

The little one, disturbed and angry, fluttered off under the sand, a moving ripple, to settle again deeper among the luin.

There was a general shifting about of others of his kind, and a jo, harmless, detached itself from its successful bark-imitation on a luin and fluttered away through the twilight.

"Drink your fill," Niun said to the distressed human, feeling pity for him, and Duncan slowly did so, while Niun made them a supper of the supplies they had brought. They would make many a meal off the burrowers themselves, meat unpalatable and tough as rubber; but this night Melein was suffering, and they had starved the night before and most of the day. He was extravagant, and gave to Duncan an equal share with them, considering that he had confiscated what of Duncan's gear was useful, including his rations.

Across the sky toward the lowlands there was continued lightning, ill luck for the regul.

And they rested with the dus for warmth, and with its ward impulse to keep the ha-dusei at bay, so that they slept secure in the luin grove.

In the morning they gathered up their gear once more; and Niun considered the matter with a gnawing of his lip and a frown, and finally, brusquely, snatched several rolls of cloth and the food from the human's burden and did them up himself.

"In the case that you do not watch where you walk," Niun said in a harsh tone, "the burrower that gets you will not have our shelter and our food."

The human looked at him, marked across the brow by a bloody stripe of his encounter with the windflower; and Niun did not think that the human would have forgotten his words of the day previous, that he would carry no burden. He glowered at Duncan, discouraging any reminder of this.

"I learn quickly," Duncan said, and Niun reckoned that among the things Duncan had learned was the art of answering a kel'en civilly.

Chapter Twenty

THE AIR was unimaginably foul, tainted by so many frightened regul. It was dark, save for the lights on the two sled consoles and the four life-battery lamps the shelter provided. Power elsewhere was out. The water plants were down. There was talk of seeking water Kesrithi style, from the land, but none of the younglings were sure that they could accomplish this; and they were not anxious to go out into the contaminated exterior, or across the seething flats.

Hulagh had not yet ordered them. He would do so, Stavros did not doubt, when he himself began to thirst.

The sleds were on battery. To this also there was a limit; but Stavros and Hulagh, elders, consumed vital power as they consumed food and water unrationed, because it was unquestioned that elders must be supported by the young. Stavros found it in him to pity the harried secretary, Hada, who dispensed food and water that remained to 300 other younglings, and likewise ministered to Hulagh and himself. They were jammed into the shelter so tightly that the youngest and least could not lie down to sleep; but the sleds were accorded their maneuvering room. The younglings gave back from them with deference that was next to worship; indeed their whole hope for survival centered on the presence of elders among them. They talked little. They all faced Hulagh, row on row of bone-shielded faces and blunt heads, and eyes glittered in the almost-dark and nostril-slits worked in a slow rhythm that seemed to Stavros, in a moment of bizarre humor, to be tending toward unison.

And in the long hours he noted something else, that there were not a few who fell asleep and did not waken.

Bai, favor, he signalled, spelling slowly in regul symbols on the screen. *I think some of the younglings are ill.*

Hulagh's great body heaved as he looked, and heaved again with a hiss of mirth. "No, reverence-human, they are asleep. They are to sleep until your assistance comes. They consume less in that state."

And in increasing numbers the young, beginning with the youngest, slipped into that state, until almost all were dormant.

And bai Hulagh himself began to drowse. He recovered from this with a jerk and a rumbled curse, and called to Hada. "Food," he ordered. "Be quick, witless."

The thick, sour-smelling soup was offered likewise to Stavros, but he declined it, almost retching. This troubled Hada, but it gave the portion to Hulagh, between whose thin lips the paste disappeared rapidly.

"You do not eat," Hulagh observed.

I do not need to eat, Stavros replied, and in honesty: *Your food does not agree with me. But I would have soi.*

Hada scrambled to accommodate this wish, feverish, almost maniac in its desire to please. It offered the hot liquid to Stavros' good hand, with a straw for his ease, and hovered near him.

Hulagh laughed, a rumbling, a series of hisses. "Go, egg-stealer, and sit with the other younglings." And Hada visibly cringed, and slunk aside, on small tottering steps.

"Hada knows," Hulagh explained, waxed almost affable under the pressure of their long wait, under the need to be pleasant with humans and human ways, "that if we are here much longer, there will be shorter rations; and Hada is greedy. I indulge this youngling. I shall keep it if it continues to please. I may keep all. I have lost," he added sadly, "my own."

With the ship, Stavros understood. *My sorrow, reverence.*

"And mine for the loss of your own youngling." The great gossamer-clad monster sighed and lapsed into a long reverie.

And Stavros, his sled nose-to-nose with that of Hulagh, hurled his temper at the weak fingers of his left hand. They gave only slightly. The right hand clenched. He had ceased to fear that the paralysis would spread or that it would affect his mind, but he was ceasing to hope that it would ever ease completely. He remained grateful for regul technology, if not for regul.

Hulagh's condolences were honest, doubtless, but it did not mean that the regul's hands were clean in the matter. Stavros regarded the drowsing regul with narrowed eyes. Now, shut in a shelter with the regul, was an inopportune moment to state the obvious, that Hulagh had had somewhat to do with the disappearance of Duncan, and that Stavros, conversely, was innocent in the loss of the bai's ship and the younglings aboard it.

In regul morality, disposing of a youngling was a serious matter, but only in terms of the affront offered its elder and its doch. A regul would as soon face an elder's wrath over the loss of a youngling as that same elder's wrath over some matter of shady dealing discovered in trade; and Stavros reckoned that the same ruthless logic just might apply to eliminating a lone elder whose doch could prove hostile, given the information which that elder possessed.

Regul did not lie, he still believed, but they were fully capable of murder, whereby lies could be rendered unnecessary. And they feared him on the one hand and hoped for his help on the other, and he fostered that hope in them as he cherished his own life.

He began to reckon the mind of bai Hulagh of doch Alagn, that here was a desperate fellow, who had suffered a very dangerous loss in the eyes of his kind. And therefore, while it seemed profitable, Hulagh, like a good merchant prince, was dealing for compromise.

It was a compromise out of which humankind could win a great deal.

But part of that settlement, Stavros was determined, would be an accounting for a certain lost SurTac, on whom Stavros had settled rather more affection than he had admitted to himself. He had not loved his own children, of whom he had seen little, locked as he was in the reclusive life of a scholar of Kiluwa, or later, while he was busy in government and at the university. He had found many other things more important than to trouble himself with the issue of several of his young passions, that had given him first an assortment of sons and thereafter grandchildren and great-grandchildren—who sought him out mostly because a Kiluwan connection was prestigious. Some of them, he knew, hated him with the same dedicated zeal with which they sought promotions based on his influence.

But he missed Duncan. Duncan had come, like others who had ridden Stavros' reputation to reach for wealth, with the motives of the others; and yet Duncan had given him a constant and earnest duty, earnest in his attempts to penetrate Kiluwan formality, simply because it was Duncan's nature to do so.

Stavros had never learned how to answer that. Nor, for the regul, did he admit to grief which they would not have understood. But in addition to an accounting which the regul owed for Kiluwa, there was that for an inconsequential Sur-Tac.

He did not, all the same, regret having sent Duncan, even at such cost. Events had damaged the regul and exacted satisfaction of them, and placed them at human mercy; and this was very much to Stavros' satisfaction. This was partial payment for Kiluwa.

It would be full payment, when he seized the reins of control from bai Hulagh, and began to bend doch Alagn into agreement with humans. This was revenge of a sort that both Hulagh and Kiluwa could appreciate—the more so when he ascertained who among regul was directly responsible for Kiluwa and found the means to deal with them. Being Kiluwan, Stavros entertained a hatred specific and logical: there was a species called regul; but the species called regul had not destroyed Kiluwa. It was one doch; and its name was Holn. It was not represented here.

There had been a decimation of Holn at their landing. This did not satisfy Stavros, who was not interested in bloodshed. It was the decline of Holn he wanted, its elimination from power among regul.

And Hulagh, controlled, an ally of humans, could become the instrument of this policy.

"Elder," Hulagh rumbled at last, "it is certain that you have authority over your people?"

Unless mri intervened and started something wider, Stavros replied. *I have authority over the force that is coming to Kesrith.*

"Favor," said Hulagh. "The mri will no longer be a factor in relations between us. They are gone. There are no more mri."

This was news. Stavros flashed a question sign, unadorned by words.

"The ship," said Hulagh, "contained all the survivors of mri-kind. We have disposed of this plague that kept our two species at war."

Hulagh had waited to divulge that piece of news. Stavros heard it, at first appalled at such a concept, the destruction of a sapient species; and then suspicious—but the regul did not lie. He began to contemplate the possibilities of a universe without the mri, and found the possibilities for human profit enormous.

"It is clear," said Hulagh, "that total rearrangement of human-regul relations is in order. Doch Alagn might find interest in helping this come about."

Stavros was shocked a second time, and recognized that dismay for a human reaction, based on a morality to which Hulagh could not possibly subscribe. There was no particular reason that doch Alagn should refrain from an offer that, in a human state, would amount to treason. Doch Alagn was in financial and political difficulty. Hulagh was seeking alignment with the powers that had control of the resources he desired.

Humanity's grudge, Stavros answered after due thought, *is with doch Holn. It would be possible to arrive at new accommodations with advantage to both our interests.*

Hulagh's lips parted in a regul smile. A slow hiss betokened his pleasure. "We shall explore this," he said. "We shall, most excellent Stavros."

And he wakened Hada and ordered soi, and remembered this time to order it sweetened, to Stavros' personal preference.

But before it was prepared, Hada came puffing back, waving his hands in agitation. "The ship," he breathed. "Be gracious, elders, the human ship, early—communications report—"

Hulagh's gesture cut the youngling off abruptly. The bai's lips continued parted, his nostrils dilated in what Stavros had learned was an expression of anxiety. The bai's total attitude was that of a man with a nervous smile, displaying good manners amid subdued terror.

"You will surely wish then," said bai Hulagh, "to greet these representatives of your people and explain the situation.

Assure them of our regret for the condition of the port, reverence."

We will manage, Stavros answered, beside himself with anxiety and restraining it, remembering how important it was that Hulagh be reassured. *Have confidence, reverence, that you have nothing to dread if your younglings will remain calm and not hamper operations.*

And he turned his sled toward the control section of the shelter, following the rolling gait of Hada Surag-gi, who by regul standards, was almost running.

The big doors of the shelter opened, and beams glared through the dim interior, handled by the fantastic shapes of suited men, who walked heavy-footed through the ranks of dormant younglings. The door was closed again, a precaution. The second man used a counter, reckoning what radiation might have gotten into the shelter. Conscious younglings scurried to clear them a path, chittering in terror.

Stavros slid his vehicle forward, faced a suited form and saw the blind-glassed head pause in an attitude of astonishment.

"Consul Stavros?"

The tab on the suit said GALEY and the rank was lieutenant.

"Yes," Stavros said, turned the communications screen by remote and spelled out a message on the basic-alphabet module, not trusting his slurred speech for complicated messages. *I am inconvenienced by an accident. Speech is awkward, but prosthetics are very adequate. Speak normally to me and watch the screen. Be respectful of these regul. It will be necessary to transfer them to safety if you cannot guarantee normal operations here in the building.*

"Sir," Galey said, seeming confused by the situation, then drew a breath and let it go again. "You're in command down here. What instructions? I'm afraid the power is going to be a major problem. We can possibly get a crew working on it, and you seem clean of contamination, but there are some considerable hot spots toward the port. The station is intact. We would rather evacuate."

Building can be occupied? Livable?

"This building? Yes, sir. It seems so."

Then we stay. Untoward weather a problem here. I have rest under control.

"The mri, sir—" Galey said. "We're not clear what happened here."

We have a problem, Lt. Galey, but we're resolving it. Kindly dispose your men so that we can resume normal operations here in the building. The communications station is accessible through that door. You will excuse me if I do not go with you.

"Yes, sir," said Galey, and gave his courtesies to the regul also, wooden and perfunctory. The marines with him began to move about various duties, on suit phones, doubtless, where regul would not be privy to exchanges of comment and instruction.

"You deal with younglings," Hulagh observed. "Favor. Are there other elders involved here?"

Other authorities, Stavros reckoned the bai's meaning, authorities who could complicate agreements made between them. *My apologies, bai Hulagh. This was an older youngling. And the elder who commands them must, as you surely remember from the treaty, defer to me where it regards the administration of Kesrith and its area. There is, however, one matter wherein his authority and mine might tend to cross.*

"And this one matter, human bai?"

My missing assistant is military personnel. The bai of the arriving ship may feel that he can settle this matter best. This would be an occasion for him to intrude his authority into my domain here. Naturally I do not wish this. I feel that it would smooth matters over if it were possible for answers to be given in this matter.

Hulagh's nostrils fluttered in rapid agitation. "Favor, reverence. We might suggest a search of the Dus plain, where there was conflict between my younglings and the mri outlaws. This is an unpleasant surmise, but if there are remains to be found—"

Stavros looked on the anxious bai without mercy. *It is then the conclusion of the bai that this youngling is dead?*

"It is most probable, reverence."

But if he were not, it is more likely that one of your staff could direct a search with more success than one of the ship's officers might. This is possible, is it not, bai? It would greatly augment my authority here and ease negotiations between us if it were possible that this lost youngling could be recovered. He is, of course, merely a youngling, and his experiences during the mri action would doubtless influence his mind to hysteria and cloud his judgments, so that no testimony he could give could be taken seriously. But it would please me if he were recovered alive.

The bai considered these things, and the understandings implicit in the words. "Indeed," said bai Hulagh, "there is such an expert on my staff, a person familiar with the terrain. With your staff's cooperation, this could be arranged at once."

My gratitude, reverence. I will see to the disposition of necessities with the ship. And Stavros turned his sled away, seeking out Galey, while his hearing caught bai Hulagh urgently summoning Hada Surag-gi.

The reaction began to strike him. He found it difficult for the moment to concentrate on the numerical signals that activated the various programs of the sled. He found his eyes misting. This was unaccustomed. He had the emotional reaction under control again by the time he swung the sled in with casual nonchalance beside Galey, who did not seem to know whether to offer condolences or congratulations on survival.

"You're alone here, sir?" Galey asked.

As you have noticed, difficulties abound. No delays. Is Koch in command up there?

"Yes, sir."

Then get me contact with him directly. I can patch this console in with the main board. Are you able to get a ship down here with sufficient personnel to staff work crews and give me office staff?

"Not quickly. The port's completely gone. But the station is in good shape. Servos everywhere." Galey bent over the console of the com unit, fingering regul controls helplessly.

"Here," Stavros said, with some satisfaction, keyed in and started the sequence of changes that put them through to the warship *Saber*, which had brought them all that clutter of personnel that would begin to make Kesrith human: soil experts, scientists.

And weapons.

His command, Kesrith, his. There was no med staffer going to rule him unfit to govern; and deep in his heart he knew that he needed that hulking merchant prince of the Alagn as much as doch Alagn presently needed him.

He saw the shock on the face of the com officer of *Saber;* and at once that face vanished, replaced by that of Stavros' military counterpart, Koch.

"Stavros?" Koch asked.

A little difficulty speaking, he keyed the answer, replacing the visual. *We have regul stranded down here. Stand by to assist us with on-world operations. We need food, drinkable water.*

"We were not prepared for regul nationals."

Unforeseen circumstances. All decisions regarding Kesrith and regul are mine. Situation here is under control. Presently seeking my aide, possible casualty of attack by mri. Hot areas reportedly confined to port. I request military personnel detached from Saber *to my command until we can clean up.*

"Excellency," said Koch, "the medical facilities of *Saber* are at your disposal if you will care to come up to the station."

Negative. Regul services are adequate. The situation is too urgent. My condition is good, considering. I am pursuing matters under my authority granted as governor of Kesrith. Send down scientists, military aides, all attached personnel and equipment as soon as area is cleared.

"It may be advisable to wait."

Send down personnel as requested.

There was a long delay. "All right," said Koch. "A medic will accompany the party."

On Kesrith, said Stavros, *medic will await my convenience.*

Koch digested this also. At last he nodded, accepting. "You have the authority, right enough. But ship's personnel stay under my command. You'll have the civs as soon as we can find solid ground for them. Starship *Flower* is attached to your personal service, with my compliments, sir. She's probe, though, not combat. Does the situation warrant immediate armed support?"

Negative.

"There is weather down there."

This is evidently frequent. Wait, then. We are pursuing operations here with available personnel. You are invited to come planetside and exchange courtesies when we get the wreckage cleared.

A sled hummed into the vicinity. Stavros heard it, and put them momentarily on visual from his side again, watching with satisfaction as Koch beheld a regul elder for the first time.

This is bai Hulagh, Stavros told him, cutting out the visual again. *A most influential regul, sir, if you please. We have achieved a certain necessary cooperation here, which is to the advantage of both species.*

"Understood," Koch said slowly, and seemed utterly taken aback: a military man, Koch, born and bred. He had been presented a situation with which he could not deal, and fortunately recognized it.

"You'll get your help," Koch said, and Stavros closed out the communication with an inward satisfaction, cast a look at Galey. *Scan the area here,* he said to the lieutenant. *And when you've made sure where it's safe, we'll start clearing these younglings back to normal duties. This is the bai's staff. All due considerations to them, Lt. Galey.*

"Reports are coming in," he said. "The whole area seems cool and secure. The building seals held very well."

Stavros breathed a sigh of relief.

"My younglings," said Hulagh, "will find means of restoring the water and repairing the collectors for the power." He waved a massive hand. "Hada will attend other matters, given use of transport. I believe some of the vehicles at the water plant may have survived intact."

Chapter Twenty-one

---•◦•——◆——•◦•---

AT THE ENTRANCE to Sil'athen a dus met them, warding with such strength that Niun's dus shied off. And there in the rocks, half buried in the sands, lay Eddan's remains; and not far away lay a tangle of black that had been Liran and Debas, and gold that had been Sathell.

Melein veiled herself and drew aside, being she'pan and unable to look upon death; but Niun came and reverently arranged the visor over Eddan's face, and it was long before he could look up and face the human that hovered uncertainly by.

He cleansed his hands in the sand, and made the reverence sign and rose. The human also made such a sign, in his own fashion, a respect which Niun accepted as it was given. "They chose this end," he said to Duncan, "and it was better for them here than for those that stayed."

And he poured a little of their precious water, and turned his back to wash, hands and face, and veiled again. When he looked up at the rocks he saw two other dusei, that began to come down from their heights; and he gave back at once.

His own dus came between, and tried to approach the three warding beasts that had formed a common front against them. Noses extended, they circled back and forth, and then the great gentle creature that had been Eddan's, or so Niun thought it, reared up and cried out, driving the dus away. But the smallest of the three hesitated between, and followed the stranger-dus of Niun, and its fellow came after.

The largest, Eddan's, gave a plaintive moan and retreated from these traitor-dusei, that he no longer knew. Niun felt its anger, and trembled; but when he moved away from this place, not alone his own dus came, but the two that had been of Liran and Debas, a tight triangle with his own. They called and moaned, and would not yet suffer Niun to come near them, but they came away from their duty all the same, choosing life, leaving matters to the dus of Eddan, who settled by his dead and remained faithful.

"Lo'a-ni dus," Niun saluted that one softly, with great respect; but he shut his heart to it, because the warding impulse was too strong to bear.

And he shouldered his burden again and began walking, his course and Duncan's converging with that of Melein.

There was no need to speak of what they had found. The dusei walked ahead of them, and now and then one would make to go back and go toward Duncan, but Niun's dus would not allow this, and constantly circled toward the rear to prevent them when they did so. Soon they seemed to understand that this particular tsi'mri was under safe-conduct and gave up their attempts on him.

They were at the entrance to the inner valley of Sil'athen, and here was another sort of warder. Niun saw it across the flat sweep of sand, and, touching the human on the arm, he bent and picked up a tiny stone. He hurled it far, far out across the flat sand, toward the central depression.

It erupted, a circumference twenty times the length of a dus, a cloud of sand from the edge of the burrower's mantle as it rose and dived again a few lengths farther.

The human swore in a tone of awe.

"I have shown you," said Niun, "so that you will understand that a man without knowledge of this land—and without a dus to walk with him—will not find his way across it. Across the great sands, there are said to be larger ones than what you saw. The dusei smell them out. They smell out other dangers too. Even mri do not like to walk this country alone, although we can do it. I do not think you can."

"I understand you," said Duncan.

They walked quietly thereafter, near the wall of the cliffs, where the safe course was, past caves sealed and marked with stones, and the strange shapes of Sil'athen's rocks one by one passed behind them, ringing them about and shutting off view of the way they had come.

"What is this place?" Duncan asked in a lowered voice, as they passed the high graves of the she'panei.

"Nla'ai-mri," said Niun. "Sil'athen, the burying place of our kind."

And thereafter Duncan said nothing, but looked uneasily from one side of the valley to the other as they passed, and once backward, over his shoulder, where the wind erased their tracks, wiping clean all the trace that men had ever walked this way.

Melein led them now, walking at their head, her hand on the back of Niun's dus, which ambled slowly beside her, and the beast even seemed to enjoy that contact. Deep into the canyons they went, by a path that Niun had never walked, down the aisle of rock that belonged to the tombs of the she'panei. Here there were signs graven on the rocks—names, perhaps, of ancient she'panei, or directions: Melein read them, and Niun trusted her leading, that she knew their way though she herself had never walked it.

She tired, and it seemed at times that she must surely stop, but she would not, only paused for breath now and again, and went on. The sun that was at noon became the fervent blaze of afternoon, and sank so that they walked in the cold shadow of the cliffs, dangerous if not for the protecting dusei that probed the way for them.

Deep in that shadow they came to the blind end of the cliffs, and Niun looked to Melein, suddenly wondering if she had not after all lost their way, or whether this was where she meant that they should stop. But she gazed upward at a trail that he had not seen until he followed the direction of her gaze, that could not be seen at all save from this vantage point. It led up and up into the red rocks, toward a maze of sandstone pillars that thrust fingers at the sky.

"Niun," Melein said then, and cast a glance backward.

He looked where she did, toward Duncan, who, exhausted in the thin air, had slumped to rest over his pack. The dusei were moving toward him. One extended a paw. Duncan froze, lying still, his head still pillowed on the pack.

"Yai!" Niun reproved the dus, who guiltily retracted the curious paw. The dusei in general retreated, radiating mingled confusion.

And in his own mind was unease at the thought of entering that steep, tangled maze with the human in their company, where a misstep could be the end of them.

"What shall I do with him?" he asked of Melein, in the

high language, so that Duncan could not understand. "He should not be here. Shall I find a way to be rid of him?"

"The dusei will manage him," she said. "Let him alone."

He started to protest, not for his own sake, but for fear for her; but she did not look as if she were prepared to listen.

"He will go last when we are climbing," he said, and gathering in his belly all the same was a knot of fear. Intel had seen the future clearly: *I have an ill feeling,* she had said the night they all died; and he had such a dread now, a cold, clear premonition that here was a point of no return, that he was losing some chance or passing something; and the human wound himself deeper and deeper into his mind.

He did not want him. He carried Duncan in his mind the way he carried the memories of the attack, indelible. He looked at the human and shuddered with sudden and vehement loathing, and found himself carrying the human's due burden, and not knowing what else to do with it. He fingered the pistol.

But he had been made kel'en for the honor of the People, not for outright butchery; and Melein had ordered otherwise, easing his conscience. He was not able to make such a decision. It was hers to say, and she had said, agreeing with his better conscience.

And suddenly Duncan was looking at him, and he slipped his fingers into his belt, trying to cover his thoughts and the motion at once. "Come," he said to Duncan. "Come, we are going up now."

He set himself first on the narrow climb, and saw at once that Melein was scarcely able to make the climb on that eroded, unused track. He braced his feet where he could and reached for her hand, and she took his fingers crosshanded, to favor her injured side. He moved very carefully, each time that he must give a gentle pull to help her, for he saw her face and knew that she was in great pain.

Duncan came after, and the dusei last of all, clumsy and scattering rocks that rattled into the deep canyon, but their claws and great strength made them surer-footed than they looked.

And halfway, the sound of an aircraft reached them.

It was Melein's keen hearing that caught it first, between steps, as she was resting; and she turned and pointed where it circled above the main valley. It could not see or detect them where they were, and they were free to watch it, that tiny speck in the rosy halflight that remained.

Niun had view not only of that, but of Duncan's back, as the human stood holding his place against a great boulder and looking outward at that ship; and he could not but think how gladly Duncan would have run to signal it, and how he might well do so if he had some future chance.

They were no longer alone in the world.

"Let us climb," said Melein, "and get off this cliffside before it circles this way."

"Come," said Niun sharply to Duncan, with hatefulness in his tone; and Duncan turned and climbed after them, away from what in all likelihood was hope of rescue.

Looking down another time to help Melein, Niun looked out and did not see the aircraft; and that gave him no comfort at all. It could as easily appear directly overhead, passing the cliffs and sandstone fingers that gave them only partial cover.

And to his relief, once they gained the top of the cliffs, they were not faced with another flat, but went down a slight decline, and followed a winding track among sandstone pillars that were now burning red against the purpling sky. There was strong wind, that skirled small clouds among the pillars and erased their tracks as they made them.

Duncan's dry cough began again and continued a time until the human had caught his breath from the climb. They were at high altitude, and it was far drier air than the lowlands. Here on the highlands, over much of the rest of the land, there was no rain, only blowing sand. A sea lay beyond, the The'asacha, but it was small and dead as the Alkaline Sea that bordered the regul city; and beyond that sea was a mountain chain, the Dogin, the mere skeletons of eroded mountains that still were tall enough to cast the winds this way and that across the backbone of the continent, and generated storms that never fell on the uplands plain, but down-country, in the flats.

The clouds that rimmed the sky now were headed to shed their load of moisture on the lowlands, affording them neither concern for the storm nor hope of water from it. All that it would bring them was a dark sky and a hard and dangerous walk without the stars.

The sound of the aircraft intruded suddenly upon Niun's

hearing: he shepherded human and dusei toward the deepest shadows, in the gathering dark—Melein had sought shelter at once. If the aircraft saw anything it would be the image of a dus, a hot, massive silhouette for their instruments, something that was common enough to see in the wilds. If they fired at every dus on Kesrith, they would be a long time in their searching.

It passed. Niun, his fist entangled in the human's robes, a grip he had not relaxed since he herded them in together, let go and drew his first even breath.

"We may rest here a moment," said Melein in a thin, tired voice. "It is a long walk from here—I must rest."

Niun looked at her, seeing her pain, that she had tried so long to hide. On the climb he had felt her every wince in his own vitals. And they were not to rest long. He was distressed with this, feeling that she was spending her last strength against this urgency to go farther.

And without her, there was nothing.

He took the cloth for a blanket, and settled her against the side of the dus, into that friendly warmth, and was glad when she relaxed against that comfort he offered, and the line of pain knit into her brow, eased and began to vanish.

"I will be all right," she said, touching his hand.

And then her eyes widened and he whirled about upon a shadow—a darting reach for a water flask and Duncan was gone, into the maze of rocks in the dark.

Niun swore and sprang after him, hearing the moaning roar of the dusei at once behind him. He came round the side of a pillar, half expecting ambush, which would have been idiocy on the human's part, and did not meet it.

Nor was there sight or sign of Duncan.

And he had left Melein, and sweat broke out on him, only to think what could happen if Duncan circled on them and attacked her, hurt as she was.

Then the sound of a dus hunting arose, moaning carried on the wind, and that cry meant quarry sighted. He blessed the several gods of his caste and ran toward that sound, pistol in hand.

So he met Melein, a pale wraith in the dark, and a dus beside her: and together they found the blind way where the other dusei had Duncan pent.

"Yai!" Niun called the beasts, before they should close in

and kill; and they wheeled in a slope-shouldered and truculent withdrawal, only enough to let Duncan rise from the ledge where he had been cornered. He would not. He huddled there, unveiled in the scramble he had made, his naked face contorted with exhaustion and anger. He coughed rackingly, and his nose poured blood.

"Come down," said Melein.

But he would not, and Niun went in after him, pushing the dusei aside. Then Duncan made to move, but he fell again, and sat still and dropped his head on his folded arms.

Niun took the strap of the water flask and ripped it from Duncan's hand, and let him rest the moment, for they were all hard-breathing.

"It was a good attempt," said Niun. "But the next time I will kill you; it is a wonder that the dusei did not kill you this time."

Duncan lifted his face, jaw set in anger. He shrugged, a gesture of defiance, a gesture spoiled by an attack of helpless coughing.

"You would have signalled the airship," said Melein, "and brought them down on us."

Duncan shrugged again, and came to his feet, went with them of his own accord in leaving the blind pocket. The dusei were still blood-roused, and confused by being set on and drawn off their quarry; and Niun walked between them and the human. Melein followed after them as they went back to the place where they had abandoned their gear in the chase.

There they sank down where they had begun to rest, doubly exhausted now; and Niun stared at Duncan thoughtfully, thinking what might have happened, and what damage might have been done them.

There was Melein, fragile with her injury.

And there was an aircraft in the vicinity that wanted only the least error from them, the least slip into the open at the wrong moment, in order to locate and put an end to them.

"Cover your face," Niun said at last.

Duncan stared at him sullenly, as if he would defy that order, but in the end he lowered his eyes and arranged the veil, and stared at him still.

The dus moaned and reared up.

"Yai!" Niun ordered him, and he subsided, swaying nervously. The dus-anger stirred his own blood. He fought it down and mastered it, as a man must, who went among dusei, be more rational than they.

Duncan shifted aside, tearing his glance from them and the beasts, fixing it instead on the rock before them.

"We will move on," said Melein after a time, and pulled herself to her feet, carefully, painfully. She faltered, needed Niun's immediate hand to steady her.

But she set her hand then upon the dus, and the beast ambled out to the fore, and she was able to walk at its side, a slow pace and deliberate—the beast the only safety they had in this dark and close passage through the rocks.

Niun gathered up the water flasks, and left the human all the rest of the burden to carry, and hurried him on with a heavy hand, in among the two other dusei, before they should lose sight of Melein's pale figure.

The dusei, their oily hides immune to the poison of wind-flowers, their keen senses aware of other dangers, were the only means that they could dare to move after dark in this place; and the dark, as Melein was surely reckoning, was friendly to them as it would not be to those that pursued them.

The long walk led them into more open areas, where they crossed fearfully exposed stretches of sand under the ragged clouds; and they made it in among the sandstone formations again as they heard the distant sound of the aircraft still in the area.

It came close. Duncan looked to the skies as if in hope, looked back sharply as Niun whipped the *av-tlen* from its sheath, a whisper of edged metal.

They faced each other, he and Duncan, standing still as the aircraft circled off again, out of hearing. Niun put the weapon back into its sheath with a practiced reverse.

"Someone," Duncan said, his voice almost unrecognizable from his raw throat, "someone knows where to look for you. I somehow don't think my people would know that."

It was sense that struck cold to Niun's heart. He glanced at Melein.

"We cannot stop again for rest," she said. "They must not find us, not here. We must be at the place before light and come away again. Niun, let us hurry."

He pushed the human gently. "Come," he said.

"Is it her?" Duncan asked, nodded back toward Melein

without moving from where he stood. "Is it somehow to do with her that the regul keep after you?"

"It could not be," he said with assurance; and then another thought began to grow in him with horrid clarity, mental process working again where for a long time there had been only shock. He looked again to Melein, spoke in the hal'ari, the high language. "It could not be that they are hunting us. They could not know that we exist. What are two mri to them, with others dead? Or how could regul have reached the edun to know survivors left it? They could not have climbed among those ruins. It is this human, this cursed human. He has ties back in the city, a master, and for his sake the regul tracked me across the flats. If it is the regul, they are still on that trail. There are regul and humans at work in this thing."

Her eyes grew troubled. "Let us go," she said suddenly. "Let us go now, quickly. I do not know what we will do with him, but we cannot settle it now."

"What are you saying?" Duncan demanded of them suddenly in his hoarse voice. Perhaps there were certain words, a sideward look, that he had caught amid what they had said. Niun looked on him and thought uneasily that Duncan did suspect how little his life might weigh with them.

"Move," Niun said again, and pushed him, not gently. Duncan abandoned his questions and moved where he was told without arguing.

And if it were Duncan that was hunted, and regul were tracking them for his sake, then, Niun thought, Duncan would ultimately have to go to the enemy in such a manner to stop that search, in such a manner that he could not betray to them the fact that a she'pan of the People was still alive.

O gods, Niun mourned within himself, urged toward murder and dishonor, and not seeing any other course.

But the aircraft did not come again, and he was able to forget that threat in the urgency of their present journey—to put off thinking what he might have to do if the search resumed.

Twice, despite Melein's wishes, they had to rest, for Melein's sake; and each time, when Niun would have stayed longer, she insisted and they walked again, at last with Niun holding her arm, her slim fingers clenching upon his against the unsteadiness of her legs.

And after the mid of the night, they entered a narrow canyon that wound strangely, dizzily, and began to be a descent, where the walls leaned together threateningly over their heads and cast them into dark deeper than the night outside.

"Use your light," Melein said then. "I think there is stone overhead now entirely." And Niun used Duncan's penlight, ever so small a beam to find their footing. Down and down they went, a spiralling course and narrow, until they suddenly came upon a well of sky above them, where the night seemed brighter than the utter black they had travelled. Here was a widening, where walls were splashed with symbols the like of which had once adorned the edun itself.

The foremost dus reared aside, gave a roar that echoed horridly all up and down the passage, and Niun swung the beam leftward, toward the dus. There in a niche was a huddled knot of black rags and bones.

A guardian's grave.

Niun touched his brow in reverence to the unknown kel'en, and because he saw Duncan standing too near that holy place, he drew him back by the arm. Then he turned his light on the doorway where Melein stood, a way blocked by stones and sealed with the handprint of the guardian who had built that seal and set his life upon it.

Melein signed a reverence to the place with her hand, and suddenly turned to Duncan and looked at him sternly. "Duncan, past the grave of the guardian you must not go or you will die. Stand here and wait. Touch nothing, do nothing, see nothing." And to Niun: "Unseal it. It is lawful."

He gave the light to her and began, with the uppermost stones, to unseal what the guardian had warded so many years, a shrine so sacred that a kel'en would wait to the death in warding it. He knew what choice the man had made. Food and water the kel'en had had, the liberty thereafter to range within sight of his warding-place, to hunt in order to survive; but when the area failed him, when illness or harsh weather or advancing age bore upon the solitary kel'en, he had retreated to this chosen niche to die, faithful to his charge, his spirit hovering over the place in constant guardianship.

And perhaps Intel herself had stood here and blessed the closing of this door, and set her kiss upon the brow of the brave guardian, and charged him with this keeping.

One of the kel'ein who had come with her from Nisren, forty years ago, when the Pana had come to Kesrith.

The rocks rattled away from the opening with increasing ease, until Melein could step over what was left, setting foot into the cold interior. The light held in her hand ran over the walls, touched writings that were the mysteries of the Shrine of shrines, convoluted symbols that covered all the walls. For an instant Niun saw it, then sank down to his knees, face averted lest he see what he ought not. For a time he could hear her tiniest step in that sacred place; and then there was no sound at all, and he dared not move. He saw Duncan against the far wall of the well, the dusei by him, and not even they moved. He grew cold in his waiting and began to shiver from fear.

If she should not come back, he must still wait. And there was no stir of life within, not even the sound of a footstep.

One of the dusei moaned, its nerves afflicted with the waiting. It fell silent then, and for a long time there was nothing.

Then came a stirring, a quiet rhythmic sound at first from within the shrine; and at last he recognized it for the sound of soft weeping that became yet more bitter and violent.

"Melein!" he cried aloud, turning his eyes to that forbidden place; and shadows were moving within the doorway, a soft flow of lights. His voice echoed impiously round the walls and startled the dusei, and he scrambled to his feet, terrified to go in and terrified not to.

The sound stopped. There was silence. He came as far as the door, set his hand on it, nerved himself to go inside. Then he heard her light steps somewhere far inside, heard the sounds of life, and she did not summon him. He waited, shivering.

Things moved inside. There was the sound of machinery. It continued, and yet at times he heard her steps clearly. And he remembered with a panic that he had turned his back on Duncan, and whirled to see.

But the human only stood, no closer than Melein had permitted, and made no attempt to flee.

"Sit down," he bade Duncan sharply; and Duncan did so where he stood, waiting. Niun cursed himself for seeking after Melein and forgetting the charge she had set on him, to mind matters outside. He had put them both at Duncan's mercy had the human braved the dusei to take advantage of it. He settled on the sand himself, at such an angle that he could watch the human and yet steal glances toward the shrine. He wrapped his arms about his knees, locked his hands with numbing force, and waited, listening.

It was a long, long wait, in which he grew miserable and changed position many a time. It seemed in his sense of time that it must be drawing toward dawn, although the overcast sky visible above them still was dark. And for a long, long time there was no sound at all from within the shrine.

He hurled himself to his feet finally, impatient to go again to the door, and then persuaded himself that he had no business to invade that place. In his misery he paced the small area he had to pace and looked down betimes at the human, who waited as he had been warned to wait. Duncan's eyes were unreadable in the almost-dark.

There was the sound of footsteps again. He turned upon the instant, saw the white flash of the penlight in the doorway. He saw Melein, a shadow, carrying the tiny light in her fingers, her arms clasped about something.

He went as close as he dared, saw that what she carried was some sort of casing, ovoid, made of shining metal. It had a carrying bar recessed into it at one end, but she bore it as she might have carried an infant, as something precious, though she staggered with the weight of it and could not step over the stones bearing it.

"Take it," she said in a faint, strained voice, and he galvanized himself out of his paralysis of will and reached forth his arms to receive it, dismayed by the weight of what she had managed to carry. It was cold and strange in balance and he shivered as he took it against him.

And he was cold again when he saw her face, moisture glistening there in the reddish light that began to spread behind her, and shadows leaping within the shrine from this side and that: she had turned once to look back, and then gazed back at him as from some vast distance.

Melein, he tried to say to her, and found it impossible. She was Melein still, and sister: but something else was contained in her, and he did not know how to speak to that, to call her back. He held out his hand, anxious at the fire behind her; and she took it and stepped over the rocks at the entry, and came with him. Her skin was cold. Her hand slipped lifelessly from his when she no longer needed him.

Duncan waited, backed a little from the both of them, continuing to stare into the light that was growing behind them. Perhaps he understood that something of great value was being destroyed. He looked dazed, confused.

There was left only the strange, cold ovoid. Niun bore it in both his arms as Melein started for the passage outward. He knew that he surely bore an essential part of the Pana, which name his caste could not even speak without fear, which a kel'en ought never to see, let alone handle.

The kel'en who had borne it here had devoted himself to die afterward, to hold it secret and undisturbed. This had been an honorable man, of the old way, the Kel of the Between; such a man would have been shocked at Niun s'Intel.

But he drew courage from holding it, for by it Melein had come into her power: he felt this of a surety. She had been only half a she'pan in his eyes, appointed by violence and necessity. But now he believed that the essential things had passed, that Intel had given her all she needed. She'pan, he could call her hereafter, believing implicitly that she knew the Mysteries. She had been face to face with the Pana, understanding what a kel'en could not. He did not envy her this understanding: the sound of her weeping still haunted him.

But she knew, and she led, and hereafter he trusted her leading implicitly.

They fled, they and the human and the dusei, out of the well, where smoke began to billow up, betraying them to the sky, where flames lit the walls with red and pursued them with heat. They entered the ascending turns of the way that they had come, into the cold dark.

Chapter Twenty-two

——◆•◆◆•◆——

THE NOM, in its first day of new operations, was aswarm with human technicians. Stavros revelled in the sound and scurry of humanity, after so long among the slow-moving regul. Reports came in, a bustle of human experts adding their agility to the technology of regul in repairs of the damaged plants, in clearing the wreckage left by the storm and the fighting.

And at a point judged stable enough to support a ship, probe *Flower* rested her squat body out on the height to the side of the city opposite the ruined port: a small vessel for a star-capable craft, a ship without the need for vast secure landing area, her design enabling her to operate in complete independence.

It had been a fortunate decision that brought several such probes on the mission, against the need for such difficult landings, despite their lack of defense against attack. *Saber* still rested up at the station, spacemade and spacebound, a kilometer long and incapable of landing anywhere.

Flower, despite the name, was an ungainly shell, without fragility, without exposed vanes, without need of landing gantries and docks, an ugly ship, meant for plain, workman duties.

She brought technicians, scientists, who were already beginning to sift through the remnant of Kesrith's records, to sample the air, the soil, to perform the myriad tasks that would begin to appropriate the world to human colonists.

"Favor," bai Hulagh had said, seeing operations begin. "We regret in the light of this new good feeling, the unfortunate destruction of our equipment in the calamity at the port. We might have been of much assistance."

Regul younglings in general were not so easily adaptive: they fretted at the nearness of humans, and preferred to work in their own groups. They made it no secret that they would gladly be off Kesrith now, to seek the security of their own kind in regul space.

But Hulagh had taken some few of them into his own office within the Nom and when the younglings came out, they had smiles for humans and great courtesy, and a powerful fear of the bai.

Until the storms descended, and the dusei returned.

The report came in first from the water plant, Galey's group, that reported to *Flower* that there were animals moving in large numbers there upon the heights; and *Flower* confirmed it, and flashed the same to the biologists, and in the doing of it, to Stavros.

Stavros locked his sled into the track that would take him to the far side of the Nom, and whisked through several changes to the observation deck, disengaged, and went on manual through the doors and out into the acrid wind.

A ruddy bank of cloud was sweeping in, and there, there, all round the visible horizon, sat the dusei.

A chill went over him, that had nothing to do with the wind, or the biting smell of Kesrith's rains. He sat in the sled, the wind whipping at his sparse hair. He saw *Flower* squatting on her hilltop; and the distant water plant, and vehicles speeding for cover as the storm came down; and airships, running for the makeshift field before the storm should hit: miracle if the crews could get them secured in time. He clenched his fist in rage, foreseeing damage, ships picked up by Kesrith's winds and hurled like toys about the field—human equipage, that, expensive and irreplaceable.

He shifted onto *Flower's* wavelength and heard *Flower* giving frantic instructions. They were warning the aircraft off, seeking means to route them round the storm to temporary landing elsewhere. He watched as lightning lit the clouds, and the clouds bred and built, and rolled in with frightening rapidity, red-lit with Arain's glow.

And the dusei in unending rows sat, and watched, and maintained their vigil. The rains began to fall.

Stavros shivered as the first drops spattered the nose of the sled. It was not a place to sit encased in metal, with the lightning flashing overhead. He backed, opened the doorway, en-

tered the Nom and sealed the door after, still hearing
Flower's chatter, with weather-radar on his receptor, a bow
of storm that clutched at the sea's edge, at the city itself.

Flower, he sent, breaking in on their communications.
Flower: Stavros.

They acknowledged, a thin metallic sound, interrupted by
static.

Flower: the dusei, the dusei—

"We have observed, sir. We are regretfully busy—"

He broke in again. *Flower: drive off the duset. Break them
up, drive them away.*

They acknowledged the order. He sat his sled feeling as if
he had lost his mind, as if all reason departed him. Doubtless
Flower believed that he had lost his senses. But the ominous
heaviness in the air persisted. His skin prickled. He could not
bear the dus-presence, watching, watching at the storm's
edge.

Responsible?

He refused to believe it. Yet in panic he had diverted
Flower to deal with them. He heard them discussing the
task—too wise to discuss the wisdom of it in his hearing. He
sat with his skin drawn into gooseflesh, his teeth near to chat-
tering, a quavering and sickly old man, he thought, a man
who had been among strangers too long.

He could countermand his own order, break in again and
bid them tend more important matters.

But neither could he rid himself of the fear of the dusei.

His screens went all to static, robbing him of the power to
communicate with anyone. The static lasted, and there came
a note over his receptors that shrilled, ear-tormenting, and
passed beyond audibility. He powered down, quickly, desperate, of a sudden consumed with the fear that the sled itself
might be malfunctioning, himself trapped, helpless to move
or call for help.

He watched, through a curtain of rain against the glass, the
line of the dusei begin to break, the beasts scattering; and still
he shivered, terrified as he saw many of them break not
toward the hills, but toward the city, entering its streets, rang-
ing where dusei were not wont to come.

Attacking.

The static continued.

A regul voice came over the loudspeaker, distorted by

static, unintelligible. The address system cut in and out sporadically. Hail rattled against the windows, shaking them dangerously. Stavros hastily tried to cut in the stormshields on the observation deck, and they did not operate. He thought to put the sled on battery, and obtained responses from it, but his screens were still dead. Somewhere there was a crash, a heavy impact of falling plastiglass: and wind and the smell of rain went through the Nom halls.

Stavros backed the sled, tried to engage the track and fouled the order sequence, began again.

It took. He whisked himself out of the area and around the corner, finding the hall a wreckage, unshielded windows lying on the carpet at the end of the hall, curtains whipping loose from their bases. Regul younglings cowered in the hall.

Deprived of the screen, he could not communicate with them. They closed about him, babbling questions, seeking any elder, even human, who could advise them. He pushed the sled through them and sought the downramp, the safer side of the building, where the offices were. The hall here was clear. The public address continued to sputter.

He found Hulagh's offices open, navigated his way with difficulty, and found the bai himself frantically attempting the closure of the stormshields.

A dus was outside. It reared itself against the thin plastiglass. The glass bowed, shook under the raking impact of the claws.

Hulagh backed his sled, fingering controls desperately; and Stavros sat still, watching the attack in horror. There was not a door in the Nom that would operate, nothing they could do if the beasts broke in. The windows quivered.

"Gun!" he cried at Hulagh, trying to make himself understood aloud. "Gun!"

And he backed, and Hulagh either understood or reached the same conclusion. They moved, as rapidly as the sleds would allow; and Hulagh rounded the desk and sought a pistol, holding it in shaking hands.

But the dus retreated, a shambling brown shape quickly lost in the sheeting rain across the square.

There were others, vague brown shapes that gathered and moved, milling nervously, and slowly, as if they had forgotten what they were about, they disappeared into the streets of the city and were gone.

In time the rain slacked, leaving only pocked puddles, and the stormshields suddenly operated all at once, too late for the storm.

The public address became clear, a constant chatter of instructions. Stavros' screens sorted themselves into clarity.

"Stavros, Stavros, do you read?"

Clear, he said. *All clear;* and cut them off, for of a sudden there was a greyness before his eyes and he was content only to stay still, to breathe, to wait until the labored beating of his heart and the roaring in his ears subsided.

There is a window out on the second floor, Stavros advised Hulagh. *Injuries there, I think.*

"Younglings will attend to it."

They neither one mentioned the dus. *Flower* was still trying to advise him what its operations were doing. He heard them talking to the aircraft, that had drawn off in advance of the storm, shepherding their lost searchers home again to the city.

And one of the aircraft answering, the rough accented voice of Hada Surag-gi. "Favor, favor, seeking return to mission, *Flower*-bai, seeking return to search."

And a human voice, also from an aircraft, cursing and demanding an explanation of the jamming.

Stavros wiped his face, cut off the chatter, and looked at the bai.

"Never in my experience," said the bai. "Never, reverence." And Hulagh jabbed at buttons and summoned a youngling servitor, ordering soi, and records; and cursed the slowness of youngling wits. His breathing was at an alarming rate. It was several moments before he seemed in control of himself. "They have all gone mad," he said.

Their world, said Stavros. *Theirs, before the mri.*

The soi came, borne by a youngling so agitated that the cups danced on the tray; and Stavros drank his unsweetened and drew the welcome warmth into his chilled belly.

At length he had the courage to touch the controls to open the stormshields again, remembering the beast even as he did so; and the square was deserted. Of a surety no regul and no humans would venture out until it was known where the dusei had gone.

He felt that he would see the apparition that had attacked

the window in his nightmares thereafter; if the regul were prone to bad dreams the bai would share it.

"I am very old," said Hulagh in a querulous tone. "I am too old for such things, bai Stavros. The regul who took this world were mad." He sipped at his soi. "The mri controlled them. Now nothing does."

There can be barriers, Stavros said. *We can build them.*

Hulagh was silent a long time, throughout most of the cup of soi. His nostrils worked rapidly. At last he blew a sigh and turned his sled from the window. "Holn," he said.

Reverence?

"Holn concealed records. I did not ask, and they did not say: and I know now." Nostrils worked in great flaring breaths of air. "Stavros-bai, you and I have failed to ask questions. Now, now, you and I, Stavros-bai, we have been handed only fragments of what we should have known about Kesrith. We are together in difficulty; and we share an enemy, Stavros-bai."

Holn.

"Holn," said Hulagh. "They were clever, human reverence; and I shall not be able to face the anger of my doch if I come back destitute. Ship, equipment, everything, reverence Stavros. I am ruined. But likewise Holn has cheated you."

Bai Hulagh, you have a purpose in volunteering this information.

"The fortunes of doch Alagn," said Hulagh, "are here, with myself, with these surviving younglings. I will not be sent back in disgrace on a human ship. We shall deal, Stavros."

An alliance, reverence?

"An alliance, bai Stavros. Trade. Exchange. Ideas.—Revenge."

Stavros met the dark, glittering eyes. *From Kesrith,* he said, *there are territories to be explored.*

"It is first necessary," said Hulagh, "to hold Kesrith."

As the Holn and the mri held it, said Stavros, *with its resources used. Even the dusei. Even them.*

And he fell to staring out the window, at the roiling sky, and saw the ruin of the port, and the rain, and considered the resources with which they had to work; and for the first time his hopes began to hold a taint of doubt.

When he shut his eyes he still saw the beast at the window,

irrational, uncontrollable as the elements: he hated them, the more so perhaps because they were without rationality, because they were, like the storm, of the elemental forces.

Antipathy to all that was regul and Kiluwan, the dusei.

But they were a part of Kesrith that could neither be ignored nor destroyed.

A combination of random elements, the world of Kesrith; and hereafter, he foresaw, was not under the control of George Stavros. He could no longer control. He shared Kesrith with beasts and with regul.

He clenched his hand on controls and listened to *Flower* again, hearing the babble of search craft that were bound out yet another time on their continuing patterns, trying to find one lost soul in all that wilderness, where dusei ran wild and the storms raked the land with violence.

Almost he bade them give it up.

But he had already given *Flower* irrational orders enough. He did not make the move. He saw one of the aircraft circle far out over the ruins of the edun and continue west, a speck quickly lost in the haze.

Chapter Twenty-three

————◦◦————◦◦————

MELEIN WAS asleep finally. Niun, wiping the weariness from his eyes, settled the heavy metal ovoid into his lap and leaned his head back against the warm, breathing side of the dus. Duncan lay sprawled in the sand, on his stomach, his tattered and makeshift robes inadequate to afford him much protection from scrapes and sand-sores. His skin, bare above the boots, was scored with abrasions and sunburn. His eyes, unprotected by the veil, without the membrane to ease them, ran tears that streaked a perpetual coating of dust, like a dus gone *miuk*.

Duncan was exhausted for the moment, beyond causing them any trouble. Niun noted that a jo had settled against the rock, its luin-camouflage a little too dark for the red sandstone, where it clung for shade in this hottest part of the day. The name meant mimic. The creature harmed nothing. It waited for snakes, which were its natural food. It was not a bad campmate, the jo.

Niun nodded over his charge, his arms clasped about it, and rested his head, and finally relaxed enough to sleep awhile, now that Melein had settled. She had almost fainted before they stopped in this shelter, overburdened and hurting more than she wanted to admit. She had gone aside from them, into the privacy of the rocks, and taken cloth with her, in long strips: "I think it will help my side," she said; and because there was no kath'en or kel'e'en to attend her, she attended to herself. The ribs were broken, he much feared, or at the least cracked. He was worried, with a deep cold fear, that would not leave him.

But she had come back, hand pressed to her side, and smiled a thin smile and announced that she felt some better, and that she thought she could sleep; and the tension unwound from Niun's vitals when he saw that she could do so, that her pain was less.

The fear did not go away.

He bore Duncan's presence, his dread of anything Duncan might do to him far less than fear for Melein, for losing her, for ending alone.

The last mri.

He dreamed of the edun, and its towers crumbling in fire, and woke clutching the smooth shape of the pan'en to him in the fear that he also was falling into the Dark.

But he sat on the sand, the dus unmoving behind him. The jo, with a deft swoop, descended on a lizard, and bore it back to his upside-down perch on the rock, shrouding his meal with his mottled wings, a busy and tiny movement as it fed, swallowing the lizard bit by bit.

Niun set the pan'en beside him so that he could feel it, constantly, against him, and leaned his head against the dus. He drowsed again, and awoke finding the heat unpleasant. He looked toward the advancing line of the sunlight, that had crept up on Duncan, and saw that it had enveloped him to the waist, falling on the bare skin of his knee and hand. The human did not stir.

"Duncan," said Niun. He obtained no reaction, and reluctantly bestirred himself, leaned forward and shook at the human. "Duncan."

Brown eyes stared up at him, bewildered, heat-dazed.

"The sun, stupid tsi'mri, the sun. Move into the shade."

Duncan dragged himself into a new place and collapsed again, ripped aside the veil and lay with the cooler sand against his bare face. His eyes blinked, returning sensibility within them, as Niun resumed his place.

"Are we ready to move on?" he asked in a faint voice.

"No. Sleep."

Duncan lifted his head and looked around at Melein, lay down again facing him. "Somewhere," he said in a faint whisper, "my people will have come to Kesrith by now. She needs medical help. You know that. If it were sure that those up there are humans—we could contact an aircraft. Listen: the war is over. I don't think you know us well enough to believe it, but we wouldn't pursue matters any further. No revenge. No war. Come with me. Contact my people. There would be help for her. And no retaliations. None."

Niun listened to the words, patient, believing at least that Duncan believed what he was saying. "Perhaps it is even true," he said. "But she would never accept this."

"She will die. But with help—"

"We are mri. We do not accept medicines, only our own. She has done what can be done under our own ways. Should strangers touch her? No. We live or we die, we heal or we do not heal." He shrugged. "Maybe our way of doing things is not even a wise one. Sometimes I have thought it was not. But we are the very last, and we will keep to the things that all our ancestors before us have observed. There is no use now for anything but that."

And he fell to thinking how Melein had planned, and that they had won this last small victory over tsi'mri, that they had gathered to themselves the holiness and the history of their kind; and his fingers ran over the smooth skin of the pan'en that he kept by him.

"I have broken two traditions," he admitted at last. "I have taken you and I have carried burdens. But the honor of the she'pan I will not compromise. No. I do not believe in your doctors. And I do not believe in your people and your ways. They are not for us."

Duncan looked at him, long and soberly. "Even to survive?"

"Even to survive."

"If I get back to my own people," said Duncan finally, "I'm going to make sure it's known what the regul did, what really happened that night at the port. I don't know whether it will do any good; I know it can't change anything for the better. But it ought to be told."

Niun inclined his head, a respect for that gesture. "The regul," he said, "would see you dead before they would let you tell those things. And if you hope on that account that I will let you leave our company and go to them, I must tell you I will not."

"You don't believe me."

"I don't believe you know what they will do, either your kind or the regul."

Duncan was silent thereafter, staring into nothing. He looked very worn and very tired. He rubbed at a line of dried blood that had settled into an unshaven trail; and he was quiet again, but seemed not apt to sleep.

"Don't run again," Niun advised him, for he disliked the human's mood. "Don't try. I have made you too easy with us. Do not trust it."

Brown eyes flicked up at him, tsi'mri and disturbing. Duncan gathered himself up to a sitting position, moving as if every muscle ached, and rubbed his head with a grimace of discomfort. "I had rather stay alive," Duncan said, "like you would."

The words stung. They were too nearly true. "That is not all that matters," Niun said.

"I know that," Duncan said. "A truce. A truce: a peace between us at least until you've got her to somewhere safe, until she's well. I know you'd kill for her; I know that under other circumstances you might not. I understand that whatever she is, she's someone very special—to you."

"A she'pan," said Niun, "is Mother to a house. She is the last. A kel'en is only the instrument of her decisions. I can make no promises except for my own choice."

"Can there not be another generation?" Duncan asked suddenly, in his innocence, and Niun felt the embarrassment, but he did not take offense. "Can you not—if things were otherwise—?"

"We are bloodkin, and her caste does not mate," he answered softly, moved to explain what mri had never explained to outsiders: but it was simply kel lore, and it was not forbidden to say. It lent him courage, to affirm again the things that had always been fixed and true. "Kath'en or kel'e'en could bear me children for her, but there are none. There is no other way for us. We either survive as we were, or we have failed to survive. We are mri; and that is more than the name of a species, Duncan. It is an old, old way. It is our way. And we will not change."

"I will not be the cause," said Duncan, "of finishing the regul's handiwork. I'll stay with you. I made my try. Maybe again, sometime, maybe, but not to anyone's hurt, hers or yours. I have time. I have all the time in the world."

"And we do not," said Niun. He thought with a wrench of fear that Duncan, wiser than he in some things, for human kel'ein were able to cross castes—suspected that Melein would not live; and it answered a fear in his own heart. He looked to see how she was resting; and she was still asleep. The sight of her regular breathing quietly reassured him.

"With time and quiet," said Duncan, "perhaps she will mend."

"I accept your truce," said Niun, and in great weariness, he unfastened his veil and looped the end of the *mez* over his shoulder, baring his face to the human. It was hard, shaming to do; he had never shown his face to any tsi'mri; but he had taken this for an ally, even for the moment, and in the rightness of things, Duncan deserved to see him as he was.

Duncan looked long at him, until the embarrassment became acute and Niun flinched from that stare.

"The *mez* is a necessity in the heat and the dryness," Niun said. "But I am not ashamed to see your face. The *mez* is not necessary between us."

And he curled himself against the pan'en, and against the solid softness of the dus, and attempted to rest, taking what ease he could, for they would move with the coolness and concealment of evening, at a time when surely regul trusted even a mri would not dare the cliffs.

There was the sound of an aircraft, distant, a reminder of alien presence in the environs of Sil'athen. Niun heard it, and gathered himself up to listen, to be sure how close or how far it was. Melein was awake, and Duncan stirred, seeking at once the direction of the sound.

It was evening. The pillars had turned red, burning in the twilight. Arain was visible through them, a baleful red disk, rippling in the heat of the sands.

Melein sought to rise. Niun quickly offered her his hands and helped her, and she was no longer too proud to accept that help. He looked at her drawn face and thought of his own necessary burden. His helplessness to do anything for her overwhelmed him.

"We must be moving," she said. "We must go down again, to Sil'athen. There is no other exit I know from this place. But with the aircraft—" Her face contracted in an expression of anger, of frustration. "They are watching Sil'athen. They believe that the place hides us—and if they have men afoot—"

"I hope they are afoot," said Niun. "That would give me satisfaction." And then he remembered Duncan, and was glad that he had been speaking in the hal'ari, as she had used with him. But it was likely enough that they were regul that they had to deal with, who would not go afoot.

"The climb down," she said, "—I think it would be best to move just at the last light, so that we can see to climb. There will not be a moon up until sometime later. That will give us some dark to cross the open place at the beginning."

"That is the best we can do," he agreed. "We will eat and drink before we go. We may not have another chance to stop."

And what that journey would cost Melein weighed heavily on his mind.

"Duncan," he said quietly, while they shared food, both of them unveiled, "I will not be able to do more than carry what I must carry. On the climb—"

"I will help her," Duncan said.

"Down is easier," Melein said, and looked askance at Duncan, as if she found their arrangement far from her liking.

It was the last of the food that they had brought with them. Thereafter they must hunt, and quickly they must find water again, in this place where luin were not frequent. Niun's mind raced ahead to these things, difficulties upon difficulties, but ones more pleasant than those most immediate.

They set out again toward the trail they had used, and when they stood finally looking down that great chasm, dim and unreal in the faded light, shading into black at the bottom, he held the pan'en close to him and dreaded the climb even for himself. When he considered Melein, he turned cold.

If she falls, he thought to warn Duncan; but it would do no good, to dishonor what small trust there was between them, and he thought that the human must know his mind. Duncan returned that stare, plain and accepting the charge that was set on him.

"Go first," Niun bade him, and the human looped the trailing *mez* across his face and secured it firmly as Niun had already done with his own. Then he set his feet on the down-slope, bracing them carefully, offering his hand up for Melein's.

"Niun," Melein said, a glance, a patent distress. It was the only thing at which she had shown fear, committing herself to the hands of a human, when she was already in much pain.

Then, her hand pressed to her side, she reached her fingers toward Duncan's, and carefully, carefully, she set her feet on the downslope, beginning the descent with Duncan's hand to steady her, he bracing his body against whatever security there was, his arm extended to give her a firm support should she slip. In small stages they descended; and Niun stood with the pan'en a cold and comfortless weight in his arms, watching while they disappeared together into that shadow.

The dusei waited behind him, shifting weight nervously.

And then something intruded on his hearing, from behind him.

Aircraft, skimming above the pillars.

He grasped the carrying-bar of the pan'en, the only way to carry it in the descent, and hissed to the dusei and started the descent, terrified lest he cause them to have been seen, lest in his haste now he slip and come down on Melein and Duncan.

The aircraft passed directly overhead, a roar of power that echoed off the narrow walls, and he crouched low against a rock, shuddering against the strain of holding position on that slope. Pebbles skidded under his outmost foot. He took the chance as the aircraft passed beyond view and slid a few lengths lower, into the shadow, and the great bodies of the dusei came behind him, sharing his fear, communicating back to him an anxiety that made his stomach heave. He began to think he could not hold the pan'en: his fingers felt cut to the bone; and after he had gone a distance more he could not feel much pain, only an increasing numbness and lack of control over his fingers. He braced himself against a rock and shifted hands, reversing his entire position on the cliffside, showered from above by pebbles and dust from the claws of the dusei. They were at such a place now that they could not stop, and he plunged down a desperate slide, until he entered the deepest dark.

And at a stopping place he overtook Melein and Duncan, and Duncan's face looked toward him in that faintest of light. Melein still held to his hand, bent for a moment against a boulder.

She moved on then, weakly, leaning much on Duncan; and Niun took the stable place they had had, braced his body against the weight he held, and waited, to stop the dusei, to hold them there, awkward as it was, until she was safely down. They came, shouldered against him, and he held them with a quiet will, an intense willing that they be still, hush, stop. They were patient, even in this awkward state, joined with his senses.

The aircraft passed again, lights winking against the dim sky overhead. Niun looked up at it, trembling with the strain, and held his place, helpless, with the growing conviction that they were lost.

They had surely been spotted, at the worst of all times, in the worst of all places.

It circled yet again.

He settled the pan'en in the right hand again and set out downward, hoping, desperately hoping that Melein and Duncan had had time, for there were no more resting places that he remembered. He went, boots sliding on the trail, bringing up against one and another rock with a force that his muscles were too tired to absorb. He came down and down until he could hardly control his descent, and dropped from the last turn to the sand, driven to one knee by the impact.

The dusei came after, clambering down with much scratching of claws and scattering of sand, safe at the bottom.

And Melein sat, a pale huddle of robes in the shadow, and Duncan knelt by her. Her hand was pressed to her lips, and the other hand to her side, and her robes were stained with blood.

He fell to his knees beside her, the pan'en in his arms, and she could not prevent the cough that she stanched with her veil. Blood came. He saw it, and the membrane flashed across his vision, blinding him. He shivered, unable to see for a moment, and then it cleared.

"It began on the climb," Duncan said. "I think the ribs gave way."

And the aircraft circled at the top of the cleft.

Niun looked up at it in a blindness of rage.

"Be free of us," he bade Duncan, and rose up, letting the pan'en fall to the sand. He looked last at Melein, her eyes closed, her face relaxed, her body supported in Duncan's arms—not even a sen'en to attend her.

He gave a sharp call to his dusei, and began to walk,

quickly, toward the end of the small valley, toward the main valley of Sil'athen.

"Niun!" Duncan shouted after him, which he did not regard.

He saw the aircraft hovering, at the valley's end. He reached for the cords at the end of the *siga's* long sleeves, and fastened them to their places on the honor belts at his shoulders, freeing his arms from the encumbering cloth; and he worked life into his hands, scored and numbed as they were from carrying the pan'en.

Duncan was running now, trying to overtake him. He heard the human—a racking cough, immediate payment for that rashness in Kesrith's thin air. He saw the aircraft on the sand, and regul descending, standing on the ramp. The dus at his side moaned a roar of menace, and the other two scattered out, flanking them—dus-tactics in hunting, the outrunners.

He saw the regul about to fire, the weapon lifted. He was not in its line when it discharged; but his eyes were clear and his hand steady when he fired; and the regul crumpled, a mass of flesh still stirring. They did not die easily, body-shot. A moment later the ramp drew up, toppling the wounded regul: coward, Niun cursed the regul flier.

And darted into the rocks and scrambled for cover as it lifted, swinging over near him, drawing off again. He was in the open now, in the main valley, and other aircraft hovered.

They would have him, eventually. He ran low among the rocks that bordered the open sands, pursued by the aircraft with their sensors, and finally, a desperate tactic, braced and fired against the nearest—all without effect for the first several shots. Then the aircraft began having difficulty, and skidded off into a great cloud of sand amid the valley.

Others swooped in. The sky was alive with the sound of them: they passed low and drew off, warned by the fate of the other.

He ran and he rested, and by now the air was tinged with the coppery taste of too much exertion in the thin air, and he could not see clearly to fire back at them. Shots tore up the rocks where he hid, and he staggered as rock became shrapnel and tore his arm, bringing a warm flow of blood.

Lights played across the cliffs, making it impossible to stay hidden. There was scant cover, and shots tore at all of it. He

ran, and fell, and scrambled up and raced for the next rock,
and what had become of the dusei he did not know: it was
not their kind of fight, this fury of fire and light.

The valley became ruin, steles and natural formations
blasted to rubble. It was the final vengeance of the regul on
his kind, to destroy the last sanctity of the People; and to
ruin the land, as they had destroyed all that they had
touched.

A near miss threw him rolling, dazed, blinded by the membrane that shielded his eyes, and he rose up and ran, too harried to fire any longer, only to run and run until they had
him a clear target.

An aircraft pressed at him, diving low, throwing sand from
the wind of its passing. And then he thought with a sudden
and clear satisfaction, and shifted left, toward the end of the
valley, toward an old, old place, under the sightless eyes of
Eddan and Liran and Debas, his teachers.

Fight with the land; make it your ally, they had been wont
to tell him; and he heard them clear and calmly through the
roar of the aircraft.

He fell, sprawling, and the aircraft continued on over him,
hovered, kicking up sand; and he lay still, still as it settled,
playing lights over the sand where he lay.

It touched; and the earth exploded, a great pale shape rear-
ing up, heaving the aircraft, catching the craft in the convulsions of the mantle: burrower and machine, entangled in a
cloud of sand, and the concussions of its struggles shaking the
earth. Niun rolled and tried to run, but an edge of the mantle
or a shock of air hurled him sprawling, and then another impact, and he saw the world go up in fire as the aircraft exploded.

And dark, thereafter.

"Niun!"

Someone was calling him out of that dark, that had not the
familiarity of the brothers; but it was a familiar voice all the
same.

Light broke over him. He moved limbs that were buried in
sand, and heard the sound of engines.

"Niun!"

He lifted his head and drew himself up, standing on legs

that swayed under him, shielding his eyes from the light with his arm.

Waiting.

"Niun!" It was Duncan's voice, from a ragged silhouette before the lights. "Don't fire. Niun, we have Melein aboard. She is not dead, Niun."

He went blank at that horrid shock, mind not functioning, and came near to falling. And then the kel-law echoed in his mind, reminding him that there was a she'pan to be served; and that above all else, he could not leave her alone in the hands of strangers.

"What do you want of me?" he cried, his voice breaking with fury, with rage at Duncan, and treachery, and dishonor. "Duncan, I remind you what you swore—"

"Come in," Duncan said. "Niun, come in with us. Safe conduct. I still swear it."

He hesitated, and the strength went out of him, and he made a gesture of surrender, and began, slowly, to walk into the lights, toward the silhouettes that waited for him, tall and human.

Better than the regul, at least.

And out of the tail of his eye, a squat dark form. He saw it, saw the move, knew treachery.

He palmed the *as'ei*, whirled and threw; and the fire took him, and he never felt the sand.

"Hada Surag-gi is dead," said Galey. "The mri are hanging on."

Duncan wiped his face, and in the same gesture, swept the head-cloth off and ran his fingers through his sweat-soaked hair. He stumbled back through the narrow confines of the aircraft and shouldered past the medic who had already twice ordered him to keep his seat.

He sat down on the deck, unsteady in the motion of the aircraft, and regarded the two mri, wrapped in white, a tangle of tubing and monitoring connections from the automed units keeping their lives by means that the mri would find distasteful if they knew.

But they would have the chance to know.

"They're going to make it, both of them," the medic said. And then, frowning, with a glance at the sheet-wrapped hulk to the rear: "That particular regul was an officer of the Nom, with connections. There are going to be some questions asked."

"There will be some questions asked," Duncan said in a still voice, and looked at the mri, dismissing the medic from his mind. He sat with his legs tucked under him, still in the tattered and makeshift robes, and with his mind elsewhere; and at last the medic drew off to talk to the crew.

They had spoken little to him after the first excitement of recovering him alive; they were put off, perhaps, by the look of him, the strangeness of a man who had come alive from the desert of Kesrith, keeping company with mri and insisting with such vehemence on the possession of a mri treasure.

He touched Melein's brow, smoothed the metallic-bronze of her hair, noting the steady pulse on the monitors that assured him of their lives. Melein's golden eyes opened, the membrane cleared slowly back, and she seemed to be exploring the curious place that she had seen in her intervals of waking, rediscovering the strangeness that had taken them in. She was curiously calm, as if she had accepted to be here. He took her long slim fingers in his hand, and she pressed his hand with a faint effort.

"Niun is all right," he told her. He was not sure she understood this, for there was not a flicker. "There is the object you wanted," he added, but she did not look; likely all these concerns were distant from her, for they were heavily drugged.

"Kel'en," she whispered.

"She'pan?" he answered: perhaps she confused him with Niun.

"There will be a ship," she said. "A way off Kesrith."

"There will be," he said to her, and reckoned that he had told her the truth.

The war was done. They were free of regul. A human ship—there would be that—a chance for them. It was the most the mri would ever ask of tsi'mri.

"There will be that," he said. She closed her eyes then.

"*Shon'ai,*" she said, with a taut, faint smile. He did not know the word. But he thought that she meant acceptance.

The deck slanted. They were coming in. He told her so.

Attention:

DAW COLLECTORS

Many readers of DAW Books have written requesting information on early titles and book numbers to assist in the collection of DAW editions since the first of our titles appeared in April 1972.

We have prepared a several-pages-long list of all DAW titles, giving their sequence numbers, original and current order numbers, and ISBN numbers. And of course the authors and book titles, as well as reissues.

If you think that this list will be of help, you may have a copy by writing to the address below and enclosing one dollar in stamps or coins to cover the handling and postage costs.

DAW BOOKS, INC. Dept. C
1633 Broadway
New York, N.Y. 10019

PHILIP K. DICK

"The greatest American novelist of the second half of the 20th Century."

—*Norman Spinrad*

"A genius . . . He writes it the way he sees it and it is the quality, the clarity of his Vision that makes him great."

—*Thomas M. Disch*

"The most consistently brilliant science fiction writer in the world."

—*John Brunner*

PHILIP K. DICK

In print again, in DAW Books' special memorial editions:

☐ **WE CAN BUILD YOU** (#UE1793—$2.50)

☐ **THE THREE STIGMATA OF PALMER ELDRITCH**
(#UE1810—$2.50)

☐ **A MAZE OF DEATH** (#UE1830—$2.50)

☐ **UBIK** (#UE1859—$2.50)

☐ **DEUS IRAE** (#UE1887—$2.95)

☐ **NOW WAIT FOR LAST YEAR** (#UE1654—$2.50)

☐ **FLOW MY TEARS, THE POLICEMAN SAID** (#UE1624—$2.50)